What people are saying about …

Greg Garrett

"An astonishingly gifted writer."

Dennis Covington, National Book Award
Finalist for *Salvation on Sand Mountain*

"Greg Garrett is a remarkable novelist who has the courage to explore in
classic terms the great theme of the human soul."

Robert Olen Butler, winner of the Pulitzer Prize for
Fiction for *A Good Scent from a Strange Mountain*

"Greg Garrett writes with intelligence, with wit, with humor, with obvious
affection for his characters, with an eye for the salient detail that brings an
economy to the writing that I particularly admire."

Elinor Lipman, author of *Then She Found Me* and *My Latest Grievance*

Praise for …

Free Bird

"A work of wit and arresting grace … a grave and hopeful story about the
battle between grief and faith."

Julia Glass, winner of the National Book Award for Fiction for *Three Junes*

"By turns harrowing and hilarious, poignant and pointed … that most rare
of things these days: a book with meaning, and with heart."

Bret Lott, author of the Oprah Book Club and
New York Times best-selling book *Jewel*

"Energetic, suspenseful, and moving … a great read with picture perfect dialogue."

Lee Smith, winner of the Southern Book Critics Circle Award for *The Last Girls*

"A fast-moving, high-octane pilgrimage to redemption, *Free Bird* offers a bumpy but unforgettable flight. You'll be glad you were around for the trip."

New Orleans Times-Picayune

"Best reason to read: For its cast of downright memorable characters, its fast pace, and its thought-provoking message."

Rocky Mountain News

"Entertaining. This wide-ranging novel makes for a very enjoyable and occasionally thought-provoking read."

Publishers Weekly

Praise for …

Cycling

"*Cycling* is a belated coming of age novel in the sexy, genteel tradition of Walker Percy and Richard Ford."

Stewart O'Nan, author of *Songs for the Missing* and *The Names of the Dead*

"Garrett creates characters who are whole and complex."

Library Journal

S H A M E

a novel

Greg Garrett

David C Cook®
transforming lives together

SHAME
Published by David C. Cook
4050 Lee Vance View
Colorado Springs, CO 80918 U.S.A.

David C. Cook Distribution Canada
55 Woodslee Avenue, Paris, Ontario, Canada N3L 3E5

David C. Cook U.K., Kingsway Communications
Eastbourne, East Sussex BN23 6NT, England

David C. Cook and the graphic circle C logo
are registered trademarks of Cook Communications Ministries.

This story is a work of fiction. All characters and events are the product of the author's
imagination. Any resemblance to any person, living or dead, is coincidental.

LCCN 2009922188
ISBN 978-1-4347-6752-3

© 2009 Greg Garrett
Published in association with the literary agency of Jill Grosjean

The Team: Andrea Christian, Steve Parolini, Amy Kiechlin,
Jaci Schneider, Caitlyn York, and Karen Athen
Cover Design: DogEared Design, Kirk DouPonce
Cover Photo: iStockphoto and Shutterstock
Interior Design: Sarah Schultz

Printed in the United States of America

First Edition 2009

1 2 3 4 5 6 7 8 9 10

022509

For Martha,
Who loves

———————

"The Lord hath given, and the Lord hath taken away;
Blessed be the name of the Lord."
Job 1:21

"What people are ashamed of usually makes a good story."
F. Scott Fitzgerald, The Love of the Last Tycoon

On the Tractor

My name is John Tilden, and this is a story about my life.

My parents always thought I'd grow up to be a doctor. I don't know how they settled on this—not through personal knowledge of one, since I don't recall any doctor ever staying in our small west Oklahoma town long enough for anyone to get to know him. Maybe it was *General Hospital,* which my mother watched furtively when she knew my father was in the fields; maybe it was simply the default dream uneducated country people have for their sons. In any case, all the time I was in high school they had this image of me ministering to the sick and, maybe, pulling down a six-figure income to provide for their old age.

My high school sweetheart, Samantha Mathis, thought I should be an architect or an engineer. I don't know why she settled on these occupations for me, since I displayed almost no aptitude in those directions, but when she sat on my lap and kissed me and sketched out our future, I was more than happy to entertain the notion, and made sure all the colleges I applied to had engineering schools, just in case she might be right about me.

I had the idea that I'd become a lawyer or a writer. I've always been good with words, on paper at least, so unlike those other notions, those options seemed reasonable.

None of these dreams came true. What I ultimately became was a farmer, like my father and his father before him, and I plow the sandy red soil of the farm where I've lived the better part of forty years. It is not, I think, what anyone expected, but life, as they say, has a way of changing your plans.

People have always told me I was a thinker, but I believe they meant different things at different stages of my life. When I was growing up, they meant that I was destined for a future far beyond the dusty confines of Watonga, Oklahoma. What they meant once I passed the age of thirty was that I thought too much for my own good.

Trouble is, going off on a mental tangent is one of those things you can't avoid if you're a farmer and you've got half a mind. Driving a tractor just doesn't require that much concentration: You chug around in an enclosed space that grows ever smaller, turning left whenever you run out of row. That's it. A ten-year-old could do it, and this isn't just folksy exaggeration. I've been driving a tractor in these same fields since I was ten years old. Hard to believe so much time has passed and only the tractor has changed: The spindly red Ford is now a monstrous red International Harvester, and here am I, still seated behind the wheel.

The hours stretch as I manhandle the tractor into a turn, shift gears, lower and raise attachments, listen to the dull roar of the engine outside the glass-windowed cab. There isn't much to do out here besides think, which is what I was doing on that afternoon last fall where I want to begin this story.

I thought about my farm: the price of wheat, currently three dollars a bushel, although it would drop back to $2.50 when the glut of harvest began in June; the calves I planned to buy and fatten over the winter on the very wheat pasture I was planting at that moment; the repairs I'd need to do on the combine before the next harvest, something perhaps to occupy me on a winter morning or two after the calves were fed.

I thought about my family: my wife, Michelle, much-loved beatnik senior English teacher at our alma mater, Watonga High; our oldest child, Michael, a moody college dropout (just temporary, he claimed); our obedient son B. W. (named Brian Wilson Tilden by my wife after her favorite rock star poet); our youngest, Lauren, twelve years old and changing so quickly in body and mind that I could scarcely keep track of her from week to week or even day to day.

I thought about the basketball team I coached, the Watonga High School students who, as soon as football ended, would take to the court under my part-time tutelage for the third straight winter: B. W., my point guard, throwing passes with the beauty and precision of geometric diagrams; Larry Burke, whom I called "Bird" because of his wispy mustache and his fadeaway jump shot; Martel and Tyrel Sparks, fast and agile forwards with a lot more talent than discipline; stolid, solid Jimmy Bad Heart Bull, long dark hair in a ponytail, grabbing another of those rebounds that seemed to appear in his hands as though willed there by the Great Spirit. A team, unfortunately, with mostly unrealized promise.

And I thought about myself, the life I inhabited, moving at five miles per hour in a field of dwindling squares enclosed inside each other like Russian nesting dolls, and the contrast with all the lives imagined for me in years long past. Those lives, the ones from which I expected to choose, vanished for reasons you will hear, and yet in some ways they were still there, always present. Maybe a phantom life is like the phantom limb of an amputee: The future I lost still felt tangible—possible, even—but whenever I reached out for it, my hand passed through empty air.

To understand that feeling completely, it's necessary to go back much further than last fall—to go all the way back, in fact, to the winter of 1974. It was the beginning of basketball season at Watonga High, the moment before my life changed for good, and—as they too often used to—that's where my thoughts drifted that afternoon last fall while the tractor toiled. The future was revealed only slowly, of course, peeling off event by event like layers of an onion, but in the winter of 1974, I still believed that great things lay ahead, that nothing bad would ever happen to me.

For those four short months from December to March, as the world outside changed from ice and snow to wildflowers and redbud blossoms, life was golden: I was in love, colleges were writing acceptance letters, and our team was playing basketball like no one in town had ever seen before.

Bobby Ray Daugherty set a single-game district scoring record that season that still stands, forty-seven points against our archrival, Thomas High School; Big Bill Cobb earned All State honors at center and went on to play college ball for Southern Methodist in Dallas after becoming one of the leading scorers in Oklahoma high school basketball history; Phillip One Horse returned from a five-game suspension for repeated and flagrant infractions of Coach Parker's team rules and pulled down seventeen rebounds against Comanche to help us advance to the state finals; Jim "Oz" Osborne threw up a thirty-five-foot set shot at the buzzer of the Comanche game to seal our victory; and I was a point guard with so many targets that I led the conference in assists for two years running, the kind of player who could always make other players look better.

Together, the five of us did what no Watonga High School sports team had done before or since: We won a state championship. For years after, whenever people from Watonga wanted to conjure us up out of the past, they simply mentioned the year we won it all—1975—and sighed, or without further clarification, referred to "The Team," and there was never any doubt on Main Street who they were talking about.

We were a team, true enough. The five of us had played together for what seemed like our whole lives. On the court, we completed each other, covered for each other's weaknesses in a way that was marvelous to behold. It's too bad that we couldn't do that for each other off the court and in the life that followed.

Because, you see, it is no easy thing for a young man to conquer the world—remember how Alexander the Great is said to have wept when he realized there were no more worlds to conquer?—and that is what a state championship means in a country town held together mostly by its school and sports. Between the five of us, I think we represented every possible reaction to early greatness: As of last fall, Bobby Ray had gone through two wives, had three corporations file for Chapter Eleven, and lost more money than I will ever be able to earn; Bill had played college ball, earned his degree in business administration, and stayed on in Dallas where he parlayed his smile, handshake, and jovial laugh into his current life as a bigwig in commercial real estate and the Texas Republican Party; Phillip robbed a Watonga liquor store with a couple of other malcontents in 1979, did ten years hard time in McAlester State Penitentiary, and after his release, hid out on forty acres north of town; Oz went to pharmacy school at Southwestern State courtesy of his pharmacist father-in-law and grew stoop-shouldered from fifteen years of hanging over the counter of that pharmacy down on Main Street, helping the elderly and indigent who are just about all who remain in a town like ours.

And me? Well, in February of 1975, when Samantha Mathis broke up with me for the first and only time, I was paralyzed with grief. Phillip One Horse was even at that early date a reliable guide to the world of alcoholic excess, so when my life's fateful moment presented itself to me early one Saturday morning in the person of cute and lanky Michelle Hooks, I was too drunk to recognize it as a fateful choice until it was too late and the rest of my life was determined.

When Samantha drove out to the farm thirteen days later and tearfully apologized for our fight, we got back together, and I thought it would be best if I didn't tell Sam about Michelle. Besides, our moment together had really become nothing more than a pleasantly foggy memory.

Sam and I got back to making plans about our future life together, talking about marriage—when it might come, what it might look like. She wanted five bridesmaids, which in those days was an awful lot, although I've seen more since.

The last time Samantha and I ever talked about marriage was later that spring when I pulled my truck over to the side of a country road in the middle of a thunderstorm and told her that I was going to have to marry someone else.

Michelle Hooks was pregnant, and I was the father.

I will never forget the silence that stood between us, an invisible wall in the tiny enclosed space of my pickup cab surrounded by the noise of falling water. First she had cried, which was bad, but then she was silent, and that was worse. She wouldn't look at me. We sat, the engine revving, "Fire and Rain" crackling in from distant WKY-AM in Oklahoma City, sheets of water pelting the roof and hood. I thought maybe it was starting to hail. A fierce ache rose up from my stomach and took root beneath my rib cage, and I had no real hope or belief that it would ever leave.

"Are you sure it's yours?" she finally asked. She was still looking out the fogged-up window toward the fields green with winter wheat.

"Yes," I said. I was sure.

"Are you sure you know what you're doing?"

I bit my lip, let out a pained sigh, shook my head. I was not sure what I was doing, supposed I would never be sure again. "But I have to," I finally said, and raised my hands, palms up, in front of me, a gesture I've performed since I was a kid, a gesture that can mean variously "I'm sorry" or "What can I say?" or both, which is what it meant then.

And that was that. My life in the wider world with Samantha, my career as doctor or architect or engineer or lawyer, someone that people might have treated with respect—all of that was gone. I never really had another choice. Maybe in some places this type of taboo would not require ritual expiation, but in Watonga, Oklahoma, in 1975, the dictates of my conscience and the mores of my community were in perfect accord; there was only one thing I could do and still call myself a decent human being.

People have always insisted that I am a good man, and to a certain extent I believe them. I have tried never to do anything in the dark that I wasn't willing to make good in the light, and my faith tradition teaches that we are called to do what is right, not what is easy.

I got Michelle Hooks pregnant, so I married her.

And that is how my life changed forever.

Michael came along as anticipated; after Michael, we had two children who were more or less planned. I took over my parents' farm out west of town near the Canadian River, and in 1991, a few years before the story I am to relate, I agreed to help out my impoverished alma mater by volunteering my time as basketball coach, an arrangement mostly satisfactory for all concerned.

When I was on the tractor and imagining my life as satisfying—for truly, much of it was—I liked to think of it in terms of the land, my family, the gorgeous *rip* of a basketball finding nothing but net, and Michelle. Basketball season, after all, was my favorite time of the year, and for more reasons than just the sport. There were, for example, those chilly winter evenings that time of year, sitting with Michelle in the fire-lit living room at the far end of our house. The kids floated in and out, depending on their homework and which of the broadcast channels was coming in visibly on our TV. Michelle graded papers, did lesson plans, or curled up with a book. I did my share of reading, and when there was room at the desk, I did my share of writing: letters to my parents in Arizona and to my little sister, to former players lonesome for mail away at college, to Bill Cobb and Samantha—for the girl I loved in high school did not stray outside our team to find a husband—in Rockwall, a suburb of Dallas, where they rubbed elbows with interesting neighbors like Marina Oswald, widow of Lee Harvey, and Olympic track star Michael Johnson, the kind of people I would never meet unless they got as lost as Robinson Crusoe.

On those winter nights, with the fire glistening in the glass of the fireplace insert, the wind whistling across the north field and into the thick stand of cedars my father and I planted along the north side of the house, some Eagles or James Taylor playing low on the antiquated turntable in the bookcase, we sat, Michelle and I, and occasionally we would look over at each other, our eyes would meet, our mouths would curve slightly upward into smiles, and I'd remind myself that things sometimes turn out for the best. Michelle and I had not always loved each other—or rather, I had not always loved her—but I did at last learn to, and wasn't it better to be unsure at first and in love twenty years down the road than the other way around?

Still, there was that night the family and I were watching an episode of *Unsolved Mysteries* about a husband and father of five kids in Galena, Kansas, who got on the tractor one morning and left it sitting empty at the crossroads of a state highway five miles away, engine still running.

"He was murdered," Lauren theorized from her spot on the love seat. "Or kidnapped, maybe."

"By aliens," B. W. said, his mouth full of popcorn. I reached down and took a handful for myself.

"He ran out on them, Lauren," Michael muttered from the floor.

"How could anybody do something like that?" Lauren shot back.

"Maybe he just thought if he plowed one more row it'd be the death of him," I said quietly, my mouth full.

Michelle glanced across at me, but with the kids present she didn't dare ask whether I spoke from personal experience. Not until later.

Not until bedtime.

One of the rules of our marriage had always been that when we talked at night, after the kids were in bed or otherwise absent, we would be totally honest with each other. I am not a compulsive truth-teller—I believe that there are sometimes situations in which a lie is less harmful and certainly kinder than the truth—but over the years, I had never told Michelle an out-and-out whopper at bedtime, and I felt confident she had been equally forthcoming with me. I would not say it had always been easy or that it had bound us together in unbreakable chains of marital trust, but certainly it had never done permanent damage to our relationship, although it might occasionally have altered—or eliminated outright—the cuddling or other activities that might reasonably be expected from a married couple at bedtime.

"J. J., what did you mean, earlier this evening?" she asked, sitting down on my side of the bed, still fully clothed. I generally went to bed after hearing the weather on the ten o'clock news, sunup coming awfully early, but Michelle was a night owl and often stayed up to read or work or listen to music.

"Sometimes," I said, "I can understand how people might want to get out from underneath all that. It's not always joy and bliss being Farmer Dad."

She ran her finger lightly down my arm. "Bad day with Michael?" It was a logical question. Our eldest supposedly had a job working the closing shift at the local Pizza Hut, which would account for his being gone all night and sleeping all day. When he was here and awake, he was surly, if he bothered to speak at all. Still, that wasn't it, and I think she knew it.

"No," I admitted. "I didn't even see Michael until I sat down in front of the TV tonight. I wasn't one hundred percent sure he still lived here." I reached up to her, tried to pull her toward me, and she did lean a bit closer, although she made me come up the rest of the way to meet her. After she kissed me once, softly, and nuzzled my cheek, she stood up, walked to the door, and hit the light, leaving me in darkness.

"You know, I do understand," she said as she closed the door, and maybe she did, although it was also true that late that night when she came to bed and snuggled close, rousing me from a light sleep and dreams of far away, she whispered into my ear, as she sometimes did at such times, "J. J., do you love me?" and I muttered back, somewhat less than half-awake, "You know I do, Shell."

And this, I swear to you, was gospel truth, for however it was that we began our life together, Michelle is a wonderful woman, and if it took me a long time to accept just how wonderful, I did learn at last. I could not have imagined a better mother for my children, or a wife who cared more for me. Michelle knew me so well, had loved me for so long, that perhaps she did indeed understand the sad, sorry, shameful impulses that could make a man imagine leaving his tractor, his home, and his family, those same impulses that make up most of the story I am to tell you.

All of these things went through my mind on that sunny September day in 1994 as I listened to Don Henley sing of forbidden love, loud and raucous on the tractor's cassette player, as a fly pattered forlornly against the inside glass of the enclosed cab, as the warming sun dropped slowly toward the far rim of the Canadian River Valley a few miles west: things from my past, present, and future. I had been around long enough to understand that, taken all together, these were the truths about life: Things had happened; things were happening; things were going to happen.

The last of these truths remained mysterious to me, as it must. But all the same, with so much thoughtful time on my hands, I couldn't help but sit and wonder.

Did my future include another twenty years on a tractor in red dirt, turning ever inward on myself? Or would there come a day when I drove straight and true toward the far horizon?

Birthdays

That horizon seemed far indeed, because to get anywhere of consequence in western Oklahoma you have to travel quite a spell. We lived twenty miles from Watonga, where we worked, went to church, attended school sporting events, and visited friends and family, but like most small towns, people seemed only too happy to escape it. Lauren already was informing me on a regular basis that to do any real shopping she needed to be taken to Weatherford or El Reno, each an hour off, and naturally she'd prefer to go to the Quail Springs or Penn Square malls in Oklahoma City, a distant City of Oz rising from the grasslands where we went once or twice a month to stock up on food at Sam's or to see a movie.

So my world was limited to what it had always been—a town that was already drying up by the time I came along and long unrelieved hours on the farm where I grew up. The farm consisted of two plots of land: 280 acres where we lived on the house my grandfather built in the 1940s—always called, not surprisingly, the Home Place—and 320 acres around the section line road where sat the remains of the house my great-grandfather built in the 1920s, which we called the Old Place. The fields I cultivated were, variously, red sandy soil or dark brown soil thick with clay. The pastures in both places were rolling hills covered by grasses and hillside clumps of cedar and scrub oak, and there were oaks and towering leafy cottonwoods in the creek beds and ravines where they could sip water. Five creeks crossed our land on their short progress to the Canadian River, and my parents had dammed up two of them to create ponds, although only one was still worthy of the name, and on Saturdays I used to take the kids down to fish in it.

Like my father, I raised wheat as a cash crop, alfalfa to make hay, and kept cattle, with some chickens to tempt coyotes and provide eggs or an occasional Sunday dinner. Over the years the kids had raised a few sheep and pigs to groom and show, but like most of my neighbors, we were pretty much a cattle and wheat operation, eating our own beef, growing vegetables in a summer garden, keeping a fruit orchard.

Both Michelle and I were raised in a culture that made do—that raised its own food, cooked it, cleaned up after it. So it almost always required a special occasion to get us to a restaurant. Two weeks after my long afternoon of tractor-bound soul-searching, Michelle and I skipped Sunday evening services at the Watonga First Baptist Church and drove out to have a steak dinner at the Roman Nose State Park lodge in honor of her birthday. We could have had grilled sirloins out of the freezer, which I told Michelle halfheartedly as we drove to the restaurant. "But it's different if we don't have to cook it," Michelle said. "It's my birthday. I want somebody to serve me for a change."

"I brought you a glass of tea the other day," I said. "I wait on you hand and foot. I am a slave to your every desire."

Her eyes crinkled when she smiled, and even though her face showed our twenty years together, it was a lovely face, and I told her that, too. "Happy birthday," I said, and I leaned over and kissed her. "May God give you many, many more."

She was wearing what for her amounted to dress-up clothes: a big crinkly skirt, a colored T-shirt with a Navajo-themed vest over it, and brown pointy-toed cowboy boots. In warm weather, Michelle attended church in a sundress; she generally taught school in faded jeans and a tie-dyed T-shirt. She refused to get with the program, and I loved her for that. I told her that when she started getting her long hair cut and frosted by the beauty operator, I would start playing dominos with the old farmers downtown.

The hostess, who was one of Michelle's former students, showed us to a good table with a window overlooking the golf course and the tiny lake—more like the size of our pond really. After taking our orders (T-bones done medium-well and charred), the waitress— another of Michelle's former students—brought salads and bread, and Michelle tore into them with the joy of someone who hadn't had to participate at all in their preparation.

"You didn't talk to me about your day yesterday. How did the sale go?" she asked as she spread some butter on a slice of bread. I had been at the weekly cattle auction in Geary the day before and picked up some calves at a little less than two hundred fifty a head. In the spring, after they'd gained about three hundred pounds on the wheat that was now starting to sprout, I'd sell those that made it through the winter for two hundred dollars profit each, God and Mother Nature willing. All I had to do over the next six months was feed them, keep them well, keep them warm, and get them to market.

"Bought seventy nine head," I said. "Some pretty good calves. If all goes well, we'll be in business for at least another year."

"What did you have for lunch?"

"Burger, fries, Coke, and a piece of pie. Mmm. Apple." The auction barn had a little café where the cook did the miraculous, whipping up roadhouse delicacies within smelling distance of tons of manure. You wouldn't think it'd be a stimulus for a healthy appetite, but all the same, I made a good meal between auction lots.

"Well, I don't remember it spoiling your dinner." And she crinkled her eyes at me again, as if to say that she knew nothing on God's green earth would ever do that. Fact is, if I didn't get out and run with the kids during basketball practice I'd look like Pavarotti, and as it is, I have a gut that never quite goes away. I've grown to accept it, like I've learned to accept the white hairs sprouting on my chest and at my temples, my own set of wrinkles around the eyes. I accept them, even though I get a twinge deep in my gut when I look in the mirror and see a middle-aged man looking out at me.

"Uh, right," I said. "Let's talk about something else." I took a deep breath, let it out, went on to another subject. "I went out and shot baskets with B. W. this afternoon before I came in to get cleaned up. He took me two games out of three. Good games, though."

"Oh. Oh." Michelle laughed and then caught herself, covering her mouth with her napkin. "That reminds me." Michelle drew herself up proudly. "National Honor Society met Friday before school. B. W. was elected president."

"This I have been told," I said, chewing my food thirty times the way my mother taught me. "What's the latest on the Lauren makeup crisis?"

"Oh, it gets better. She wants to know if she can double-date."

"Maybe with us. Was that her intent?"

She gave me a look of derision, and deservedly; what junior high kid wants to be seen with parents or even wants to acknowledge their existence? "I think not. Let's present a common front. What do you think?"

Cherry, our waitress, came back to ask us if things were okay, which they were. "I think the usual things," I said when she walked off. Where Lauren was concerned, I was against makeup, against double-dating, against the onset of puberty itself. Like the progressive parent she was, Michelle tried to keep me up-to-date on Lauren's physical changes, but to be honest, I didn't want to hear about that, didn't even really want to learn secondhand by pulling training bras out of the dryer or carrying in grocery sacks containing feminine hygiene products. Ideally, I would have preferred for Lauren to remain prepubescent until the moment before her wedding.

I didn't have my head in the sand. I mean, I watched the news, I talked to my buddies over coffee every morning at McBee's, and I heard firsthand from Michelle that girls Lauren's age were having sex, that these days twelve-year-olds were having babies. And as somebody whose entire life was changed by becoming a parent, I was scared to death that Lauren would accidentally screw up her life and not the least bit sure I knew how to keep her from doing it. Although at the time it would never have occurred to me, I think I longed for Rocket Ron Reagan, for the bad old days of the cold war; I missed the looming specter of nuclear destruction and the knowledge that the AWACS base at Tinker Field—not far away, outside Oklahoma City—was a primary target for all those Soviet ICBMs.

Back then I could submerge my purely personal fears; how could you obsess about kids and crops when the world as we knew it might disappear any moment into mushroom clouds? But now that the Berlin Wall had come down, I was forced to think about too many other things.

"I think we probably need to give her The Talk," Michelle said after the waitress cleared off our salad plates and set down our steaks. We had wondered when to say what to Lauren about sex, although she probably knew more about sex as a seventh grader than we had in high school.

"Forget that," I said, cutting up my baked potato so the butter and sour cream could fraternize more freely. "I say let's confine her to her room for the next eight years. And what do you mean 'we'? I didn't notice you anywhere around when I was giving B. W. and Michael The Talk."

"Well, let's think about it." This, or something similar, was Michelle's way of deferring action I had spoken out against. She actually would think about it; I'd forget about it, and the next time she brought it up, I'd have to try to deflect her reasoned arguments with bluff and bluster.

"Oh, that reminds me," I said. That, or something similar, was my way of changing the subject. "I had a talk with Bobby Ray over coffee this morning." My old friend and teammate Bobby Ray was now another of the group of farmers and farmer types who met daily at six or seven for caffeinated rural fellowship. Despite his round of business failures over the years, he had amassed enough personal capital to get elected to the school board, so my talks with him were sometimes farmer to farmer, sometimes lord to vassal. "He said the money was iffy for new uniforms this year."

Michelle was chewing vigorously, but she managed to curse around the steak before turning bright red and looking left and right to see if anyone had overheard. "They don't pay you a cent for coaching. And those uniforms have holes in them. How can he say such a thing?"

"We did get in some new basketballs this week." I sighed. "Leather balls at forty bucks a pop. But, Shell, it's not like we're talking about football here. They'd find the money for football uniforms."

"Football." She raised her eyes heavenward and shook her head. "Football is a stupid game. It's a game for human tractors. It doesn't require grace or stamina—"

"It's the only sport people in this state care about anymore," I said, and it occurred to me that, free coach or no, as far as some folks were concerned, Watonga High School basketball could disappear, could sink into the swamp, leaving only a few disconsolate bubbles behind to mark its passing.

"Oh well," I said. "That's life."

"Hey," she said, laying down her knife, "we should hold a benefit concert. Basketball Aid. I'll invite Jackson Browne and the Boss."

"Right. I'll give Paul Simon and Peter Gabriel a call." I checked my pockets. "I think I've got their numbers right here."

"Sting."

"Oh, right. And Bonnie Raitt. And John Mellencamp." We were both laughing again, and the evening went on its appointed way. It was a good birthday.

So I forgot about the impending fiscal crisis in boy's basketball to concentrate on nursing eight sick calves back to health. It wasn't until practice actually began a few weeks later that I remembered Bobby

Ray's warnings, and then it was only because before our first practice I took a look in the closet where our game jerseys were hanging and got a good look at them; they had so many holes in them they were starting to look like our mesh practice jerseys. But that was a problem for later; I had my mind on the here and now.

As always, on the first day of practice I had a mixture of old hands and new talent. Most of the young kids hung back around the edges as the lettermen shot. Tyrel Sparks was the exception—only a sophomore this year but totally fearless. I'd been watching him play schoolyard ball for three years. Jimmy Bad Heart Bull and one or two other boys would be joining us after football ended, but for the most part, these twelve would be my team. I stood back for a moment, caught up in the possibilities of a new season, and watched them shoot, listened to the sound of basketballs thudding dully against the hardwood floor and echoing off the upper reaches of the old gymnasium, breathed in the dim odors of decades of perspiration and floor wax.

When they'd had a few minutes to shoot around and get warm, I blew the whistle and gathered them all together for the first time, an event I had anticipated for weeks, an event I had lost sleep over for days.

I had never really thought of myself as a coach. I was once a smart player, and I loved the game. But I never planned on being a coach; fate dropped me into the position. I read the few books on coaching basketball available at the Southwestern State University library in Weatherford, books written by coaches of NAIA champs in the 1950s, books that extolled the virtues of the two-handed set shot, books illustrated exclusively by line drawings of white players with crew cuts. They added nothing to my knowledge. Everything I knew about coaching came from my own high school years under Von Parker and from repeated viewings of Gene Hackman in *Hoosiers*.

I had coaching philosophies: I favored good aggressive man-to-man defense, transitioning from defense to offense by moving the ball upcourt quickly, and, on offense, a mixture of crisp ball movement and individual initiative. But even with some idea of what I wanted, it was all I could do to speak when I stood in front of a team at the first practice, whistle around my neck, clipboard in my hand. On this afternoon, I lifted my head, looked briefly at each of them—including B. W., who was grave and only blinked at me—and forced the words out in a low, neutral tone.

"My name is John Tilden. Some of you I already know. The rest of you I'll get to know if you stick around. You can call me 'Coach' or 'Mr. Tilden.' I don't care much which."

I paused for a moment. The boys stood in various degrees of nervous discomfort, standing arms crossed or not meeting my eye, waiting for me to go on. Their anxiety gave me extra confidence. Pitiful, wasn't I?

"Twenty years ago I played on the team that won that state championship." I pointed to the faded banner hanging proudly on the wall of the gym next to the scoreboard. "I can't promise you the same kind of success. All I can promise is that we're going to work hard, we're going to get in shape, and we're going to have fun. We'll win as many games as we're supposed to if we do all of these things."

Then I started them on drills—dribbling to the foul line and back, to midcourt and back, to the other foul line and back, to the far inbounds line and back. I had them do touch-pass drills, bounce-pass drills, baseball passes. I had them dribble to the far end of the court and back, alternating dribbles between their legs.

"Between your legs, Frank," I called to one of the new boys. "Not off your legs." B. W. and the seniors could do this without thinking, but some of the new boys always had trouble. "It's not a hot dog move," I shouted out as they struggled slowly upcourt, sometimes bouncing the ball off their feet and chasing it off the court, sometimes bouncing it off more sensitive parts of their anatomy and doubling over. "It's a way to keep part of your body between the ball and the man guarding you." In a week or so I'd change the drill so that they guarded each other on the way upcourt, all to demonstrate what it was good for; while it wasn't always an appropriate move, they could do it when they needed to if they'd done it repeatedly, and that was the idea behind all of these drills—repeating actions until they became second nature, until the body had memorized them like the brain memorizes a face or a line from a song.

We worked on some very basic plays: screen and roll, backdoor passes, dribble penetration, and passing out to the perimeter. Kids these days don't think much about passing thanks to watching the NBA, people playing one-on-one even when it's five-on-five.

After we'd done drills, I let them scrimmage full court, four-on-four, winners keep the court, until all of them had had a chance to play at least once. They played hard, with exuberance if not always great skill, and there were some nice moments: Tyrel faking his brother off his feet and Martel returning the favor on his end of the floor, Micheal Wilkes driving the baseline, Bird Burke dropping in the fadeaway jumper from twenty, B. W. directing traffic. They were pretty much done in by the time everybody had played, drenched with sweat and bent over, clutching their shorts and puffing for air, the sure signs a player has given it everything he has.

They were almost finished.

"Okay," I said, checking my watch for effect. "Twenty laps around the court. Winner doesn't run after practice tomorrow. Go!" And off they went, shoes squeaking, jostling for position, an initial pack like the starting line of a marathon. Micheal Wilkes or one of the Sparks kids would probably win; they were the best natural athletes on the court. But sometimes B. W. or one of the others, someone with less pure physical ability but more want-to, would get caught up in the contest and surprise everyone. That, too, was part of whatever strategy I had.

While they ran, I shot baskets, starting off with one at the free throw line, a daily ritual, and then around the perimeter at about twenty feet.

"You ready?" came the voice from behind me. Carla Briggs—tall, her long brown hair in a ponytail—stepped around the hard-puffing Ramiro Garza, already mired toward the back of the pack, and joined me on the court. Carla was three years out of college, our high school girls' basketball coach; she also taught history. I liked her, although I knew she was too bright and too intense for us to keep for long. She brooded over each loss as though it were a battle fought over actual territory, as though actual human lives were lost. Because of her, the girls played miles above their potential, and they won more games than anyone had a right to expect given the middling pool of talent we drew from, which meant that someday soon Carla would move on to some 5A basketball powerhouse or maybe a college assistant job and I'd be left to break in a new one-on-one partner.

Until then, I had a partner in crime. She would often come by after her sixth-hour class and shoot with me once my practice ended. Usually we'd end up playing one-on-one as the boys finished their laps and either collapsed into the bleachers to watch or trudged back to the showers. We also sat together on those occasions when both teams went on a road trip, but at such times, even though it was harder for us to talk, I draped myself across the seat behind her instead of sitting next to her in the narrow confines of the bus. You see, despite the fact that Michelle sometimes dropped by after school herself to shoot with us or to chat with Carla, I had to be careful not to spend too much time alone or in conspicuously intimate circumstances with Carla. Rumors started easily in a small town. Even though my civic spirit in coaching the team had been noted and applauded and I had been largely forgiven for my one youthful indiscretion, the past always seems to be sitting within easy reach of anybody who wants to pick it up.

"How do your kids look this year?" she asked, launching an effortless arc from the top of the key.

"God only knows," I said. I rebounded her made shot and bounced the ball back out to her. "Yours?"

"Better and better," she said, shooting again with the nonchalant flip of the wrist that I ached to pass on to my kids. "We could win a few games this year."

"I don't doubt that," I said, passing it out to her again. "You warm?"

For answer she drove the baseline, gave me a head juke to get me in the air, and stepped around me to lay it off the backboard.

"Ah," I said, passing it to her to check. "New move."

"Had to do something," she said, giving ground slowly as I dribbled back into her. "You waxed my butt the last couple of times we played. I couldn't stand for that." And, of course, she couldn't. That was one of the reasons I liked her.

Michelle called my name when we were tied at ten and distracted me enough that I practically gave Carla a seventeen-footer.

"I'm going home to fix dinner," Michelle called from the sideline; she was wearing boots and knew I wouldn't allow her on the court proper.

"I'll be along in a second," I called back, dribbling as Carla watched warily. "Just as soon as I—" and in mid-sentence I cut to my left, then stopped to pop a jumper "—finish this game."

"Sneaky," Carla said.

"Learned it from you." I waved as Michelle exited.

I won seventeen-fifteen, and dinner was ready and on the table when I got to the house, thick juicy fried hamburgers for everyone but Lauren, who had a bowl full of green stuff in front of her and a paranoid look on her face as she looked around at her dining partners.

"What's up?" I asked.

"I am now a vegetarian," Lauren said. "I will no longer be a party to the beef conspiracy."

"The what?" I looked across at Michelle, who shrugged. Not her idea, this.

"The beef conspiracy," B. W. said, already three bites into his second burger.

Lauren speared a slice of cucumber. "I've decided to quit FFA," she said, crunching happily. "Or at least stop showing cattle. I refuse to be party to their exploitation."

"Okay, now you're just quoting somebody," B. W. said.

Lauren stuck out a green-flecked tongue at him.

Future Farmers of America, blue jackets, and livestock contests had been a part of Lauren's life since she was conceived. Before, even. I stood staring at her. Something must have kidnapped my sweet, beef-eating daughter and replaced her with this Stepford Vegetarian.

"Beef is high in cholesterol," Lauren explained to me, crunching. "And Mrs. Anderson said cows overgraze the land and release millions of tons of ozone into the atmosphere, or something like that."

B. W. shook his head. "It's methane, or something like that."

"Whatever." She arched her eyebrows dramatically. "Anyway, now you know. What are we going to do about it?"

I sat down and picked up my first greasy burger, a slab of thick melting Watonga cheddar on top, spread top and bottom with Selmon Brothers barbecue sauce, just the way I liked it. "Lauren, we raise cattle. Our family has always raised cattle. That's what we do." I took a bite, and dear Lord, it was good. "Anyway, people love hamburger. They love a good steak."

"Why don't we at least raise emus?"

"Emu?" I blinked a couple of times like the poleaxed steer I was, looked at Michelle as though to say, *she's your daughter*, and tried to turn my attention back to my food. It almost worked; I was almost able to block out the ode to emus that followed.

It was pretty sad; not yet forty years old and I was already hopelessly behind the times. Either that or I was being treacherously undermined by some kind of secular humanist seventh-grade science teacher. Why didn't Mrs. Anderson spend more time teaching them that life in a one-horse town could be hazardous to their long-term development instead of turning my daughter into an advocate for flightless birds?

Of course, that night when she couldn't go to sleep, whom did she call? Her cow-murdering father.

"Tell me a story," she said, as she still sometimes did when I looked in on her and found her still awake, and I went into her darkened room, the vague outlines of teen love gods whose names I didn't know peering from posters on the wall.

"Doesn't it ever get spooky to have all those guys watch you undress?" I asked. "The correct answer, by the way, is yes. It will always be spooky to have a guy watch you undress."

"Oh, Daddy," she said as I sat on the edge of the bed and she wriggled away so as not to be pinned down by the comforter. "Try not to be so strange."

"What kind of story do you want?" I asked, knowing that it didn't really matter, that all she really wanted was the sound of my voice. The next morning she never seemed to remember the stories I told.

"You pick," she said, and yawned.

So I told her a story I'd recently heard Robert Bly tell a gathering of men on a PBS special on television. It was supposed to symbolize something about manhood, I guess, since that was what the special was about, although I had just watched it because Michelle wanted to listen to Bly, one of her favorite poets. Anyway, it was the only story I could remember just at that moment.

"Once upon a time there was a king and a queen. They lived in a castle, and near the castle was a vast and dangerous forest." As she settled farther down into her pillow, I told her that the king had sent a small group of hunters, then ever-larger groups of hunters into the forest, and none of them had ever returned, and soon nobody went near that forest. Her eyes closed, and she began to breathe regularly. "When a young man came along looking for adventure, the king told him that if he was looking for adventure he could point him in the right direction, and so off he went into those woods alone, except for his dog." By then I could hear her snoring, but sometimes if I stopped she would jerk back upright and demand to know what was wrong, she was listening, so I kept going.

"The young man walked deep into the forest and it became darker and darker, and ominous shapes moved all around him as he walked through a murky bog. Then all of a sudden, a monstrous hand reached up from the water and yanked his dog under."

Her breathing was deep and regular. I thought about stopping—but I was close to the end, and I didn't want her to sit up and say, "What happened?"

I patted her reassuringly. "Now, the young man didn't panic. He just stood there for a moment, reflecting, and said, finally, 'Well, this must be the place.'"

I sat there watching her chest rise and fall. I counted to three hundred—five minutes, or thereabouts. I placed my hand gently on her forehead, prayed for her safety and for wisdom. Then I got up and slipped out of the room, pulling the door shut behind me.

Michelle and I had adjourned to the living room after dinner, and while I had been telling Bly's story, she had put on the Eagles' *Hotel California* and was listening to "Wasted Time."

"Everything okay?"

"Lauren wanted a story," I said, as I leaned over her shoulder and nuzzled her cheek.

She turned her head to kiss me fully on the lips. "What story did you tell her?"

I went around and sat across from her. "I told her the plot of that Mickey Rourke movie we saw that one time. You know, the one set in Brazil, with all the naked women?"

She rolled her eyes and went back to her grading. I got out my pen and paper and started writing letters.

I wrote my parents, happily living out their golden years in Arizona.

I wrote my baby sister Candace at the University of New Mexico, lovely Candace, who came along as a menopause baby (although of course my mother would never use that word, referring as it did to a bodily function) after Michelle, Michael, and I moved into this farmhouse and my mom and dad were forced back into the same bedroom for the first time in my awareness.

My folks were inclined to regard Candace as some kind of miraculous replacement for my big brother, Trent, who graduated from Watonga in 1967, joined the Marines to fight communists, and was killed during the Tet Offensive at the siege of Khe Sanh. Most of the time I was inclined to agree with them, although, of course, even the most wonderful children can't replace those you lost, something those who think that the book of Job has a happy ending just don't understand.

I even wrote one of my rare letters to Samantha and Bill in Rockwall, Texas, a letter addressed to both of them although I didn't like Bill and imagine he returned the feeling. Still, it let us preserve the illusion of lifelong friendship.

Everyone tells me that letter writing is a lost art, and all I can say about that is, if it's true, it's a shame, a crying shame, as Oz would say. I never liked the telephone and would rather have had a few heartfelt lines penned as the mailman approaches than an hour of telephone talk, the voice in my ear a parody of intimacy.

Maybe it was true that I had never been farther than Dallas—well, I'd once been to the ocean at Galveston on a youth trip—but it wasn't true that I never got out of town. I left almost every night, transported on the broad backs of words. While Michelle graded her papers and made out lesson plans, I wrote letters, little bits of myself carved paper-thin and stuffed in envelopes that would wing across the country, carrying me to all those places—all those people—I couldn't see in person.

Michelle said she did not believe in letters. She said that with computers and the information superhighway coming, paper would be as obsolete as Pop Rocks, the Oh Henry! bar, and the record player.

But, of course, she said this while a turntable in the cabinet behind her filled the air with sweet music.

I just smiled at her and kept on writing.

Michael's nineteenth birthday fell not long after Michelle's, and she and I crossed our fingers that with his teen years almost left behind he would now become a model son and citizen. Hey, it was worth a shot; we didn't see anything else on the horizon with much of a chance of changing him short of an exorcism or a lobotomy.

The whole family—Lauren and B. W. with various low degrees of enthusiasm—prepared to throw him a party. We called those friends of Michael's we knew and could stomach and invited them to come out to the house for dinner; we even called Michael's girlfriend, Gloria, a twenty-four-year-old woman with black hair, clothes, and fingernails. I always thought she looked like the consort of Satan in an old Hammer horror film, but Michelle liked her, since Van Morrison and U2 both wrote songs entitled "Gloria."

Michelle arranged with Mike's manager at Pizza Hut to give him the evening off. I gave my team the afternoon off and set out a dozen thick T-bones to thaw. Lauren baked a chocolate cake. B. W. did Michael's chores, although it wasn't really to recognize the birthday—he had been doing most of Michael's chores for years.

About six, I went out to fire up the charcoal grill and was joined by our old hound dog, Frank, not much of a help with charcoal but something of an authority on steak. I saturated the charcoal with lighter fluid, stepped back, and flipped in a match. There was an eyebrow-singeing *whoomp*, a miniature Hiroshima fireball, and I walked back inside to season the steaks while the charcoal burned down.

I met Michael coming down the hall from his room and ventured some conversation. "You want to come outside and help me with the steaks?"

He stepped around me as though I were a street person who had wandered into his path and walked out the back door, straight toward his truck, my last Chevy except for one.

I had a bad feeling about this exit. I followed.

"Where you headed?" I asked brightly. He turned to look, and his keys jangled in his hand as he prepared to get into his truck.

"Out," he said, and he climbed in and slammed the door behind him.

A miniature Hiroshima went *whoomp* in my gut, and I was around the front of the truck in a flash, grabbing the door handle and pulling it back open. "Just where do you think you're going?" I asked.

"Wherever I want," he said. I could feel my pulse pounding in my temples, and I was sure that at that moment I didn't present the most pleasing sight. Maybe if I'd been a little angrier a long time ago, things could have turned out different.

I kept my hands tight at my sides, struggled to pronounce these words calmly: "We're having a party. For you. Your friends are coming."

"No, they're not," he said, a touch of impatience in his voice now. "I told them to blow this off and meet me in town."

I tried one last time. "Michael, we're having a party for you. Here. Now. Your family has planned it."

He wouldn't look at me, just leaned over so that he could turn the key when I was finished. "I didn't ask you to do that," he muttered, and then he spoke a vile word, just loudly enough for me to hear, and he cranked the engine to life.

I leaned in some myself and cocked my head sideways. "What's that?"

He revved the engine.

I took his arm above the elbow, none too gently. "Michael, what did you say?"

"I said I don't want a birthday party," he said, snatching his arm out of my fingers, and now he looked up at me and his eyes burned with hatred. *Hatred.* "Do I look like that big a loser to you?" He snorted. "A birthday party? Dad, are you *trying* to ruin my life?"

Maybe you should never ask a man questions when he's angry, or maybe some lunatic germ of errant truth-telling betrayed me. "Why not?" I said. "You ruined mine."

And it was out, impossible to take back, impossible to pretend that I hadn't ever thought it.

Impossible that I hadn't meant it.

"What?" he asked, and for a second his eyes were wide and his face was more stricken than angry.

"I'm sorry," I said, and I was, sorrier than I could ever express. Shame burned in my cheeks now instead of anger. "I'm sorry I said that. It's not true."

"I know it's not true," he said, and his voice rose into a higher register. "You screwed up your own life." He pointed a finger. "You did it. You were so hot to get into each other's pants that you didn't think about anything else, did you? You didn't think about me, didn't think about how my whole life people would talk, point their fingers."

"No," I said, and the fireball was gone, and I suddenly felt very tired and very old. "We didn't think at all." I turned to go.

"You didn't want me, did you?"

I looked back at him. His gaze was direct, piercing, and I was not used to it, not from this young man who hadn't met my eyes for what may have been years. I wished I could lie, tell him that I had been excited, tell him that I looked forward to his birth with the anticipation shown by the shepherds in Judea.

But that was a lie.

"No," I said. "Not when your mom first told me. I had other plans."

He smiled now, a horrid smile, maybe because for the first time he had found a place of congruence with me. "I guess you thought that your life was just totally screwed." He didn't say this, exactly; he actually used that same vile word, and while normally I' would have told him that such language was not welcome around me, it seemed like the least important thing in the world at the moment.

"Yes," I said. It was true. "That's what I thought then."

"And what do you think now?"

I took a deep breath. "I think it all turned out for the best."

He shook his head, smiled as though I amused him. "That's pretty weak, Dad."

I felt a momentary smolder at this, but it was quickly gone. It *was* pretty weak. Still, I had to say something. "This is the only life I'm going to get, far as I know. And I did get something good out of it, after all. I got this family." I actually managed something like a smile. "I got you."

He was unconvinced. Maybe what I had to say didn't matter; maybe he'd had this conversation or one like it in his head so many times that now he couldn't hear anyone else.

"You would have been happier without me," he said.

I put my hand on his arm again as he prepared to close the door, but gently this time. "I thought so once. Not now."

He shrugged off my hand and shifted into reverse.

"Michael, please don't go," I said, and again felt shame washing through my veins, a father reduced to pleading—pleading—with his son.

He looked at me, and now there was nothing in that gaze, not anger or fear or even pity; there was just nothing, like he was looking at a tree or a mailbox.

I stepped—almost fell—away from the truck, and Michael slammed the door shut and sped off. At the end of the driveway, his truck became a wispy cloud of dust rising from the road to town.

I walked to the barn, climbed up into the bales about twenty feet off the floor, and leaned back on one, the hay bristling against my back and neck, the smell of dust and decay strong in my nostrils. The smell brought to mind another fall afternoon I'd sat in this barn.

Years back, Michael had decided to stop playing junior high basketball. He wasn't good at it; he'd gotten other things from his parents besides athletic skill, I guess, but still it hurt me to hear him say he was giving it up. "I hate it," he had said then, his lip curled with contempt. "I think it's a stupid game." And nothing I could say in the next few days could convince him to just have fun with it. He turned his head away, walked back into his room, and turned up his heavy metal.

But there was an afternoon a week or so later when I had pulled the truck around back of the barn to load some hay, and I heard the sound of the ball bouncing on the slab of concrete my father had poured as a makeshift basketball court. I walked through the back of the barn and stopped far enough inside that I couldn't be seen. I sat down on a bale of hay and just watched as Michael shot and missed, shot and missed, his form awkward and ugly. He stood there at the free throw line, missing shot after shot, and he was sobbing like his heart would break.

I can't say for sure why he was shooting baskets when he thought I wasn't around any more than I can say why it made him so sad that he was no good at it. All I really knew was this: I had struggled to love Michael since the day he was born, and maybe I didn't do such a good job of hiding it. At the very least, he must have noticed that we didn't have much in common. Maybe Michael thought I would love him more if he were a basketball player.

Sad.

What's even sadder is that he was probably right.

After awhile, he checked his watch and dragged himself off toward the house, the ball bouncing behind him. And I just sat there in the hay and watched him go.

Michael probably didn't remember that afternoon. But I always would, and I had always kicked myself for not talking to him, for not trying to build some kind of bridge between us.

It was hard, and never got easier. How could people so alike not understand each other in the least?

Did he think he was the only one who had ever had the desire to get in his truck and run?

I had had my share of those impulses over the years: to stop farming and find a vocation, discover what I could have made of myself; to find out whether Samantha still felt any of the things that had led us once to talk about a life together; to leave Michelle and the kids and a twenty-year accumulation of responsibility, disappear forever, become an unsolved mystery.

But I never acted on any of those temptations. Any of them.

Whatever else I was or had done, whatever words I might have used to describe myself—disappointed, stolid, intelligent, quiet—the words I most wanted to apply to myself were simply these: decent and honorable. At times in my life, that decency had seemed an almost intolerable weight to bear, but who knows? Maybe at other times, without my knowing it, it may have buoyed me up, floated me across raging rivers that otherwise might have dragged me under.

Maybe in trying to do what I believed to be the right thing, I had actually done the right thing, at least on occasion.

This, at least, was my fervent hope.

When I heard Michelle calling from the house, I got down from my perch in the hay. I walked across the yard to the patio, where she stood looking down at the charcoal, now nicely white.

"I think it's ready, J. J.," she said.

"He left," I said, and my voice broke. Michelle put her arms around me, and I bit my lip to keep from betraying anything else.

"I know," she said. "I'll bring the steaks out." And she pulled back to look at me, and I could see the sadness—my sadness—reflected in her eyes. But she brought out the T-bones on the platter where I'd laid them out after rubbing them with cracked pepper and I put them on the grill, and you know what?

The sound of them sizzling and the smell rising up with the smoke didn't just make me hungry. They were some of the best steaks I ever ate.

Lauren's cake was pretty good too.

I could almost feel glad there was more left for the rest of us.

Almost.

October 7, 1994

Miss Candace Tilden
P.O. Box 97443
University of New Mexico
Albuquerque, NM 87106-7443

Dear Candy,

Hey, kid! How goes it? Know you're setting the curve in your classes. You always do. What's your favorite this semester?

Are you still seeing Arturo? Is it still serious? More importantly, have you told Dad about him yet? You know you're going to have to one of these days. You can't just show up on their doorstep and say, "Hi, this is going to be your new son-in-law," although come to think of it, that's just about what Michelle and I had to do. But one such trauma in your parents' lives is probably enough, so avoid that method if you possibly can. See if you can't find a way to introduce him into conversation; maybe they'll surprise us.

I like to hear you talk about him, by the way. It seems like I can hear in your voice what he means to you. I can hear pride and affection and—if you'll permit the observation—passion. Just be smart, and be prepared. I don't begrudge you your fun, God knows. Just be careful.

Have you been out hiking lately? I also like the way you talk about those Sandia Mountains. It makes me want to hop in the truck and head out your way. Maybe someday I will.

Mom and Dad seem to be feeling okay, if you can trust them. How did they look when you saw them last? Let me know if they're not giving me the whole truth.

Michael has moved into some new transitional phase, and we're not speaking just now. If you can, will you call and check on him for me so I know he's okay? I think he just might talk to you.

In any case, call or write soon. Your big brother always loves to hear from you and know that you're all right.

Love,
John

October 7, 1994

Mr. and Mrs. John Tilden
7743 Sunny Acres
Phoenix, AZ 85372

Dear Mom and Dad,

How's life in the desert? Had a letter from Candy, and she says she's visited recently. I'm sure that was a nice homecoming. She's turned into a beautiful young woman, smart and capable. Know you're proud of her, and you certainly should be.

Basketball started today, Michelle's classes are going well, and the new calves are putting on weight. Speaking of cows, remind me to tell you a funny thing that Lauren said recently about cows. You're going to love this, Dad, I know you are. Just remember that she didn't get this idea from me.

Then again, why don't I let her tell you when you see her next? Yes, I think that would be best. Let her take credit for her own ideas, I always say.

Michael's just as moody as ever. I don't have the slightest idea what to do with him, about him. Was I ever like this? I don't think so. At least, I like to think I was like B. W., quiet, hardworking, studious, obedient.

And yes, now I can hear you laughing all the way from Arizona. Okay, okay. Maybe I wasn't quite as wonderful as he is, continues to be.

Alma Cooper asked after you at church Sunday. Told her you were well, just growing cactus instead of wheat these days. You should have heard her cackle. Glad I didn't tell her during the sermon. Hope I was right in assessing your state of being, that your ticker isn't giving you any more trouble, Dad, and that you've been sleeping better, Mom.

Did you ever suppose we'd be sharing these kinds of details with each other? I sure didn't. But then, life is a constant and ongoing surprise to me.

Write soon with some wisdom. I always appreciate your advice, even if I never seem to take it.

Your son,
John

Philanthropy

We stayed mad at Michael for some time, all of us, and I suppose I should have taken some parental action right away, although I don't know what that action might have been. Anyway, something else came along that promised to distract us from purely familial difficulties for awhile. I got my first notion that something out of the ordinary was up when B. W. rushed into a stall at the back of the big barn, followed closely by the dog, Frank, who had stopped to snuffle some particularly choice manure.

I was working with one of the calves that had a stubborn case of pneumonia and was probably going off on wobbly legs to that great salt lick in the sky, but the sight of B. W. in a hurry, which he rarely was anywhere off the basketball court, shook me. My first impulse was that he brought news of some tragedy: my parents, Michelle's parents, some friend dead or dying.

"Don't kill me," he panted, his breath clouding in the early-morning chill. "I'm quoting. Mom says you need to get your butt in to the phone. It's important."

"How do you know?"

"She put her hand over the phone and hissed at me. And that's what she hissed."

"Okay," I said, and I got a little unsteadily to my feet, maybe from the blood rushing out of my brain. Hissing. Rarely a good sign. "Okay."

I hurried off after him, past the old chicken house—now a storage shed—past the barren site of next year's garden, and into the house through the back porch.

In the kitchen, Michelle had the receiver to her ear and was saying "Uhn-huh. Uhn-huh. Sure." As soon as I came in, she put her hand over the mouthpiece, whispered, "It's Bill Cobb," and made a sort of "Why on earth is he calling us?" face, one eyebrow raised, her other features squinched. I let out a sigh of mingled relief and resignation. While I was glad there was no tragedy, I didn't want to listen to Bill talk about his wonderful expense account, his wonderful house, his wonderful life.

"Here he is now," Michelle then said brightly into the phone and gladly surrendered it to me, for which I probably made a "Thanks a lot" face if there is any justice in the universe.

"John," Bill Cobb said in his big, hearty Republican businessman's voice. "Only have a moment, but Sam said that in your last letter you talked about some financial problems in the old hometown."

"I may have," I said.

"Something that affects the basketball team."

"Ah," I said, remembering my last letter. "Currently it's uniforms." Moth-eaten jerseys. "Next year it'll be something else. But this year it's uniforms." And I made Michelle's "Why on earth is he calling us?" face right back at her as she finished packing her lunch across the counter from me—an apple, celery, and some low-fat yogurt with wheat germ liberally sprinkled over it.

"Exactly," Bill said. "This year it's uniforms. Next year, who knows? So here's my proposition. I'll donate the money for the uniforms. I think I can write it off as a charitable contribution. But I can't be expected to bail out the school year after year."

"No," I said. "Of course not."

"The community is going to have to chip in. Some kind of fund-raiser. And I have a wonderful idea along those lines. Simply wonderful."

"I don't follow you," I said.

"It's very simple," he said very slowly, speaking with the kind of tolerance that always let me know he thought I was stupid. "I'll donate the money for your uniforms. And you help me get the team—our team from seventy-five—back together to play a fund-raiser. We'll use the proceeds to set up an endowment for future expenses for the basketball team. Maybe we could play against your current varsity. That has a nice symmetry to it. What do you think?"

I thought that perhaps Bill Cobb didn't understand precisely what the word "symmetry" meant, but that was no kind of an answer.

I looked around. Michelle had kissed me on the cheek and was gone with Lauren; B. W.'s tiny truck had already putt-putted away; Michael, if he was even in the house, was sleeping soundly. There was no one left to make faces at, for which I was heartily sorry. There were things I wanted to say and knew I shouldn't.

One thing I longed to say was, "You know, Bill, not all of us are that anxious to be reminded of the past. Not all of us feel that our lives have proceeded in quite so orderly a fashion as yours." But what would be the point of it? It would be like trying to convince my Cheyenne friends that white men had always had their best interests at heart, like telling my farming friends hereabouts that we should all raise emu.

We all see reality in a particular way, generally for pretty good reasons, and things that clang against our vision of that reality usually ricochet off again without doing serious damage to it.

"I think," I said finally, when the long-distance hum on the line became apparent and speech became impossible to avoid, "that it would be generous of you to help us out. But I don't see how we could possibly get our team together. I'm sure you're still in pretty good shape, but we've got a couple of guys who'd be courting heart attacks. And maybe Sam mentioned to you that Phillip One Horse doesn't seem to be feeling particularly social these days."

"Oh, I'm sure you can bring him around," Bill said, and even from four hundred miles away I could see him making that dismissive rising hand gesture I always hated. "Anyway, that's my deal. Call me back and let me know what people think."

We needed those new uniforms—needed them, that is, if we didn't want to be the laughingstocks of the conference. I didn't see how any of the rest of what he proposed could work, but the thought of his hand sweeping up like a backhanded slap, brushing difficulties and objections from its path, drove me back out into the yard, slamming the back door so hard it rattled in the frame.

Maybe nothing would ever come of it, I thought on the way back out to the barn, my sick calves, and the smells of manure and dust, but once we had his check in our mitts, I didn't much care what happened afterward. I wouldn't feel sorry for taking his money. Bill could afford to be magnanimous; he won. He got everything: the girl, the car, the house, and whatever is behind curtain number one.

"I think it's a great idea," Lauren told me that night while we shoveled feed for the calves. "Could I bring a date?"

"I'd like to play," Oz said at coffee the next morning. "And it'd be great to see the whole team together again."

"Phillip won't come," Bobby Ray growled, "and even if he would, I'm not sharing the court with a criminal."

"If you'll just act like we'll do it," I told him, "I think I can get my uniforms. Nothing else actually needs to happen."

Or so I thought. This was one of the many miscalculations I made that fall.

When Oz and his wife, Caroline, came out to the farm for lunch that Sunday after morning services, he had cooked up a plan that was going to elevate Bill's half-baked idea to a different plane: completely baked.

We were loitering over cherry pie and coffee and making small talk while the dishes soaked in the sink when Oz turned to Michelle and said, "I've got an idea about the reunion, but if you like it, we'll have to get on it right away."

Michelle raised an eyebrow. Although she and Oz were both on the Watonga High Class of '75's permanent homecoming committee and we were slated to have our twentieth anniversary that next summer, she had already set up a dinner catered by End of Main, one of the few dining establishments left in town. That was her responsibility, she had carried it out with distinction, and I could see by her expression that she wasn't particularly keen on changes or further complications.

"It would take a lot of work," he went on, oblivious, "but Bill's idea for a fund-raiser made me think of it. What if we moved our reunion to coincide with the game between our team and the Watonga varsity, moved it from summer to Christmas vacation? Don't you imagine that people would come back to town to see The Team play again?"

"But they have seen us," I said. "Even with Bill in Texas and Phillip in exile it's not like any of us are dead or living on another continent."

"Ah," he said, smiling, and he raised a long, thin pharmaceutical finger, "but have the five of us been together since graduation?"

I took a sip of the dregs of my coffee and realized he was right. At our last reunion, the warden at McAlester Penitentiary had requested Phillip's presence. When it came down to it, the five of us had never really even hung out together in school, although some of us had been social off the court.

"I guess we haven't," I said. "But this game is never going to come off. Don't hang the whole reunion around it. It'll just be a disappointment."

Caroline sat forward and spoke for the first time in quite awhile, maybe since we'd sat down to dinner; if Oz could rightly be considered quiet, she was a conversational black hole. "But, John, if it could happen—did anything happen that year that was more important than the state championship?"

Oz nodded forcefully.

Michelle and I each, without consulting the other, glanced quickly down the hallway toward Michael's room, where he may or may not have been in attendance.

"Maybe for some people it was momentous," I said, finally. "But it's just not going to happen."

"And why not?" Oz asked. "You can schedule the varsity for an exhibition like this. We can surely find a night during Christmas break when the gym isn't in use."

I looked over at Michelle to see what she was thinking. Her bottom lip was in between her teeth and she was worrying it like she always did when she was trying to decide something. "The game could work," she said, looking back and forth between Oz and me, "if you old folks will agree that it doesn't mean anything, that it's not a way to reclaim your lost youth or something ridiculous like that. Because you can't. John's high schoolers will beat you, no matter who you were twenty years ago."

"Maybe," I said. I hoped they would. While much of what Michelle said made sense, I wasn't sure yet that my kids could beat somebody's seventh-grade varsity on a good shooting night.

But there was more: "I also thought we could have a dance the night before the game," Oz said. "Decorate the gym, all that. We could have rock, disco, country from the seventies. The game could be open to the public, but the dance would be just for the reunion folks."

"A dance?" I asked in mock—but barely mock—horror. "What will the pastor think when he hears that two of his deacons are planning a dance?"

"I think that's probably low on his list of worries," Oz said dryly.

Michelle's teeth were still worrying her lip through this exchange, but at last she said, "I'll talk to Sharon about it, see if we can get the information out in time, get some reaction. If we set this up for sometime after Christmas, we've got about three months." She sighed. "That's not much time, but if people really want to do this, I guess we ought to give it a shot." Sharon was Bobby Ray's first wife, yet another member of the class of '75 marooned in Watonga, and as former head cheerleader, nobody had a better finger on the pulse of the student body, then or now.

"Everybody I've talked to has been wild for the idea," Oz said.

"You haven't talked to Phillip One Horse," I muttered.

But it was clear that I was outvoted. I was just the court leader of one team and the coach of the other, so what possible weight could my vote carry?

"A dance," Michelle said later as I was climbing into bed and she climbed in after me. "I love to dance."

"I know," I said. I myself did not. I could not scoot a boot, cut a rug, do anything on a dance floor that someone would recognize as rhythmic motion except maybe line dance, and there I could get by because mostly people were too busy to pay attention to what anyone else was doing. I could slow dance, for what that was worth. In fact, I preferred to, since my idea of dancing was that it should be something closer to passion than aerobic exercise.

"I love to dance," she said again, in a lower, throatier register, and she threw one leg over me, and bent low to nibble at my ear.

"I know," I said again, although by that point I didn't really know anything except my fingertips moving across her body and my lips meeting hers and my body rising to greet hers and a lot of sweet movement, noise, and sensation.

Maybe there was something to the idea after all, no matter where it came from.

The next time I saw Bobby Ray, a few mornings later at coffee, I threw in the towel, threw up my hands, threw out the baby with the bathwater: "Why don't you call Bill Cobb and officially accept his offer to send us some money?" I said, although before I'd uttered the last word he was shaking his head.

"You're the coach, you made the contact, you're going to have to make the arrangements. Besides, I've never liked the son of a gun."

"Oh, and I do, right?"

But I said I'd do it.

That night, while the family watched *Murphy Brown* in the living room, I, with pulse racing—have I mentioned that I can't abide the telephone?—dialed the number on our old rotary phone, the line crackling with the background noise common to rural connections. My heart began to speed up as the first ring burred through the miles between us, and then the second. My finger tapped at the cradle, and I wanted to hang up, but I let it ring a third time, a fourth, and then there was a click and a tinny version of Bill's voice, strange and almost funny without the deep baritone, crackled into my ear.

"You've reached the Cobbs. We're unable to come to the phone right now, but if you have business with us, please leave your name and number—"

Business. No thanks. I hung up before the message concluded.

"Any luck?" Michelle swung around the corner to check the refrigerator.

"Nada," I said. "Nobody home. Hey, how was school today?"

She turned and gave me a floodlit smile. "Wonderful. The seniors are getting ready to start bringing in their music. I played 'Tomorrow's World' and talked about what I want them to do with their reports." "Tomorrow's World" was a song by Joe Jackson, one of the only songs about the future, Michelle said, that saw it as something worth looking forward to. "I still get choked up when I listen to it."

Her enthusiasm was always contagious, at least for me. "Do the kids get choked up?"

She scarfed a carrot out of the crisper. "Who cares?" she said as she exited, the commercial break timed to perfection. Michelle's classroom philosophy was that, as long as mama was happy, the rest would follow, and she was generally right.

As she got settled back in front of the television, I could hear laughter—Michelle, B. W., Lauren, and a simulated studio audience. The din from down the hall, the direction of Michael's room, was Guns 'n' Roses, *Appetite for Destruction*. I guess all of us have a golden age, and for Michael, maybe it was 1987; maybe this music reminded him of better times.

Maybe, or maybe it reminded him of satanic rituals. Lately Michael's behavior was making me believe in the possibility of demonic possession.

I toyed with the idea of going in to tell him to turn it down, but I'd heard it louder, and it seemed wise to save such an interruption for something more serious, since the "while you're under my roof, young man" gig was never one I played very well. It must be God's judgment on rebellious children that they almost always become the parents of even more rebellious children.

So I closed the door in the hallway, walked back to the living room, poked the fire, settled into my chair, and picked up Scott Turow's *Pleading Guilty* where I'd left off.

Practice the next day got off to a slow start. The kids had been hearing rumors about some kind of exhibition game over Christmas, and they had a zillion questions.

"So we gonna play some old guys?" Tyrel Sparks asked, one eyebrow arched skeptically.

Martel Sparks elbowed him and hissed in his ear.

"I mean," Tyrel said, his eyebrow dropping and a cheesy grin spreading across his face, "four old guys and you, Coach?"

"That's about the size of it," I said, laughing. "If it ever comes off. Red team—get in here." I passed the ball in my hands to B. W., who was going to run a new play I'd drawn up.

"If we're gonna have to play an extra game, I think we should go on strike for more money," Micheal Wilkes said as they were walking onto the court; God help us, they were already thinking like the pros.

"C'mon, you guys," B. W. called, bouncing the basketball once for emphasis. "Less talk, more action." And at that, the five on the court got serious. B. W. passed from the top of the key to Micheal posted low and to the left of the basket. Micheal could either take the shot, pass off to Martel coming back door, or whiz the ball back out to B. W., who looped on around to the baseline for what we hoped would be an open jumper if he could shed his man on Bird's screen.

They ran it again and again while I shouted off instructions: "Roll and shoot. Hit B. W. Back door. Set it up out front." Then after they'd gotten some feel for all the different ways the play could flow, I called the second five onto the court to run it and pulled the first five to the side to watch. It looked different, of course; Albert Heap of Birds didn't have B. W.'s graceful jump shot or keen passer's eye, but still it was a decent play.

Then I put the two squads out there together and had them try to defend against what they'd just learned to run. The second five had a rough time of it, both ways. Except for Jimmy Bad Heart Bull, still playing football, this was all I had, and it wasn't encouraging to see what was actually out there once you got past the first four or five boys. One time, though, Albert Heap of Birds actually succeeded in shaking B. W.—Ramiro Garza managed to successfully set his screen by stepping in front of B. W. at the last second (illegal, last time I checked)—and Albert popped a fifteen-footer and raised his fist in triumph.

B. W., meanwhile, shoved Ramiro Garza so hard that he tumbled backward and down onto one knee. Before Ramiro could get up—one of the few times I was grateful for his slothlike speed—I was in between the two of them.

"Step back," I said to B. W., planting a hand firmly in his chest to stop his forward progress. "What's wrong with you? Have a seat."

He dropped his head and walked off the court. I checked my watch, sighed, and shouted, "Okay. Do your laps. I want to see you running, every last one of you." And before B. W. could get up, I raised one finger to stay in place.

"I'm sorry, Coach," he said, eyes down. "I don't know what got into me." When we were on the court together, he said I wasn't his dad anymore, and I should treat him the same as anyone else. Well, here was my chance.

"A ref might have called a moving screen there," I said, my voice barely carrying over the trample of feet as the pack passed in front of us. "And he might not. You have to keep playing. You know that. Remember how mad you and I used to get when Scottie Pippen was standing under the Bulls basket arguing with the ref while his man was scoring at the other end?"

"Yes, sir." Apparently Lauren was the only child still willing to look me in the eyes; I hoped she'd keep that ability, although I didn't have much hope, given my experience with the other two. If we didn't resolve the homecoming double-date controversy soon, she'd probably run off and join a circus or whatever it is kids from unhappy homes do these days.

"Okay. Hit the floor," I said. "And I want ten extra laps for your display of temper. This whole team looks to you to see how to act. You can't lose control out there. Ever." As the words came out of my mouth, I realized that this kind of leadership was a lot of responsibility for a seventeen-year-old, but he had to shoulder it, both for his sake and for the team's. There was no way around it.

"Yes, sir," he said, and he joined the thundering herd without a look backward.

I wondered what he was thinking as he ran.

He didn't talk to me at dinner or afterward, although I couldn't tell whether that was from embarrassment or anger. Michelle tried after supper and at bedtime reported that she couldn't crack him either. "Not a word. It's like we suddenly grew another Michael. Perish the thought."

"I've got to get out of this house and away from Lauren before it's too late," I said with a sigh as I pulled off my jeans. "She's the only one I haven't screwed up yet."

Without warning, Michelle wound up and slugged me in the stomach—hard—and I doubled over and fell backward on the bed, my feet tangled in my Levis.

Then Michelle—a Baptist deacon's wife, another deacon's daughter—cursed and said, "Don't you ever say something like that again. Ever. Do you hear me?"

"I was just kidding," I gasped, quickly, since she had her fist raised again.

"I don't care," she said. "You're a good father, John. A very good father. And what's more, you are not responsible for everything that happens on this planet. Do you hear me?"

I heard, if only distantly; my breath was starting to whistle back into my lungs again. "Ugh," I muttered, experimentally. I tried a groan. "Why did you do that?"

Her fists unclenched, and although I flinched, she dropped her hand softly onto my stomach. "You made me mad," she said, patting gently the site she'd just excavated. "I'm sorry. But that was a terrible thing to say."

"I was just kidding," I repeated.

"Some things aren't to kid about," she said as she sat next to me on the bed, and then she sighed, and I could see that she wasn't angry anymore, only sad and sorry. "You've made some mistakes, sure. We both have. But Lauren really loves you. No, she *adores* you. And I think they all want your approval, in their own ways, but Lauren really wants you to be proud of her."

"Lauren thinks our cattle are contributing to some worldwide ecological catastrophe. Maybe I should check into her emu idea. Although it would change our whole way of life." I felt the corners of my mouth threatening to turn upward. "Imagine the rodeos. Those birds could peck some poor cowboy to death."

She snorted, and a wisp of a smile began to spread across her face. "Emu wrestling," she suggested.

"Emu roping."

"Hot emu action," she said, doing an echoing voice like the

tractor pull announcer. "Vicious Mexican fighting emu, bucking cowboys to their doom." She wasn't mad anymore, and her face bore a sad smile. "I love you," she said. "I'm sorry I got so mad."

"Punching people bad," I said in my best *Hulk smash* voice.

"I know," she said, and then her smile turned into something that wasn't the least bit sad. Frisky, maybe. "Shall I kiss it and make it better?"

"Oh, by all means," I said.

And for once, she let me have the last word.

Bass Fishing

Michael and B. W. were both sitting at the breakfast table when I stepped into the kitchen after feeding the calves the next morning. I thought at first that this togetherness boded well, that it might be an omen of something good for the family, but then I walked into an atmosphere so thick you had to push your way through it, something like wading thigh-deep in the pond, and I knew my hope was futile. B. W. was at the opposite end of the table from Michael; both had taken refuge behind cereal boxes.

I sat down between them, asked for the Raisin Bran, in front of B. W., and the sugar, closest to Michael. They passed these requested articles across to me without looking up from their bowls, without even varying the upward and downward rhythm of their spoons.

"It's going to be a beautiful day," I murmured as I poured an untidy heap of flakes into my bowl, "just beautiful," and instantly regretted having opened my mouth. The glance I got from B. W. was indecipherable and could have gone either way, but the look from Michael was pure scorn: a beautiful day. What Sesame Street reality, exactly, was I stepping out of?

I might just as well have launched into "Oh, What a Beautiful Morning" and done a snappy dance with trained emu. He would not have found me more ridiculous.

So we sat, nothing but the sound of our crunching—and, eventually, our spoons clattering against the bottom of our bowls—to break the silence. Then each of them rose without another word to go in their different directions: B. W. to school, where he would be arriving early, Michael to bed, where he would be arriving late.

And I just sat there in the silence they left, looking for some sort of key to unlock it and not finding one.

When I got up from the table, rinsed out our bowls, and put them into the dishwasher, I stood for a long time looking at those three lonely bowls in the bottom rack, and I decided that I needed to do something to get some perspective.

I thought I knew where to go.

There was a place down at the pond I always liked to go, down in a hidden valley where the sun warmed the red sandstone bluff in the winter and a breeze could find me beneath the big red cedar in summer. Everybody has favorite places, and this was mine: With the sun sparkling off the water and the smell of cedar in my nostrils, I would drop my line over the bluff, five feet to the water and sometimes thirty feet under it, where descendants of the largemouth bass stocked long ago by the Oklahoma Department of Wildlife lounged in tangles of brush, waiting for something edible to drift down their way.

Ours was not a beautiful pond. The water was greenish brown (except after a rain, when it was tinged red with the runoff from the sandstone), and the gray gaunt tips of cottonwoods that once grew along the now dammed-up creek still stuck through the surface in places. The fish were mostly gone, since relatives and freeloaders had been sneaking down there without permission for years. But all the same, that bluff on that pond had been my special place for almost—good God, could it be true?—forty years. This is where I always went when I felt life crowding in around me, and after I had the calves settled, the ones on cows suckling, and the ones on feed happily chomping, I tossed my rod and tackle into the truck, drove the short distance to the dam, and climbed over a hill and down to reach my bluff.

There I sat at the edge, a heel braced against a protruding root, just in case. I'd almost been pulled in more than once by a fast-escaping bass, even if it was more surprise than anything else. Still, it was best to be prepared. Wouldn't do for me to fall in, whatever the season. My boots would fill with water and I'd probably sink like a stone, down through the layers of warm and cold that varied by season—during summer, hot as bathwater at the surface, chillingly cold four feet beneath; during winter, cold through the first five feet and warm enough beneath to support life all through the winter.

On that morning, I tossed my line into the water, baited with a pink wriggling earthworm from the washtub full of earth I kept in the old chicken house, where the worms fed on coffee grounds. Leaning back against the red rock, which over the years had either in reality or in my fancy conformed itself to my shape—or maybe vice versa—I let my line float, red and white bobber drifting about ten feet above the hook.

A hundred yards away, out of sight but not out of my hearing, the creek that fed the pond fell over the red rock into the standing water beneath. Wherever I went on the farm, I liked to think that I was within range of the waterfall, and sometimes, on spring nights when we slept with the windows open, the sound floated to us through the

screens, borne on the wind, soothing, calming, the silky sound of
magic waters. On those nights, I slept like a baby.

But now there was a slight tug on my line, my bobber dancing a
little jig, and I set the hook, or would have, if there'd been anything
there. Something had been nibbling at Mr. Worm—actually it's not
a good idea to anthropomorphize your bait—and I had a pretty
good idea what that something was. I cast again and lay back, one
tiny piece of my mind on the bobber, the rest drifting. It wasn't that
important to me whether I caught anything; I often threw back the
perch or sunfish I hooked and even the occasional bass or catfish.
The fish I caught were often simply the punctuation at the end of a
beautiful sentence.

Someday, I thought, I'd like to reach the point of Zen-like
harmony where I could be like one of those fly fishermen who catch
and release, the experience of fishing amidst the burbling waters being
the only purpose, but at that time, I didn't see much hope for it. The
previous winter Michelle and I had watched *A River Runs Through
It*—the tape rented from the Four Corners convenience store where
Michael's Gloria worked, in fact—and I had felt the waters pulsing
in my veins as I watched it. When the movie was over, Michelle
turned to me and said, "Someday, we'll go there."

"Where?"

"Montana."

"Sure," I said, although I didn't have the slightest faith that such
a thing would ever happen. Bass fishing would have to do.

There was a stronger tug on my line, and this time I set the hook
with a jerk and felt a tangible presence on the end, could almost
see the flash of tail and the line trailing downward. The rod bent

only slightly as I alternately reeled and raised it skyward, so it wasn't any monster down there, but all the same he was a fish of some substance.

I wanted to get him to the surface before he had a chance to play any games with the sunken brush, and I thought I was reeling him in with sufficient speed to do that, but I guess my thoughts had been drifting a little too far, because with a sudden alarming curve of the rod, my reeling stopped and the solid feel of fish had been replaced by the even more solid feel of tree trunk.

I whipped the rod side to side a few times experimentally, gave it some slack and tried again, but nothing happened.

"Oh man," I muttered, and I could feel disgust bubbling in my stomach. It wasn't the loss of hook or worm, or even the loss of fish. It was just a further symptom of my recent inefficiency; if I'd been a car, I could have been taken in for a tune-up, but people usually just go on idling rough until they stop running completely.

I hoped that at least the fish had gotten free, that after winding my line around and through a branch or two he had taken off for the deep to tell some fish stories of his own. But I feared that he, my line, my hook, and my worm were still intimately connected, snarled through his natural actions in trying to escape his fate, feared that his last moments would be the realization that his universe had collapsed to limits he could not thrash his way out of.

Like I said, it's dangerous to start assigning human qualities to things when you're out fishing.

I cut my line and my losses, trudged back up the hill, down the other side and around the bank to my truck, and then I drove on into Watonga, although practice wouldn't start for hours. On the way, a Harley passed me, bearing an old man in ostrich boots and a Levi jacket and a woman I presumed was his wife, who certainly was the largest old woman I'd ever seen on the back of a hog, wearing an electric blue jumpsuit. They looked like they were having a great time, off on some kind of adventure. I wondered where they were going, when they would get there, and if I would ever be bound someplace like Montana—someplace besides church, school, the pond.

I couldn't imagine what it would feel like. But I guessed it would make you feel like wearing electric blue.

I pulled into the parking lot behind the gym as the sun went behind a cloud. When I got out of the truck there was a noticeable chill in the air, and I rolled down the sleeves of my denim shirt and buttoned them at the wrists. I thought I might wander by Michelle's classroom to see if she could get away for lunch, so I crossed into the main building and down the long hallway, empty except for the echoes from my boots on the tile.

Outside Michelle's partially opened door I heard her voice and paused to listen. "This next poem is a prayer." A communal groan followed. "Now, don't lose your cool. You know I'm not here to preach to you. But this is beautiful and should make you think. And I'll bet you can't guess where it comes from."

"I'll bet you're right about that," a girl muttered, and everyone laughed.

I heard Michelle walk back to her desk, and without seeing her, I knew she was sliding up onto her desk, crossing her legs at the ankles, looking out at her kids, and preparing to declaim. "New Hymn," she said, cleared her throat, and began to recite.

Halfway through, when wild men were clawing at the gates for bread, a male voice said, "That's dark, man. It don't sound like no prayer I ever heard."

"Hush up, Tyrone," said a female voice, not Michelle, and then Michelle said, "Give it a chance. There's more," and she went on, ending with an invocation to whatever Presence and Maker there might be to be here—now.

There was a hush as she finished. I felt the moment too, and there was some kind of wetness in the corner of my eye through the last eight lines; the woman could recite a poem, and this was a fine one.

She let the silence last as long as it would, and then when some rustling and shuffling began to surface, she asked, "Anybody want to guess who wrote this?"

"U2?"

"Amy Grant?" asked a sweet voice.

That suggestion was hooted down.

"Reynolds Price," I said quietly into the silence. But it was loud enough to be heard inside, if just barely, and then there was the sound of footfalls proceeding purposefully toward the doorway, the sight of Michelle's smiling face, and the tug of her hand urging me to follow her back into the classroom.

"The ultimate result of a life lived in close proximity to poetry," she said, presenting me to her class. "This, ladies and gentlemen, is an educated man."

"One of my many skills," I said, while inside, I winced. *Uneducated, you mean.* "How is everybody?"

A chorus of replies drifted back, ranging from "Okay" to "Cool" to "Hey, Coach!"

I looked around, saw some kids I knew. "I thought maybe I could drag your teacher off to lunch. When is lunch, anyway?"

"Now," Michelle said, looking at the clock with a rueful expression. She turned back to the class. "I wanted to talk about the song. Tell you what: I'll play the James Taylor recording for you tomorrow and we'll get back into it that way. Okay?"

If there was acquiescence, it was granted en masse and in motion as the bell rang and within seconds the room was empty, leaving just the echoes of their departure, the smell of chalk dust, Michelle, and me.

I gave her what I hoped would come out as a smile. "You have time to go downtown?"

"Sure," she said, pulling out her keys to lock up and beckoning with her head toward the door. "A choice between lunch with you and grading papers on my planning period? I'll take you any day."

"You say the nicest things," I said, and she slipped her hand into mine as we worked our way down the hall against the flow of boisterous kids. "How did poetry go today?"

"They liked Don Henley," she said. "I had them write short response papers to 'Dirty Laundry.'"

"Ah, the planning period papers," I said, and she nodded. "Was this an all-male day then? What happened to gender equity?"

She punched me—but gently. "We did Indigo Girls yesterday. And Shanezia Wylie brought in something from one of those female rap groups about black men not giving black women any respect. The women were hooting and the guys all picked out floor tiles to stare at."

We got into the truck and headed for the Hi-De-Ho diner, which we'd frequented since we were kids, the kind of place that calls cut-up iceberg lettuce and Thousand Island a salad, where the gum-snapping waitress pours endless glasses of tea into colored plastic glasses full of ice that looks like rabbit pellets, where the jukebox is stocked with songs that haven't been on the charts for decades, yet nobody complains, or should.

Once Eileen, an angular woman with peroxide hair teased skyward, took our orders—the daily special, which on this wonderful day was chicken fried steak with cream gravy—Michelle took a sip of her tea, folded one hand over the other, and sat looking at me.

"What?" I said after about fifteen seconds of this.

"You didn't call Bill this morning, did you?"

I slapped my forehead in exasperation and hoped it would look like a genuine symptom of consternation.

It didn't. "You never take me to lunch unless you're feeling bad about something. You're transparent." She speared a chunk of lettuce. "Work on that."

"I'll call this afternoon," I said.

"Maybe you think you're going to put this off until someone else does it for you," she said, smiling. Actually, I did sort of think that. "It's not going to happen. He made the offer to you, and only you."

"You answered the phone when he called," I said hopefully.

She shook her head forcefully. "Nope. Not a chance."

I sighed and tossed my lettuce around the plate so it would get coated with Thousand Island. "Okay. I'll call this evening. When he gets home from the office. If I can stay up that late."

She patted my hand. "Good for you. I'll stand right behind you."

I had a momentary flash of irritation. "I believe I can at least manage a conversation on the telephone."

We sat in silence for a bit; I think she felt that she had pushed a little too far. Maybe she had. I might be a social misfit, but I was capable of dialing the telephone, even if I didn't want to.

I finally said, "How'd you get from 'Dirty Laundry' to 'New Hymn'? That's quite a stretch."

She looked up and made a rueful smile to acknowledge the uncomfortable moment and its passage. "Well, we've been talking about how a lot of poetry deals with social issues. You know, men and women, the environment, politics, the media. We're starting to move into the section where I want them to see how literature addresses individual concerns."

"Including finding out where you fit in with the man in charge?"

"Something like. If it is a man, which I have my doubts about."

"Heretic," I announced to the diner at large. "Grab some stones." The only woman who looked up just rolled her eyes and returned to her food.

Our orders came then, and I launched into my chicken fried steak, not exactly tender, but certainly edible. "I do like that song," I said. "'New Hymn,' I mean. I'm not sure I've ever really listened to the words before. I feel that way sometimes, like I'm calling out and He doesn't hear me."

She nodded vigorously, her mouth completely full of lettuce, and I couldn't help myself.

"You're beautiful," I said, and she stopped chewing, the edges of her mouth curled up slightly, sadly, and she brandished her fork at me in mock threat. "I mean it," I said. "You are. With your mouth crammed with lettuce and a spot of dressing on your chin."

"Oh." She took care of the dressing with her napkin. "Did

B. W. speak this morning?" she asked, and watched me closely as I responded.

"Not to me," I said.

"Ah," she said. "He will. You'll see."

But he didn't talk to me at practice, and he didn't talk to me at dinner that night. Which was just as well, because Lauren and I launched into a spirited but amicable discussion concerning the minimum age for dating. She maintained that perhaps cavewomen had waited until sixteen to car-date, but women at the end of the twentieth century were considerably more advanced. I contended that her mom was the only woman at the table, and that perhaps a dating novice could try her hand with an occasional parentally sponsored evening of entertainment.

"Dad," she said, with a snort, "I would feel like a complete loser if you guys drove us around." She paused. "No offense."

"None taken," I said, trying to live up to that sentiment.

"Do you even know any guys with cars?" Michelle asked.

"Not the point," she said through a mouthful of greens.

I looked at B. W. "Any opinions?"

He shrugged and dropped the full piercing intensity of his gaze onto his steak, as though cutting a T-bone required his complete and undivided attention.

That was the most we got out of him. In fact, right after dinner he got up from the table, went back to his room, and would you believe that loud music began to issue forth. Bryan Adams, I think, "Summer of '69."

Michelle and I exchanged a pursed-mouthed glance. "I'm going to call Bill after dinner," I said, finally, shifting us from one pleasant topic to another. "We're going to try and put that game together."

"Good," Lauren said brightly. "I like seeing B. W. play. Now I'll get to see you both play at the same time."

"Who said you're going to the game?" I said, and smirked at her when she looked up in dismay.

"You're a stinker," she said, but then she smiled, and I could tell that she still loved me. Michelle and I smiled at each other; Lauren pretended not to see that, but she kissed both of us on the tops of our heads as she gathered dishes.

"You're the best," she said.

"God help us," I said.

Morning Time

Although B. W. remained tight-lipped, after a few days—unlike Michael—he at least returned to speaking to me, and I got the sense that although he was upset about something, whatever that something was, it wasn't primarily me. Maybe a truly good parent would have rooted out the cause of his melancholy like a terrier burrowing after a gopher. I have to admit I was willing to let things ride for a bit rather than take the risk of sending him back into silence.

We conversed at the breakfast table again, at least when Michael didn't join us, which anyway was about every morning. We talked about practice. B. W. shrugged when I asked how he thought it was going.

"Okay, I guess. You're the coach."

While Michelle bustled around getting ready to leave, we talked about colleges, and he got a gleam in his eye when we talked about forestry. He had spent part of the last few summers after we'd finished harvest with other FFA kids at the Cimarron camp in the Sangre de Cristo Mountains in New Mexico, and he hoped to work as a ranger this next summer, taking groups out into the wilderness for two-week backpacking trips. While it looked like he would probably go to Oklahoma State, which had a good reputation for forestry, he really had his heart set on the high-powered program at the University of Montana in Missoula, and he said so again this morning.

"Well," I said, "let's hope you have another good season." There had been some interest from college scouts the previous year. "Maybe you'll get a basketball scholarship or get some help if you keep your grades up."

"Maybe." He sighed, and I sensed a danger spot, an open pit looming ahead, and eased cautiously around the edges of it. Instead, I asked him about Jennifer, his current girl, and he smiled big before catching himself. "Oh, she's good, she's fine," he said, filling his smile with a spoonful of cereal.

"Which one? They're not interchangeable, are they?" asked Michelle, dashing back into the kitchen to scoop her keys off the counter with an exasperated I'm-running-late groan.

"Yup," he said, and took another bite so he wouldn't have to say anything else.

"Okay," Michelle said, "I'm off to save Western culture. Any encouragement?"

"All memorable events transpire in morning time," I called after her, and was answered by a laugh and a slamming door. Henry David Thoreau said something of the sort, I believe, in *Walden*, and since Michelle annually taught him to her seniors and implored them to listen to his advice on life, I had sought out a few pungent quotations to employ on appropriate occasions—which is to say, when they worked to my benefit, which is the only reason anyone ever quotes anything.

B. W. and I were the only members of the family who happily followed Thoreau's admonitions to rise early and greet the dawn, unless you count Michael, who sometimes greeted it coming home, which I don't think was exactly what the bard of Walden Pond had in mind.

"Got to go, Dad," B. W. said, rising from the table with his bowl and juice glass.

"I'll see you at practice," I said, patting his shoulder as he went past.

He grunted, put his dishes in the sink, and departed, leaving me to bask in the auroral glow of morning by myself. Actually, I'd already been outside and it was brisk out there, wind out of the north, mid-forties according to the thermometer outside the kitchen window, which was probably about right for a low temperature in October. I was content to remain inside for awhile, and was thinking about going into the den and pulling Henry David off the bookshelf instead of driving into town for coffee when the phone rang.

I figured it was probably one of my coffee buddies wondering where I was, so I picked it off the cradle and said, "Yeah."

"Since when do the only two men in my life conspire behind my back?" Samantha Mathis Cobb purred in my ear. I knew that voice in the same way I knew the contours of the face I shaved every morning, but knowing that voice and being prepared to hear it were entirely separate matters. My breath left me like a covey of quail exploding out of a stand of tall grass, and my insides, whether straining to follow or exposed to the partial vacuum thereby created, knotted.

"S-Sam?" I stammered.

"The very same," she said. "Surprised?"

"Uhmn," I said, not yet trusting words. At least I was breathing again.

"What is this thing that you've talked Bill into doing at Christmas? A basketball game? What kind of middle-aged macho nonsense is that?"

"It's not *my* middle-aged macho nonsense." I felt I should point that out.

"Well," she said. "I thought not. So do you, uhm, like the idea?"

"No," I said.

"I don't either," she said. "So. What are we going to do about it?" We were planning the future again. Her voice was still soft, conspiratorial, and it sent a thrill shivering up my spine; it made me want to promise that we would stop the game somehow, that I would chain myself to the doors of the gymnasium, that at the homecoming dance the night before the game I would spike the punch and disable the team with food poisoning.

But what I said was, "It's a done deal. They changed our reunion to December because of the game. You should have already gotten something in the mail. Oz and Michelle sent things out a week or two back."

"Yes, I got something about that," she said. She paused for a moment, emitted a sound like a low hum, and finally said, "Well, a dance. I suppose something good could come out of this." She hummed again. "Save a dance for me, Johnny? I loved our dance at the last reunion. Do you remember?"

Oh, dear God. She would have to bring that up.

Did I remember?

Of course I did.

It had been one of the last dances at our tenth anniversary get-together. The Cars' "Drive" was playing, and as they sang, "Who's gonna drive you home tonight?" and I held her close, the years melted away, and it might almost have been that younger me, that younger her. While my hands stayed respectfully above the curve of her hips, my fingertips remembered and rememorized the small of her back, and I discovered that the smell of her hair still made me stupid, still made my heart catch in its steady progress toward middle age.

"Right. I remember it." I paused, spoke when my voice seemed steady. "I think I can set aside one dance, seeing as how we've been friends forever."

"Forever," she said with a sigh. "Has it been that long? Sometimes it seems like just yesterday. But I look at the girls, and they're fifteen and thirteen, and I've seen them grow, so it's not like the record skipped somewhere, jumped ahead. Oh, John, how did we get so old?"

"Two ways," I said, cribbing from Hemingway. "Gradually, then suddenly."

"No, it was all gradual. It's just the recognition that's been sudden," Sam murmured.

It was my turn to sigh. Before I could say anything else, she leapt in again, and the tone of her voice had gone from sharing secrets to making plans. "Johnny, one of these days we really need to talk about some things."

"We're talking right now," I said, although the hollowness in my chest told me she was speaking of something different, something considerably more involved than what we were presently doing.

"In person," she said firmly. "I think some things can only be said face-to-face."

The severity or importance of such talks is almost always directly proportional to the pause between "We need to talk" and the eventual conversation. So is the level of anxiety of the person so warned. Want to make someone sweat? Say, "We really need to talk. See you in a few months."

But I couldn't let myself think about any of that. "I've got to go, Sam," I said, and I seized on the first excuse I could conjure. "I've got to haul a dead calf off to the canyon."

"Well, that's a fine way to end a conversation," she said, but she was laughing, and the sound of Samantha Mathis Cobb's laughter was still as beautiful as the sound of my waterfall dropping musically into the pond. "We'll talk soon. Take care of yourself, Johnny."

"You, too," I said. "So long." I hung up the phone, stood up, then dropped my hands back onto the top of the cabinet to steady myself and shook my head so hard I thought I could hear something rattle. A nocturnal presence—Michael—passed on the way to pour himself a glass of orange juice and disappear again into his inner sanctum.

He glanced in my general direction and then back at the ground as he passed me on the way out. "Who died?" he muttered, although he didn't stop for any answer.

If even Michael saw how shaken I was, it must be pretty bad. "Come on, man," I whispered. "Shake it off."

Or, maybe, more properly, "Walk it off," which was what my coach Von Parker used to say, his remedy for any disaster that might conceivably befall a human being.

Twisted ankle coming down with a rebound?

Walk it off.

Your heart broken?

Walk it off.

Mysterious phone call from your old flame?

Walk it off.

So I walked. Out to the barn, where I pulled on a pair of battered gloves. Into a pen at the back of the barn, where the ex-calf, dead from pneumonia, lay on its side in its own sickly yellow manure. Out to my pickup, dragging the calf, which weighed at least what I did, by his legs, my own legs straining, boot heels slipping as I backed to the tailgate where I half lifted, half wrestled it into the truck bed, my old dog, Frank, snuffling delightedly around behind me. Out to the canyon, where my father and his father before him used to dump trash—there is no curbside pickup for farmers, let me assure you—where I backed the truck to the rim, climbed into the back, and pushed the body out unceremoniously. The deceased calf hit once, rolled partway over, and caught on some debris halfway down the canyon wall.

Maybe Lauren was onto something when she talked about bailing out of the beef conspiracy. I had just provided a meal for a coyote, a worthy project, maybe, but still the sight of the calf's stiff limbs sticking out into cold, empty air was enough to complete the job of ruining my morning.

And I'd had such high hopes for it, too, because I knew the afternoon was going to be ridiculously hard. Oz and I—Bobby Ray completely washed his hands of it—had agreed to meet at McBee's for lunch and then drive out to Phillip's place before practice to talk with him about playing in December.

"Think he'll shoot us?" Oz wondered when we decided to do this, and although he had called me from home, I had a vision of him hunkered down behind the pharmacist's counter at the drug store while bullets flew.

"He wouldn't shoot us," I said, with a confidence I did not feel. "We're old friends."

"No, we're not," Oz said. "Never were. Certainly aren't now."

He was right. I had been closer to Phillip than any of the other guys, been out drinking and driving with him, even tried to help him, but I didn't know what demons drove him, didn't know what had sparked him down the trail that eventually led to armed robbery and the penitentiary.

And yet we were going out to talk to him, to trespass on his turf, and as much as my body told me it wanted to put things off—or at least wanted more time to recuperate from my morning shock—the clock on the dash of my Chevy said 11:00, and we were supposed to meet in town at noon.

I went back and changed clothes, threw the ones I'd been wearing into the washer. I didn't want Phillip to think I was putting on any airs, so I wore another faded pair of Wranglers, another pair of work boots, and an old blue T-shirt under my jacket. Oz must have had a similar idea, because underneath his pharmacist's smock, which he untied before he climbed into my truck and then wadded between us on the seat, he was wearing an old pair of Converse high-tops, Levis, and an ancient gray sweatshirt, arms tugged up to the elbow, with "Watonga Eagles" across the chest.

"Couldn't hurt," he said when he saw me glance at his shirt and smile.

"Might help," I replied.

After lunch, we drove in silence out of town, past the entrance to Roman Nose State Park, and then down the dusty section roads toward Phillip's place. I had directions that my closest neighbor,

Michael Graywolf, had given me. When I'd asked him if he wanted to guide us personally into his cousin's house, he said, "No way am I setting foot on his property."

"Why not?" I had asked him.

He pulled off his black Stevie Ray Vaughan hat and rubbed his forehead. "Man, that Indian's in a world of hurt. I think our Grandma Ellen is the only person he hasn't shot at."

"Thanks for that encouragement," I said.

"Good luck, John," he said. "But you may be all right. He's not as good a shot if he's been drinking. Of course, he's more likely to want to shoot you then." He stopped and looked at me in what I hoped was mock seriousness. "You did tell Michelle to rent me your pasture if anything ever happened to you, right?"

"Thanks," I said again. "Let's hope it doesn't come to that."

It hadn't rained in town for what seemed like weeks, although I knew it couldn't have been that long. The dust billowed out from behind and under the truck, and once, when we passed another pickup, we drove in his dust for a quarter of a mile, the fine white powder coating hood and windshield and settling finally to earth again in the fullness of time.

Up ahead and to the left was the barbed-wire gap, and once we crossed it, we would be in Phillip's territory. I stopped in front of the gap. Oz looked at me, took a deep breath, let it out, and got out of the truck to let us in. He pulled the gate post out of its upper and lower barbed-wire loops, carried it back and in, and when I'd pulled the truck far enough inside, walked back to the loops, dragging the gap across the dry grass behind him and raising a miniature cloud of dust. Then he seated the post back in its lower wire loop, and with a slight nudge from his shoulder, eased the gap tight until the upper loop would fit back over the post.

"Bad fence," was all Oz had to say when he climbed back in. I had seen it too. The strands of barbed wire as far as we could see were loose and sagging, and some of the posts had broken or were rotting. No self-respecting farmer would present such a face to the world.

We followed a twin-rutted track through the dead grass, down a rise, and into a stand of cottonwoods. In amongst them nestled Phillip's small mobile home: white corrugated tin siding with aqua trim, old tires arrayed on the tin roof to hold it on during high winds, a protective grouping of junk cars guarding any approach with the assistance of some old appliances, a century-old plow, a pile of bottles, and a big black half-Brahma who raised her tail and delivered a powerful yellow stream of urine to commemorate our arrival.

We sat for a moment in the truck after I shut off the engine, and not, I assure you, because we were afraid of the big black half-Brahma heifer. But then I saw a curtain pull aside slightly in the front window, and I opened my door and got out, hands wide of my body so he could see that I came in peace.

Oz reluctantly followed my lead, and even from the far side of the truck I could see his huge Adam's apple rise and fall as he gulped.

Then the door opened with a screech of ill-fitting metal on metal, and the barrel of a .30-30 slowly emerged, rose, and looked me right in the eyes. I may have gulped then as well, although I don't remember it. All I remember was looking into the dark opening of that rifle and thinking that if Phillip One Horse was crazy or drunk enough to put eight pounds of pressure on the trigger, I was a dead man.

"Phillip, it's Oz and John," I heard Oz call, a catch in his voice. "Can we talk with you for a bit?"

The rifle did not move. I saw the bluish sheen of the barrel and observed that while everything else on the farm might be falling down around him, Phillip was still taking good care of this rifle. He always did love to hunt. He was a good shot, too, when he was sober.

These were the thoughts that finally propelled me to join Oz in hailing the castle. "Hey, Phillip, we just want to talk to you for a second. Can we come up to the porch?"

The porch was actually just four steps leading up to the door, but I wasn't willing to stand on formalities at that moment.

The rifle dropped, the door screeched open wider, and Phillip One Horse filled the doorway, as tall and broad-shouldered as I remembered him, and despite the passage of years, no bigger around the waist. The only real difference I could detect was that his long black hair was streaked liberally with gray.

"What do you want?" he asked softly, and his voice was not angry, but it was colored with sadness and weariness.

"Long time no see," I heard myself babbling, and in that moment wished he hadn't taken the gun off me; the resulting relief had pushed rational thought from my head.

"Yes," he said. "What do you want?" He seemed pretty sober to me.

"I don't guess you'd believe we just dropped by to say howdy," I said.

"You haven't been to see me once since I got out of prison," he said. "Why start now?"

"We've come with a proposition," Oz said, which may not have been an improvement, but then again you didn't have to be God in heaven to see that I wasn't getting anywhere. "We're getting our old team together to play a fund-raiser for the school. Against John's high school team. In December, during the holidays. Our twentieth reunion." The strain of talking so much wore on Oz; if he'd had to utter one more sentence it would have been about one word long.

Phillip turned to me. We were about ten feet apart—the height of a basketball goal—and his eyes looked out of a face that I could now see was worn and lined beyond his—our—years. We held each other's gaze for a long moment. I could feel his questions, feel his sadness, and I was ashamed that I had come.

What was a stupid game compared to this kind of sadness?

At last, he looked down at the top step. "No," he said. He turned to go inside, and Oz turned to go back to the truck.

"Phillip," I called, and I stepped forward to the base of the stairs. "Do you remember that Comanche game? Remember those rebounds? Seventeen of them. Maybe Oz made that last crazy shot, but he wouldn't have had the ball if you hadn't pulled it down and passed it out to him."

"That's right," Oz said, as though he had just remembered, and maybe he had, although I doubt it; when a man is renowned all his life for one exploit, he tends to know it inside and out, although it may be embellished, polished up, as the years pass. "When my man put up that jumper, I peeled off and headed down court."

"That's right," Phillip repeated. He turned around, and there was something new in his face as he groped for that memory. He raised the first two fingers and thumb of his right hand to his lips as though he were getting ready to insert a pinch between his cheek and gum, but he just left them there, tapping gently. "Guy shot from the top of the key. It hit the front right of the rim and I outjumped their center for it. It came off the rim funny. Cleared it out over half-court to you with a baseball pass." And as the light of remembrance took over his face, something that was almost a smile flickered across it.

"Right to me," Oz said excitedly. "A great pass with something on it, or I never would have got the shot up to beat the buzzer."

"But you did get him the ball," I said, stepping forward. "We won that game and went on to the finals that year because of you. Couldn't have done it without you. And it won't be the same playing again without you. What do you say?"

He looked at me and then across at Oz, and in the process, his gaze took in deceased washing machines and the broken-windowed carcass of a '66 Chevy Impala. The light across his face flickered and then went out.

"It's *not* the same, John," he said quietly. "Playing a game is exactly what it would be. It's just pretending." He took a deep breath, shook his head, and turned to go again.

"Wait," I said. "Phillip, let me say one more thing." And to my surprise he stayed where he was, although he did not turn around. "It must seem silly to you, and you've got no reason to want to come. I know that, and I don't blame you. It seems pretty silly to me, too." The shame was deep, washing over me as I spoke the truth: "But this isn't silly—we didn't stand by you. I didn't stand by you." I raised my hands, palms up. *Mea culpa.* "We weren't good friends. You're right. But if you want to come to the gym Sunday afternoon at three to shoot around with us, we'd be proud to have you. No matter what's happened in between, no matter how we let you down."

It was a pretty good speech, certainly heartfelt, and I guess maybe I expected him to turn around and smile and maybe we would all have driven into town together for a celebratory chocolate shake at the Sonic or something. But when he looked back, his face was even graver, and what he repeated was, "You were not good friends."

"No," I said, and I bit my lip, and then went on. "We were not. I hope you can forgive us. That maybe we can start over."

He didn't say anything, make any gesture, answer in any way that I could see except to step back inside his trailer and pull the door shut with a screech. Oz and I stood there for a moment, the only sound the snorting breath of the Brahma heifer. After a time, the two of us got back in the truck and returned to town.

We didn't talk until we reached the city limits, and all I said was, "Well, Bobby Ray'll say 'I told you so.'"

"Maybe," Oz said, some moments later, as I pulled back into the parking lot. "But anyway, I'm glad we went."

We shook hands, and he tied his smock back on and walked down the street toward what remained of downtown, toward his polished counter, his orderly plastic bottles, although I sensed that he'd find little satisfaction in them today.

Basketball practice wouldn't start until 2:20, but I drove to the gym, changed into practice clothes, and played full speed by myself for an hour, rebounding my misses, chasing down errant shots, driving, juking, jumping, pushing myself until my shirt was heavy with sweat and my eyes stung, until weariness crept pleasantly into my legs and shoulders and upper arms. Finally I draped myself across the first row of bleachers while my players filed in from their last class of the day.

And that's where I sat for the remainder of practice. "Full court scrimmage," I called. They'd earned a day just to play; they had worked hard. So for an hour, I let them run the floor, let them execute the plays we'd drilled over and over, let B. W. find the open man, as he could do better than anyone I had ever seen, far better than I could on the best day of my life, and while I had the whistle in my teeth and was supposed to be calling fouls, what I ended up doing was watching B. W. and realizing for the first time—even though I'd coached him for three years, even though I'd watched every game he'd played since junior high, even though I'd played him myself hundreds of times since he was old enough to loft the ball as high as the basket—that he was the real thing. He had the physical gifts, but there was more to it than that; he had the intelligence to know he'd have a cutter coming back door, to loft a pass to Micheal Wilkes when Micheal's defender shifted around to front him and left the path to the basket open, to penetrate the lane and dish the ball off to Bird for an easy jumper when the defense collapsed to cut off his drive.

It was more than intelligence; basketball intelligence can be learned, but instincts are something you can't teach, and that's what he had.

So maybe I fell down on my duty as referee. It was not a huge failing; they called their own fouls, mostly, and I caught the most flagrant that went uncalled. What was important, what stayed with me, was what I saw that day, what I learned.

I learned that my son was something special, the basketball player I always wanted to be and never was, and I don't think he realized it any more than I had.

So when B. W. popped a jumper from the top of the key with Albert Heap of Birds right in his face, his arms raised, when that beautiful high arc passed through the net like a diver cleanly knifing into the water, I whistled practice to an end. I wanted to keep that image, and so I exercised the power I possessed to preserve it unsullied. "Take your laps," I called. "Then hit the showers. You played hard. Tomorrow we'll go back to drills."

They took off like the tired but happy kids they were. But before B. W. could hit his stride, I dropped my hand to his shoulder to detain him, patted him awkwardly a couple of times, and said, finally, "It's a joy to watch you play."

He smiled—almost sadly, then said, simply, "Thanks, Dad." And he sprinted off to catch up to the others.

I watched, shaking my head and smiling. It was a day when I learned much, not the least of which was that not all memorable events transpire in morning time.

October 20, 1994

Mr. Bill Cobb
Cobb and Associates
12344 N. Preston Road
Dallas, TX 75231

Dear Bill:

The Watonga school board has asked me to convey to you our appreciation for your generous donation to the school's basketball program. As you directed, your money will be used to buy new game jerseys for the high school varsity team, and I am pleased to inform you that your gift will be acknowledged by a plaque in the lobby of the gymnasium and by a presentation made during halftime of the fund-raiser exhibition played between the 1974-75 varsity and the 1994-95 varsity teams in late December.

Again, thank you for your generous contribution to the success of our basketball squad.

Sincerely,

John Tilden, Coach
Watonga High School Eagles basketball team

October 20, 1994

Mr. and Mrs. John Tilden
7743 Sunny Acres
Phoenix, AZ 85372

Dear Mom and Dad,

Good to hear about your plans to come home for Christmas, although it seems silly to come all this way even for such an awe inspiring event as the Bill Cobb Commemorative Basketball Game. I hope we'll get to spend plenty of time with you on either side of that august occasion. Is Candy coming, or does she have other plans? She's welcome, of course, if she wants to come, although she may have to sleep in the hay.

Of course, I could put Michael out there, or she and he could trade off, since they would never be occupying the room at the same time. He's not any better and maybe a lot worse, and it seems to be rubbing off on B. W., believe it or not. I thought I had him, at least, figured out. Now I wonder how completely I may have misunderstood everyone in my life.

Did you guys ever feel like this (or have I gone over the edge anticipating how much I'll be on display in preparing two equally hopeless basketball teams to play each other)? I'm not even sure I understand myself, and I thought I had me pretty much doped out at this stage in my life. Now I find out that there's a whole lot I've assumed to be bedrock-solid about myself that turns out to have been shifting sand.

Forgive me. I'm babbling, and probably to no effect. It is getting late, and I should be in bed. When I see you in December we will solve all my child-rearing problems, get the farm's books in order, see a well-played game between basketball titans, and play dominoes until we drop. That last, at least, is a promise I think we can keep.

Take good care of yourselves. We miss you and look forward to your visit.

Your son,
John

October 20, 1994

Miss Candace Tilden
1425 E. Fifth
Albuquerque, NM 87106

Dear Candy,

Hey, Kid! Thanks for the letter and for the update on important events in your life. I have, as you see, noted the new address, as I'm sure Mom and Dad will do when you next write them, which I hope you will do soon (hint, hint). Like you, I don't know how they're going to react, seeing as how they don't even know Arturo exists yet (!!!), but as I see it, the possibilities are limited to three: there will be shock, surprise, and dismay (although I hope not, and maybe I have eased the way for you a little thanks to my scarlet past); there will be grudging acceptance, with a suggestion that you two find your way to the altar as soon as practical; or there will be absolutely no reaction, since you are twenty years old and capable of making your own decisions. Like you, I hope for the last and fear the first. I suppose we'll see what we shall see.

Don't let connubial bliss or whatever you call it interfere with your studies, or with Arturo's. Is he still on target to graduate in May if he finishes his dissertation? I think it's an impressive accomplishment, and I hope you'll relay that on to him. I once thought I might be doing something like that, but at least I can enjoy his achievements, and yours too, of course. I'm proud of you both, and I've realized recently that I don't say those words often enough to the people I love. Forgive me for that.

Anyway, the time is now. Break the news. If Mom calls, I won't just up and tell her, but if she asks, I'm not going to lie to her. Don't put me in that position, okay? Even if telling them is hard, putting it off won't make it easier.

Ask one who knows.

Lots going on here, but I don't feel capable of writing about it just now. Maybe with some distance I will look back on all of it and laugh. But right now, it feels like I'd just like to go back and start over again from the beginning.

Dangerous thoughts, I know. Try not to do things you'll regret, okay?

Love,
John

Communal Raccoon Suicide

Since it was Sunday morning, I had my church clothes on underneath a pair of manure-stained coveralls and had pulled on some knee-high boots to take me through the black primeval morass that the cow pens had become after a cold fall rain. It was those boots—and the cow bog—that kept me from getting to the house as quickly as I should have, because when Lauren came to the back door screaming for me to come quick, they were killing each other, it seemed like it took a superhuman effort to slurp through the mud and manure, and once out, I ran lead-footed across the backyard, my boots weighed down by pounds of clinging muck.

I did not spend much time considering the question of who could be killing each other; with Michelle already gone to Sunday school like the loyal teacher that she was, it could only be B. W. and Michael, and although Michael and B. W. hadn't had an actual fight since they were little kids, when Lauren's words shrilled across the distance between us, it suddenly seemed to me not only logical but inevitable.

I panted through the back door, boots and all, and on into the kitchen. I arrived between rounds, but I could see well enough what had already happened. A cereal bowl was upended on the table in a small pool of milk; Michelle's antique crockery butter churn had been knocked over; a slow drip of orange juice plopped from table-edge into a growing puddle spreading across the tile floor.

B. W. stood at the far end of the kitchen in church clothes, his tie pulled savagely to one side, his oxford shirt untucked and stained with orange juice. Michael, in sweats and a T-shirt, his back to me, raised his hand to his face, brought it down with a smear of crimson on the fingertips, and looked at it in silence for a moment. Then he said, "I'm going to kill you."

"I don't think so," B. W. said, and they stood and glared at each other.

Somewhere in here, both of them became aware of my presence, but in a peripheral way, as though I was a threat of less immediacy, which I suppose I was.

At last, Michael whirled and brushed past me in the narrow hallway. Once in his room, he slammed the door with considerable force, rattling his graduation picture on the hall wall sideways.

The noise continued from inside the room—things being thrown, yanked—as I raised my hands in disbelief, palms up, and asked B. W., "What on earth has got into you?"

At first he dropped his eyes to the puddle on the floor, and I thought we were headed back to universal silence and gloom. "B. W.? Son?"

He looked up at me, shook his head, and said, "I just got tired of it. That's all."

"Tired of what?"

"Michael was calling him names," Lauren said. "I heard from the bathroom."

"I'm not asking you, Lauren," I said. From Michael's room, the sounds of violence committed on inanimate objects stopped cold, and I turned to assess this new development. "Stay right where you are," I called back over my shoulder.

"We'll be late for church," B. W. said. "Mom will think something has happened."

"Something *has* happened. And anyway, you can't go looking like that," Lauren was saying as I headed off to befoul new sections of the house. I met Michael coming out of his room with a full duffel bag slung over his shoulder. A black shirtsleeve was hanging out the opening, incompletely stuffed.

"Where are you going?" I asked.

"I'll be back for the rest of my stuff," he muttered without meeting my eyes. He tried to push past me, but it was a narrow hall. Only when he couldn't get past me did he look up. "I'm getting out of here. This is a family full of lunatics and losers." He raised his voice so the last part would carry back toward the kitchen. "Losers," he repeated, in case we hadn't heard.

"Maybe so," I said, biting my lip. "But all the same, I don't want you to go."

"You can't stop me," he said, and he shouldered his bag as menacingly as a young man of his slender build could.

And I sighed, because he was right, at least short of physical force—he didn't respect me as a person enough to do what I asked, and he didn't revere God enough to honor his father just because it was a commandment. I stepped to one side, he brushed past me, and I settled for talking to his back, a conversational maneuver at which I was becoming disturbingly proficient.

"Michael, you're making too much of this," I called after him as he pulled the door open. "You don't have to go. We sure don't want you to."

And, of course, his answer was to slam the door behind him, to slam it, in fact, hard enough to jar the family portrait completely off the wall. It hit the ground with a thud, and the glass cracked from one corner to the other. I picked it up, looked at it: Michael was ten years old in this picture, and he was smiling.

We all were.

I walked back into the kitchen, sank into a chair next to the orange juice ocean, and looked up at B. W., still standing obediently next to the butter churn, his eyes down.

"I'm sorry, Dad," he said. "I didn't mean for this to happen. Really I didn't."

I raised my hand in a gesture I recognized with some discomfort as being at least second cousin to Bill Cobb's wave of dismissal. "It's not your fault," I said. "Are you okay? Are you hurt?"

"He caught me good a couple of times," he said, and now I could see the beginnings of a shiner under his left eye. "But I'm okay." He blinked rapidly a couple of times. "I'm really sorry."

"Lauren," I called, and she appeared, hovering at the edge of the living room. "I'm prepared to hear your testimony now. What in the world happened?"

She put her hands behind her back, assumed a posture appropriate for recitation, and declaimed. "Michael was making fun of B. W. for going to church. He called him a Baptist wussy. When B. W. told him to shut up, Michael threw orange juice on him."

"Who threw the first punch?" I asked the room.

"I did," B. W. said, before Lauren could decide what version of the truth she wanted to honor.

I sighed. God knows I never asked to be a parent: combination judge, counselor, mess cleaner. I sat in silence as they waited patiently for me to hand down a ruling. The clock chimed eleven, the time at which we should have been in our pew in Watonga. The opening hymn would be happening right about now, and I was supposed to help take the offering midway through the service.

"Dad, you should take off your boots," B. W. said finally. "I'll clean up."

"I'll help you," Lauren said.

"We'll all help," I said. "Let's at least get the house looking decent before your mom gets home." And for the next hour, we wrestled with messes, the biggest of which was the traveling brown storm spread by my boots. But with some hands and knees scrubbing, I felt like the rug would at least pass muster, even if my fatherhood wouldn't.

Michael's room didn't take much time to set right. All the noise had come, not from furniture being overturned, but from closet doors and drawers being flung open. In fact, it wasn't noticeably messier than the last time I dared to enter, a few days before. All the same, already, there was a trace of absence in the air. His stereo was still on, the headphones dangling from his bedpost. I pulled the headphones out of their jack and was greeted by the blare of vintage Judas Priest: "You've Got Another Thing Comin'."

Michael couldn't have been more than nine years old when this album came out. For a moment, I wanted to believe all the fundamentalist horror stories about rock music.

Then I decided to take it as an omen. I did have another thing coming.

And probably another thing after that.

When Michelle's Lumina cleared the rise and headed down the driveway toward us at around 12:40, I sent the kids to their rooms. "I'll handle this," I said, although I wasn't at all sure how I was going to. For the first time, I started to look forward to our three o'clock senior basketball practice at the high school, a miserable hour or two where Bobby Ray and Oz and I would stand around and throw feeble shots up at the backboard and finally shake our heads and go home.

"Hey," Michelle called out as she came in from the garage. "Family? Where are you? What's up?"

"Here," I called from the kitchen, which looked surprisingly good considering the abuse we'd subjected it to about an hour previous. She walked in wearing a red and purple crinkly skirt, a silver concho belt, and a purple jacket, and she saw disaster in my face before I could even open my mouth.

"What happened?" she asked, and she dropped her purse on the table and rushed around the table to me. "What's wrong?"

"Michael and B. W. had a fight," I said, and before she could ask, I assured her, "Neither of them got hurt bad. But Michael stormed out of here with a bag over his shoulder." I looked down at the floor. "I don't think he's going to come back."

"Well, why didn't you stop him?" she asked, her eyes glistening. "How could you let him walk out?"

I was willing to give her a moment or two to register the enormity of the situation before holding her accountable, but the words stung. "I tried," I said. "I asked him not to go."

"And he did anyway," she said, and now her face had shifted from anger to sadness to resignation. She sat down across from me and slumped, her head dropping forward. "What did they fight about?"

"I didn't see it," I said. "But it sounds to me like they fought about everything. About their whole lives." I stood, went around to her, took her into my arms, and she wept into my midsection, great racking sobs that shook us both. I murmured the usual ineffectual things, "Everything's going to be all right," and "Hey, hey," and "We'll figure things out," but it wasn't anything I said that finally calmed her. I could feel her take a deep breath, and then she pushed me back a step, stood up, and wiped her eyes.

"What are we going to do?" she asked. "Go after him?"

"I don't think so," I said. "We can let him know that we love him and we want him to come back, but I don't see how we can do anything else."

"Oh, I think we can do more than that," she said. "Have you called Gloria's yet?"

"You think that's where he'll be?"

Even in the depth of her despair she had a little energy left for eye rolling.

"Be my guest," I said, and she sighed and nodded.

"Okay," she said, resting the phone in the crook of her neck and opening her address book.

"Luck," I said as she began dialing, and I stood beside her and took her free hand in mine. I heard the far-off buzz of the ringing, then the sleepy "Hello"—Gloria worked nights, same as Michael—and Michelle said, "Gloria, this is Michelle Tilden. Is Michael there?"

I watched Michelle's face as she listened. She began worrying her lower lip with her teeth. When she spoke again, it was with rigid control. "Okay," she said. "Thanks, Gloria. Tell him that." And she wearily hung the receiver back on its cradle.

"What?" I asked.

"He's there," she sighed. "Asleep, she says. Also says he told her we'd call and to tell us he's not coming home."

"Great," I said.

"But she said she'd tell him that we loved him, and that we should call her anytime if we wanted to see that he was okay."

So Gloria was actually some kind of okay. But still: "Big hairy deal. We could just go to Pizza Hut and order a Meatlover's Pizza if we wanted to do that."

She gave me a rueful smile, and then she lost it. I gathered her into my arms, and we stood there a long time, by male reckoning, before she looked up at me and asked, "So what do we do?"

Like I knew. "Give it some time," I said. "He'll be back or he won't. Either way, we can let him know we love him."

She let it sit for a bit—and decided she would let it sit a little longer. "How's B. W. taking it?" she asked.

I snatched a look back down the hall to make sure both the kids' doors were still shut. "Not well," I said. "I thought I'd drag him off to the gym with me so he wouldn't brood."

"One brooder is enough," she agreed. She put her hands on my shoulders. "Hey, are you okay? Are you sure you want to go to practice?"

I shrugged; the weight of her hands felt good. "Hey," I said, trying to make my voice light, "I've envisioned worse scenarios. I had one where Michael killed us all for the family fortune."

"You're awful," she said, leaning in to kiss me. Her face was still moist, and when she raised it to mine, I tasted salt. "Besides, he knows there's no family fortune."

I remembered Michael's words. "Yes, I think he's well aware we've been complete failures." I looked at the clock. "You want to go back in with us when we go?"

"Rain check," she said. "I'd like to sit and think. Say a prayer or two. Maybe listen to some loud music."

I nodded. It was the equivalent of what I planned to do on the basketball court.

We fixed sandwiches, a tiny meal for B. W. and me since we'd soon be running hard. We ate mostly in silence, and Lauren asked, "We're not mad at each other, are we?" and Michelle shook her head and said, "No, honey, the four of us are all right. Don't you worry."

In the truck on the way into town, B. W. was silent. I asked, "How do you feel?" figuring that would give him an opening if he wanted to talk, but he said, "Not so good," and stared out the window as we turned onto Highway 270.

The leaves were starting to change, the various light and dark greens of elm, cottonwood, blackjack, river willow, and walnut turning to golds, browns, the occasional yellow or orange, the red cedars still standing out dark green on the hillsides.

B. W. stared out the window. I stared out at the road.

As we crossed the first of the bridges over the North Canadian River, I saw the body of a raccoon on the shoulder of the road, flat on his back, his paws crossed on his chest. Not twenty feet farther there was another, sprawled on his stomach, limbs extending in every direction. Just before we reached the other end of the bridge there was a third, curled in a fetal ball. Despite appearances, I knew they hadn't actually committed communal suicide; they had probably just come up onto the roadway to find an easier way across the river and individually gone to meet their Maker at the powerful recommendation of fast-moving vehicles. Likely they were family members, come to check on the fallen—and falling themselves.

"Three coons," B. W. murmured without looking across at me. "That's a shame." In earlier days, B. W. used to go out with a group of boys and dogs and hunt coons or possum all night long, but that was one thing, a fairer contest, maybe. He was right; this was just a sad waste.

We pulled into the parking lot and walked into the darkened gym, the jingle of my keys echoing into the vast blackness.

"I love the gym when it's like this," I said. "When I was your age, I had my own key."

"Students aren't supposed to have a key to the gym," B. W. said. His face broke into a wry smile. "My dad broke the law."

"Well," I said, as we reached the light switches, "I guess you could say I got punished for it." I smiled when he looked at me quizzically. "Your mom and I met here late one night after the girls and boys teams had both beat Okeene. We were feeling pretty good to start with—we'd both of us had good games that night—and this guy had bought me some booze. So after everyone left, we went down to Coach's office and sat drinking Everclear and Gatorade, and eventually we ended up making your brother."

It had been stuffy in that office, and I recalled the smells of sweat and wintergreen from the Atomic Balm that Coach used to dispense to rub into our sore muscles. The carpet was worn and was little comfort from the concrete floor, but I don't recall that discomfort stopped us or even made us pause.

"Dad," B. W. said after a bit. "I absolutely did not need to know that." He seemed a little embarrassed—at least, his face was flushed—but then he was laughing. "That's how it happened? Oh, man. I thought it happened in a pickup truck."

"Ah," I said, "that's what everyone thinks. Now you alone know the truth." I opened the closet and wheeled out a ball rack. I picked up a ball, felt it for pressure and texture, liked the grain, and stuck it under my arm. "I always thought Michael was going to turn into the basketball player. I mean, you'd think with a start like that—" I took the ball from under my arm and dribbled it once to complete the sentence.

B. W. fiddled around with a couple of balls, made faces at each, and finally pulled one off the bottom of the rack. "So where did you guys make me?" he asked. "I mean, if you remember. If you don't mind telling me."

"Not in a car," I said, thinking hard. "And not here, although you play like you've got the gym in your blood. Probably the same old boring place."

We dribbled over to the west goal, closest to the door we'd opened. "I think it's neat," B. W. said, raising the ball to his chest and pausing before he shot. "About how Michael got here, I mean. Have you ever told him?"

"No," I said. I'd never told him anything about that night. I sighed. "Maybe we should have. Or maybe that would just have made him madder." We both shot at the same time, and the balls arrived in the cylinder at the same time and crowded each other off to either side of the basket.

"Hey," Bobby Ray said as he entered. "You boys are getting a head start."

"You know it," I said. "Grab a ball and join us."

The three of us shot for about ten minutes with surprising success. Although Bobby Ray was always a streak shooter, he had a pretty shot when he was on. And when he was on, he could shoot the lights out. I remember once in the second half of a game against the Clinton Red Tornadoes in the Tornado Dome when he scored from deep outside—NBA three-point land—twelve straight times down the court. It broke their backs. They'd been up eight points, but a streak like that can take your mind off your game. They started double-teaming him, they tried to foul him when he went up, but we freed him on a couple of screens—I passed it to Bill in the post and then he would dish back out to Bobby Ray for the shot, and finally the Clinton players got so flustered and focused on him that any of the rest of us could have walked the ball up to the basket and shot, which is basically what we did the rest of the night. I've never seen anything like that game, although I knew what he was feeling, could see it in him, that sensation of being one with the flow, like a surfer maybe, completely in tune with the wave and completely in control as a result. He knew that if he shot, it would go in. It was as simple as that.

Who cared if he went one for twelve the next game against the Seiling Comets (as they used to be called)? Even the forty-seven points he later scored against Thomas that year didn't compare in my mind to that twelve for twelve, a dozen shots arcing in perfection toward the net. That game against Clinton made up for a multitude of Bobby Ray's sins, and believe me, there was a multitude.

Oz arrived precisely at three in a T-shirt and a pair of baggy blue sweats that were almost falling off his narrow hips.

"Get in here, Scarecrow," Bobby Ray growled and passed him the ball as soon as he got on the court. "Let's see your shot."

"I'm not warm yet," Oz protested. His first shot from about twelve feet missed everything. He flushed beet red and ran after his miss, which B. W. had retrieved.

"Here you go, Mr. Osborne," he said.

"So are we gonna practice or not?" Bobby Ray asked. "Time is money." Bobby Ray sometimes gave me the sense that, while he might have failed over and over again, at least he got there in a hurry.

"No Phillip?" Oz asked.

"I don't think so," I told him. "That's why I brought B. W." It seemed like a valid excuse; no use airing any more of our laundry in public than we had to.

"Of course he won't be here," Bobby Ray said. "Jailbird wouldn't dare be seen in public, and I don't blame him."

"That's our teammate you're talking about, Bobby Ray," Oz said, his usual quiet voice tinged with an edge.

"John?" called a voice from the hall to the girls' locker room. Carla Briggs walked out onto the court in abbreviated red shorts and one of those black sports bras. I had seen women jogging and playing sports in them, but they were probably a violation of our community decency standards. "What are you boys doing up here?"

"Practicing for the big game," Bobby Ray said, pulling a ball from the rack and walking across to present it to her. I didn't blame him; she did look fine. All of us—except for Oz, so happily married that he had already turned back to our goal—had spent a moment gaping.

"I was just going to shoot around some," she called over to me. "Will that bother you guys?"

"We'll try to keep our minds on the job," I said, before Bobby Ray could say something less tasteful.

"Well," Bobby Ray said loudly as he arrived back under our basket, "are we going to practice or not?"

"We are practicing," Oz said. "I haven't had much of a chance to shoot lately." His next shot slanted off the backboard and in, and although I don't think he'd planned it—he smiled sheepishly at me when I complimented him—he ran down the ball with new vigor.

"When we've had a few minutes to get warm and shoot," I said, "we'll play some two-on-two. Then we'll work on our wind. Maybe run some."

This apparently satisfied Bobby Ray, although I could tell from B. W.'s quick glance that he had no intention of participating in the running portion of our program on his day of rest and wanted to make sure I knew that. I did.

We chose up for two-on-two, Oz and me against B. W. and Bobby Ray. The first game lasted for maybe fifteen minutes, and we only played half-court, bringing the ball back out to the top of the key at each change of possession. B. W. and I played tolerably well, but our teammates were not only not at the top of their games, they were not even the masters of their own bodies. They lost the ball dribbling, passed over our heads, or imagined we were cutting in directions that we had never had intentions of cutting and threw the ball out of bounds. The one bright moment for the old folks was when B. W.

pulled up to shoot, gave Oz his standard head fake, and Oz stood like a block of salt and blocked his shot without leaving his feet. Bobby Ray doubled over laughing and told B. W., panting as he clutched the hem of his shorts, "Kid, when you're as old as we are, you don't go for fakes. Takes too much energy."

We broke for a few minutes to get a drink, and I wandered down to the other end of the court, where Carla stood sinking free throws.

"You guys stink," she said, smiling in commiseration before making another, and I could only smile back.

"Don't I know it. But what do you expect from a bunch of old men?" I passed the ball back out to her at the line.

"B. W.'s not old—" she began. Then at the far end of the court, the outside door swung open with a bang, and Phillip One Horse stepped hesitantly into the gym wearing a pair of faded jeans, a jean jacket, and his own pair of ancient Converse high-tops. Phillip looked left and right before sighting me at the far end of the court, but he didn't move from the spot just inside the door. Bobby Ray stopped dribbling, picked up the ball, and likewise just stood there.

No one made a move to welcome Phillip; I think for a moment none of us could quite believe he existed.

But there he stood, his head down, eyes darting from neutral corner to neutral corner, until I realized that if nothing more happened, if nobody said anything, he would disappear out the door and back down the road, probably for good. I stirred myself into action and called his name.

He recoiled at the sudden sound, his shoulders jerking, his head rising. I advanced quickly toward him with long strides to cut off his escape. "Hey, Phillip," I said when I got closer. "It's good to see you."

Oz followed when he saw me stretch out my hand and saw Phillip slowly take it. "Thanks for coming," Oz said, and knowing the difficulty of that utterance, Phillip gravely inclined his head to him.

"Am I too late?" he asked me quietly, and I could catch a whiff of something that smelled like bourbon when he spoke.

"No," I said. "No, you're not. We're just taking a break. We were playing some two-on-two. B. W. can take a rest and you can get right into things if you want."

"Could I maybe see a ball for a second?" he asked. "It's been a long time." He pulled off his jacket. Underneath he was wearing a ragged tank top that advertised Winston Lights.

"Bobby Ray," I called. "Ball." But he'd turned back to shoot, and so B. W. passed me his.

I walked over to Bobby Ray while Phillip took the ball and ran his hands across the leather cover. I could see now that Bobby Ray's turning away from Phillip was intentional; his total indifference to Phillip's amazing presence flew in the face of our involvement. Oz saw it too, and he followed me over, leaving Phillip and B. W. standing quietly on the far sideline—as though those two could stand any other way but quietly.

"We're going to add Phillip and play some more two-on-two," I said when I was close enough for Bobby Ray to hear me. "B. W. is going to sit out."

"I'm not playing with that convict," Bobby Ray said, his back still to us, although his voice was loud enough to carry.

"For Pete's sake, Bobby Ray—" Oz said, and was about to say something undeaconlike, but I jumped in.

"Okay," I said. "We'll go three-on-three. Oz and I'll pick up Phillip, and we'll ask Carla to join you."

Bobby Ray got ready to protest again, either because he didn't want Phillip on the court at all or because of the indignity of sharing the court with a girl. Assuming it was the latter and feeling my guts knot at his stubbornness, I said, "Carla can beat you four games out of five, Bobby Ray, and you know it. I think she'll be good enough to play on your team." And I turned my back on him to walk back over to Phillip, who was taking a few tentative dribbles as B. W. stood by.

"Phillip, you're with us. We'll take it slow." Then I invited Carla over, introduced her to Phillip, and suggested they guard each other. I thought that might make it a little harder for Bobby Ray to communicate his distaste to Phillip.

B. W. took the ball out, and I dropped back a little, conceding the outside shot for the moment because I knew B. W. would try to involve the others and also because if I played him too close he'd be past me in a flash and into the lane. He passed across to Bobby Ray, who tried to dribble around Oz and lost the ball. Phillip picked it up and fired it out to me, and I nodded my approval. He had always had a nose for the ball, and even if he wasn't in any kind of condition to play—his tank top flapped on his skinny frame—he still had good basketball instincts.

I passed it down to Oz, who passed it over to Phillip, and the ball slipped through his hands and out of bounds, to Bobby Ray's barely suppressed snort of amusement. Phillip turned to look at him with genuine puzzlement and then gave his attention back to Carla, who was bringing the ball in.

Unlike B. W., who knew this wasn't his practice and had generous instincts in any case, Carla was a scorer, pure and simple, and in her college days she had been a shooting guard. She drove the lane, and Phillip gave way and let her take it in, to the accompaniment of another snort from Bobby Ray.

Phillip stiffened, took a deep breath, and I wanted to be on another planet.

I passed down to Oz and went to set a pick on Carla so Phillip could roll free. Oz bounced him a pass, which he was juggling as he stepped toward the basket, and then Bobby Ray came across the lane and body-checked him into next week with only the barest attempt to look as though he were going for the ball.

"You stupid—" I started, getting ready to say something undeaconlike myself, and caught myself, seeing B. W.'s jaw drop.

"For Pete's sake, Bobby Ray," Oz said again.

Bobby Ray stepped forward to look down on Phillip, who was getting up slowly, without looking at him.

"That's enough of that," I said, shoving Bobby Ray backward, and I'm afraid I got up in his face, even after all I'd told B. W. about losing his temper on the court.

I don't know what would have happened then. It's true that I'd been mad at Bobby Ray more than once in the years I had known him, and that I'd still never taken a swing at him or he at me, but I can't promise that nothing would have come of this. We glared at each other, our faces about four inches apart, both our jaws set and temple veins standing out.

Then the gym door banged shut again, and we turned to see that Phillip was gone.

"Look what you've done," I said without stepping back. "I didn't think he'd come out to practice with us in a million years. And you've sent him packing."

"Good riddance," Bobby Ray said. "He doesn't deserve to play with us. He let us down. He disgraced the team."

"Well, you would know about disgrace," I said. I let out a loud sigh. "He made a mistake. God knows, it happens to the best of us." I turned to Carla. "Could you run B. W. out to the house?"

She shrugged. "Sure, John, I guess. Why?"

"I'm going after Phillip," I said, and turned to Bobby Ray. "If he doesn't come back, then you can go out and find yourself two new players, because I won't be coming back either."

Bobby Ray looked at me with dismay, as though I'd just told him I was an IRS collector come to slap a levy on his tractor. "You can't do that, John," he stammered. "You're the guy who holds this team together."

"That's exactly what I'm trying to do," I said, and I shrugged on my coat and was out the door. The day had grown chilly, and the wind was blowing hard out of the north. I climbed into the truck, started it up, and turned toward the parking lot exit in the direction of Phillip's place. It was then that I saw him beside the road not more than three blocks down the street, walking fast, his arms swinging as he went, his breath a gray cloud floating behind him.

I gunned the engine, slinging gravel as I left the parking lot, and rolled down the passenger side window, letting in the howling wind. When I pulled alongside him, I braked and called out to him, "Can I give you a lift?"

He walked on, not even looking at me. If anything, he sped up.

"Phillip, please," I said. "Get in."

"I'm not going back," he said.

"You don't have to go back," I said. "I don't blame you for not wanting to. Bobby Ray is an idiot. But you don't have to walk home, either. If I'd known you didn't have a way in, I would have come after you. The least I can do now is drop you off."

He stopped, looked down the road, where a walk of close to a mile still separated him from the highway, which was only the first step on his way home.

He took a deep breath. He was thinking about it.

I leaned across and opened the door.

He got in.

"Roll up that window," I said. "It's gotten nippy."

He did, and then we sat inside the cab in silence while outside the wind whipped past and the engine rose and fell as I accelerated away from a stop sign or eased up to the next one.

Phillip sat close to the door, one arm on the armrest. He looked down at his feet, or maybe at the floor mat.

"You shouldn't let Bobby Ray get to you," I said finally. "You know what he's like. What he's always been like. He hasn't changed." We turned onto the highway and headed past the airport and out of town. The airport's windsock was stretched parallel to the ground in the stiff breeze.

"I never should have come today," he said at last, when I thought no one on earth would ever speak again. "You'd be better off forgetting about me. I'm an embarrassment."

"Don't think that way," I said, shaking my head. "Since when does anybody worry about what Bobby Ray thinks? Oz and I were glad to see you."

He looked over at me then. "Bill probably thinks the same as Bobby Ray."

"Also an idiot," I reminded him.

"Anyway," he said, staring back down at the floorboard. "You don't need me there to fight over."

We passed the entrance to Roman Nose Park, so I slowed and put on my signal, which clicked loudly in the silence.

"I told them I wasn't coming back if you didn't," I said, looking across at him, and then I turned onto the washboarded dirt road.

"Why would you do that?" he asked after the road had smoothed out and we'd driven on about a quarter mile.

I slowed as I approached Phillip's drive, such as it was, stopped, put the truck in park, and looked out the windshield at Phillip's sad fence. "I've been thinking a lot lately," I finally said. I sat with it, thought about what I wanted to say out loud. "If it's possible to make up for the past, somehow. To fix things that I should have done right in the first place." I rolled my shoulders upward in a slow shrug. "I'd like to think maybe you could. This seems like a good place to start."

Outside, the wind whistled through the sagging barbed wire and the overhead telephone lines; the engine idled like the purr of a big cat. When Phillip spoke again, the unexpectedness of it made me jerk.

"You know the last time you and me rode someplace together? It was twenty years ago." He looked out the window, but his eyes were focused on the past. "It was that night you and me went out drinking in your old man's truck," he said. "It was after the Canton game. You remember?"

I had a dim memory of headlamps lighting a triangle of dirt road and adjoining pastures, the dimness a result of drinking half a dozen beers on a deep dark starless night. I remembered an ice-flecked Coors nestled cold against my crotch as we drove—where?

"Is that the night we climbed the bridge?" I remembered us on one of the big iron bridges over the Canadian River, remembered him climbing up high—

"Climbing," he snorted. "The night you kept me from falling off. I've never forgot it. You saved my life."

"That was pure luck," I said, although he was probably right. I had saved his life.

What he didn't say—and I didn't either—was that Phillip had not fallen.

He had jumped.

I had grabbed him as he fell, pulled him back onto the bridge, even though it almost tore me off with him, and when he was on solid ground, we held onto each other for a long moment to make sure we were both still there before we pulled ourselves slowly, carefully back onto the roadway, one foot at a time. He never told me why he tried to jump. Maybe I wouldn't have understood.

I was just a kid, and I didn't know yet how life could chew somebody up.

"I was drunker than you were," I said quietly. "I was just lucky. I was in the right place at the right time."

"I almost pulled you off after me," he said. He turned his head slowly to me. "You know, John, when I was in prison, down in

McAlester, I thought about that sometimes. You didn't let go. I don't think for a second you thought about not trying to catch me."

"Hey," I said, trying to keep it light, "it was my job, keeping the team together and all that. Coach would have killed me if I'd let you fall off the bridge. Besides, you would have done the same for me, right?"

His fingers and thumb rose to his lips and tapped gently, and he looked back out the window for awhile before he answered what I had thought was a rhetorical question.

"I don't know," he said. "I'm not sure." He looked across to see my reaction. I didn't have one yet; I just met his gaze and waited to see if he had anything else to say. "I don't know that I would have. I gave it a lot of thought, like I said." He stared out the window again, at the field just sprouting with green shoots of winter wheat. "And what does that make me?"

"I don't know," I said. "Human?"

"No," he said. He dropped his hand to the door lever, his eyes darting across to mine and then back out the window. "You should have let me fall."

He opened the door to a whirl of rushing wind, leaves whipping past, blowing dust.

"So long, John," he said, and he started to slide out.

It was instinct, not any conscious thought, not anything I might have planned. But I leaned across and just managed to catch the sleeve of Phillip's jacket as he was stepping out.

"Come home to dinner," I said, not relinquishing my grip on his jacket. We stayed like that, joined tenuously for a moment, and then he looked back at me with a look that was not anger, or curiosity, or sadness.

I could only describe it as gratitude.

He nodded.

"Maybe you're right," he said, as he climbed back in and we were driving away from the chilling gale. "Maybe this is a good place to start."

We drove home into a wondrous sunset, high clouds turning orange and red and purple, toward my wife, my kids, and my ever-surprising life.

Dreams and Murmurs

Everything in the dream feels at once so familiar and yet so strange; maybe it's not surprising that I take a moment to recognize where I am and with whom. It takes me a second to place the song on the radio, since I haven't heard it in years; the Spinners' "Could It Be I'm Falling in Love" probably came out in '71 or '72. Likewise, it's been years since I've been horizontal with a girl on the bench seat of a Chevy pickup truck on a cool, rainy night.

And of course it's been years since that girl was Samantha Mathis.

But it's just as beautiful as I remembered it: the rain tapping at the roof, the far-off splash of lightning and rumble of thunder, the fog on the windows becoming droplets, rivulets of water, the faint green light from the radio dial illuminating the territory I've already explored. Sam whimpers as my lips flit across her skin, as my fingers cup her curves. Way back—at the farthest reaches of conscious thought—I recognize the insistent low stomach tension of fear. I suppose it's the fear that we're going to get stuck in the mud if it keeps raining, because we once did and it was a hard thing to explain to her father, but memory or fear, it is shouted down by the desire to stay right where we are, the desire to touch Sam's pale, thin body, the desire to feel her lips on mine again.

Her eyes look up at me, wide and dark, and I see the glint of her teeth, her lips drawn back in a smile, or pleasure, or both. The rain picks up, a patter becoming a pounding that duplicates the sound of my heart.

In a flash of lightning, we are revealed in our nakedness, and with that flash and the following boom of thunder, foreboding again rumbles through my gut. What if someone sees us this way? If someone comes along and catches us: my folks, her dad, Michelle?

Michelle.

I can't be doing this.

I shouldn't even be dreaming this.

I'm married. Married to Michelle.

That life is over and gone.

And so I forced myself awake, swam up to consciousness, to a chilly bedroom and the light patter of early-morning rain against the windows—woke, bathed in sadness and shame, woke to a gnawing in the pit of my stomach that I knew was not hunger but guilt, big-time, capital "G" guilt, like it must feel to get caught doing the babysitter.

"It wouldn't have hurt to sleep just a little longer," I muttered to myself as I rolled out of bed—hung for the goose, hung for the gander. Behind me Michelle stirred and murmured, "Wha's that, honey?"

"Go back to sleep," I said. "Nothing." Guilt or love—or both— impelled me to pull the comforter back up over her shoulders and gently adjust it at her throat to protect her from the farmhouse draft we never quite succeeded in preventing. She was instantly asleep again—oh, to be so at peace with the world and with myself—and

I stood watching her snore as she lay on her back, mouth open, face pointed toward heaven.

I dressed quietly and went into the kitchen to start a pot of coffee, meditate on my night, and contemplate the coming day.

Some fun. And it got better as the day wore on.

"So how are things going?" was what Bill Cobb asked when Michelle called me in to the phone hours later. I had been out doing early chores and cracking a thin layer of ice from a light freeze on the stock tanks. The calves had been jostling me thankfully. I bet trying to break ice with a warm moist nose is no fun.

I came stamping into the house, took off my boots carefully on the back porch, and deeply inhaled the warm dry air of the kitchen once before picking up the phone—and inhaled once again after hearing Bill's question.

"Things," I said, at last, "are going like you would not believe."

"Good practice the other day?"

"There was a lot of action."

"Who ran my spot? One of the kids?"

"You know there's no one who could fill your shoes," I said. I foresaw a future of communication with Bill in which he could fill in the blanks however he wanted; it was actually kind of liberating.

"When's the next practice? This Sunday?"

"Probably," I said. And maybe we would practice again. When I dropped Phillip off after dinner, he said he would think about coming back. I guess all that was needed now was to work on Bobby Ray, maybe with a lead pipe. "When are you coming up?"

"I might be able to get up for one practice before the game," he said. "Lots going on here. It's crunch time in the elections, you know, and I've got a good friend running for Texas governor." A good friend, I recalled, whose father used to be the president of the United States. All this delivered in the I-don't-want-to-brag tone that I always hated Bill for; maybe he didn't want to brag, but somehow he always managed to.

"Uhm," I said. "Well, we'll try to manage without you somehow." This delivered in my sweetest and most secretly ironic tone, a voice that has always worked on Bill.

People who take it as an article of faith that they are smarter than you never pick up on any clues that the exact opposite might be true.

As quickly as I reasonably could I hung up, anxious to quit talking about Bill's stupid basketball game and get back to the more important things I'd been thinking about. Things such as Michael, of whom we had neither seen nor heard a thing for weeks; things such as the mysterious call from Samantha some time back, still unexplained, although it began to take up more and more space in my head; things such as my varsity team, which still seemed woefully unprepared for the pending season, and, unless Jimmy Bad Heart Bull made a remarkable difference in our starting lineup, would spend this winter looking at the other team as bewildered as a cow at a new gate; things such as the upcoming Watonga homecoming game which marked Lauren's first date (if you could call it that—said date consisting of she and her beau riding to the game with me and then riding with me and Michelle to the restaurant afterward).

In any case, enough things on my mind to make me want to go somewhere to think seriously, to think without interruption, down by the pond, which was what I did, although it was too cold for fish to be biting and I had to bundle up with my jacket collar upturned.

It was a gray day, intermittent drizzle, the sun occasionally threatening to break through. I sat staring at the lightly wind-rippled surface of the pond and the low clouds reflected in it, and I was so deeply lost in it—like you might lose yourself in the sight of the crackling gray static of a television set or the lulling tumble of clothes in a dryer—that I didn't even hear the rustling of the wind high up in the cedar trees on the hillside.

I did hear a displaced stone bounce first with a hollow thunk on the red rock beside me and then with a hollow plunk into the pond, and I prepared to get up to shoo a cow away from the steep incline and back to safety. Then a pair of battered ropers descended, followed by black Wranglers, until gradually B. W. was revealed. He sat down next to me with a sigh and stared down into the water I had so recently sent my mind swimming in.

"How'd you find me?" I asked, and he glanced over at me and gave me a slender smile.

"Looked for you," he said.

"There are times you're too smart for your own good," I said.

"Maybe." He looked back out at the water. "Not many, I'd guess."

The wind picked up a little bit and bent the treetops, riffled the water so we lost our reflections. He put his arms around his knees and hugged them close, and I could see that it was going to be up to me to do the talking, at least until I could guess what had brought him down here.

"You still feeling bad about Michael?" Because I was certainly feeling bad, and Michelle was pestering me to try and confront the issue more forcefully.

B. W. shook his head, then picked up a small, flat rock beside him, aimed it experimentally a few times, and skipped it across the pond with a flick of his wrist.

"I feel bad, I guess. And I miss him, even. But I need to talk to you about something else," he said. "I've been thinking about this for a long time, only I don't know how to say it, and I know you're going to be upset, and so I haven't said anything."

"Okay," I said.

"But it doesn't go away. Not talking about it just makes it worse."

Well, that was true enough. "So now you're here to talk about it," I said.

He nodded.

I waited. The last concentric circles of the rock he had skipped had disappeared.

"Okay," I said at last. "Did *you* get somebody pregnant? Become a vegetarian? What?"

He didn't laugh, just flashed another brief, mouth-only smile that died on his lips. Nah. "Dad, I've decided I don't want to play college ball. I don't want to play basketball, period. I'm not having fun anymore." Then he looked back down and away.

"What are we going to do about college?" I hadn't meant to say that out loud. But now that it was out, I starting thinking about the balance in our savings account, about the feed bills coming if we had a tough winter, about new parts for the combine, and my stomach knotted with something that felt very much like fear.

He held up a hand, perhaps to try to forestall that whole panicked line of thought. "I'm still going to college, Dad. I've been accepted into the forestry program at Montana."

"Montana," I repeated.

"I got the letter last week," he said. "And I want to go. I'll work to pay my way there if I have to."

"If you have to," I repeated. If he'd said, "When I get there, I'm going to become a moose," I probably would have repeated that, too.

"So I guess I'm asking your permission," he said. "To quit."

Quit. I never did like the sound of that word, and I didn't repeat it. Instead I turned to him, and there was an edge in my voice I couldn't help. "B. W., don't you know that basketball could be your ticket out of this town? More important, don't you know what a gift you have?" I dropped my hand onto his knee and clamped on tight. "Don't you know what some people would give to have the talent, the instincts you have? If I'd had what you've got, I would have ridden it as far as I could go. I would have left Watonga and never looked back."

He looked at my hand for a second. I was probably hurting him, but he didn't pull away.

"Dad," he said. "I'm not you. And you can't live my life."

I lifted my hand. "Right," I said. "You're right."

He looked away from me, his mouth drawn in a grim line. "I'm sorry," he said, finally, looking up. "I didn't mean to make you worry. It's okay. We'll make it work somehow. I can take out loans. Maybe get some grants."

I mentally calculated our savings again, the possible income from the winter calves, from next summer's harvest; the numbers did not lend themselves to much optimism. But I looked at B. W., my obedient boy, the boy who had always done what we asked.

The boy who had never been anything but decent and honorable.

Didn't such a boy deserve every chance at the life he wanted?

So I looked at him and I nodded, and what I said was, "We'll find a way, I guess." But my limited optimism didn't get too far down the road before some other things sidetracked it. I wasn't just a father here, although maybe I should have tried to be; I was also a coach from whom people expected great things and in a very short time. Which meant I had another problem.

"If you quit now," I said, "you'll be leaving me and the team in a real fix."

He nodded.

I brought my hands together as if I were praying, brought them to my face, thought for a moment. "What if we compromise? I won't bug you about college ball. But play for me. Finish the season. It's not like we'll be going to regionals, be playing playoff games into the spring. It'll be a short season."

He smiled sadly. "I think you're right about that," he said. His shoulders relaxed. He had decided. "Okay, Dad, I can do that. For you."

"And if it starts being fun again, well—"

"Dad," he cautioned, and raised that warning hand.

Okay," I said. "Okay."

He pushed himself to his feet. "I got to get on to school." He brushed off his butt, then held out his hand.

"I think I'll stay," I said. "For a bit."

"I'm not trying to help you up," he said. "I'm trying to shake your hand."

I reached my hand up, and he took it in a firm grip. "Thanks for talking to me."

"Likewise," I said. We shook once and he turned to climb up the hill.

"See you at practice," he called from the top. "Don't forget you wanted to try Todd Daugherty at guard today."

"I won't forget," I called after him.

I waited a moment to make sure Lauren wasn't in line behind him, then I turned back to look at the water.

I had known B. W. was unhappy, but I misjudged the cause of his unhappiness. I was reminded what I had said in my letter to my folks; if I misunderstood even B. W. so completely, how had I misunderstood the others in my life, the other people I should know best?

I didn't want to think about that any further. It didn't seem productive for anything except paranoia.

It was cold, and the day was growing grayer, with clouds blowing in from the north. I decided I didn't want to stay, so I got up, dusted myself off, and walked to the truck.

When I got back to the house, I made my early-morning phone call to Gloria's place—a new habit I'd developed since Michael had left—and Michael, if he was there, was exercising his new early-morning habit of not answering the phone. After that, unless I lingered for hours over coffee with my farming buddies up at McBee's, my calendar was depressingly clear until basketball practice.

Come November, I'd just as soon be anything besides a farmer.

November can bore the life right out of you, make you want to sleep forever or run screaming through the fields.

Come November, I start to feel the life I lost, a life somewhere out there in the big world, trying to break out of my very bones.

I couldn't do it—sit around reading, or worse, thinking, until practice.

I got cleaned up and went on into town. For a moment, when I got to the Four Corners, I thought about going to McBee's, sitting with all the other bored farmers, listening to their tired jokes and laughing like I was in a good place.

I turned left instead, turned left again on 2nd Street, Gloria's street, and, heart pounding, parked in front of her house, the engine still idling, the heater blowing.

It was a beat-up frame house, covered with what I guessed was old green asbestos siding. After a bit, I saw a flicker of movement from the bedroom window—the shades drawn open for a moment, then falling back into place.

"All right," I said. The movement didn't come again, but it seemed like a sign of some kind. Anyway, someone knew I was here, and if I just sat there, I'd look like an idiot, or worse—stalker Dad.

I turned the engine off.

I got out.

I walked to the front door.

I knocked on the wooden frame of the screen door. It echoed into the house.

And then I just stood there on the doorstep, the cold wind whipping around me, whispering up my sleeves.

I knocked again. I thought I heard movement. My heart still pounded.

Then the deadbolt was drawn, and the front door cracked open ever so slightly.

"He doesn't want to talk to you," a sleepy voice said. "I'm sorry."

"Hey, Gloria," I said. She waved, yawned. "I'm sorry I woke you."

She yawned again. "He doesn't want to talk to you," she repeated. "I'm sorry too."

And then the door closed and the bolt turned behind her and I was left standing on the doorstep, listening as steps receded into the house and disappeared.

I stood there for awhile longer, not hoping for a change of heart, but not knowing what to do next.

And at last I understood that what I had to do next was climb back in my truck to get warm.

I started the truck, turned the heater on high, and raised a forlorn wave even though I was pretty sure nobody was watching.

Then I put the truck in gear and drove away.

That night we entered negotiations with Lauren for her homecoming date. It reminded me of those World War I armistice talks in railroad cars, with Lauren wanting to be French marshal Foch and us to be the poor bewildered Germans making concession after concession. Unfortunately for her, she was riding our railroad.

I don't think it helped that we negotiated over cards, either, especially during a partners game of Spades, since our family takes cards seriously and responds angrily to distractions.

"Can I stay out 'til midnight?" was her opening volley. Her curfew was ten.

"Play," B. W., to her left, said.

"No," Michelle, her partner, said. "You may not."

Lauren led with the ace of clubs and B. W. immediately trumped it with the two of spades.

"Uhn!" she protested, mouth open—she'd counted on taking that trick—and he shrugged.

"No clubs," he said. "Sorry."

He did not seem particularly sorry.

After we'd tossed out low clubs, B. W. gathered up the trick and laid down the ace of hearts. Michelle threw a six of hearts and I threw a two.

Lauren tapped her cards on the table. "Then can we ride to Pizza Hut with Martin's brother?" Martin Amos, Lauren's homecoming date, was okay—a junior high boyfriend is sure a lot less threatening than someone who shaves and listens to Nine Inch Nails—but Billy Amos, who had spent three days in basketball the year before as a sophomore, was not okay. That kid had a temper and a miniscule attention span, neither of which boded well for him as a driver.

"Play," B. W. said.

"No," Michelle said. "You may not."

Lauren made a face and threw down the queen of hearts, and B. W. smiled and raked in another trick. He led next with the king of hearts, and Michelle and I again threw lesser hearts.

"Drop us off at the Pizza Hut then come back and get us?" Lauren looked up at us plaintively, her bottom lip tucked beneath her top one.

"Play, stupid," B. W. said.

"Don't call me stupid."

Michelle looked at me. I looked at her.

"Don't call your sister stupid," I told B. W. "And you. Lauren. Yes. You don't budge from the restaurant before we get back, on peril of death."

Lauren nodded at me, then laid down a three of spades on B. W.'s king of hearts and brushed B. W.'s waiting hands aside to collect the trick.

"Yeah, don't call your sister stupid, Bret Maverick," Michelle said. "Did you think she played a queen last time because she didn't know better than to waste a face card when you already had it won, or because it was the only heart she had left?"

"I plead the fifth," B. W. said, and Lauren punched him in the shoulder.

Lauren ended up beating us all, and we retired to the bedroom grumbling. Before we went to bed, Michelle said, "I had a long talk with Gloria when I stopped off at the convenience store today. She says she thinks Michael is starting to miss us."

"Sure he does," I said, around my toothbrush. He hadn't shown much sign of it that afternoon.

"What?" She poked her head around the corner into the bathroom, as if that would make me more intelligible. "Grape Nuts?"

I rolled my eyes, leaned over the sink, and spit. "Sure he does," I said, enunciating each syllable carefully. "He's stricken with remorse. He can't wait to come home, hug us all, feed the calves, slop the hogs."

"We don't have hogs," she said. "Really. I mean Gloria would know, wouldn't she?"

Although Gloria was slowly growing on me, I still was a little unsettled by her Goth appearance. "I consider Gloria an authority in the fields of cult rituals and anorexia. Maybe personal hygiene, if you'd consider defining it by negation. When was the last time she washed her hair?"

"She's not that bad," Michelle said, sliding a nightshirt on over her head, her voice momentarily muffled by flannel. I rinsed, dried my face, sat on the edge of the bed. "You should give her a chance. After all," and she stood, watching closely as she delivered this last, "she's going to be the mother of your grandson."

I blinked at her.

She quickly added, "Or granddaughter."

I stood up, then sat back down again. "You mean, of course, that they're going to have a baby eventually, like, after marriage or some other meaningful ritual."

No reply.

"Or do you mean that they are in the process of having a baby even as we speak?"

"You're mad," she said, and she leaned over and took my hands in hers. "I told Gloria you might need a little time to get used to the idea."

"I'm not mad," I said. "I'm upset." Which I think was a proper interpretation of what I was feeling. And anyway, why hadn't she told me, too? I mean, I was the one who woke her out of prenatal sleep. "What kind of a way is that to start a life together?"

Michelle dropped my hands and turned away from me. "Maybe they're happy about it. Maybe *he's* happy about it. Not everybody has to feel the same way you do. Or did."

Ouch. "Okay," I said, and tried to pull her to me, but she would not be pulled. "I'm sorry. But what kind of future do they have? He works at Pizza Hut, she works at a convenience store, they live in a house that's falling down around their ears—"

"What kind of future did we have? We didn't have any prospects. My parents helped with my college and we saved and slaved to get me through. I think we've done all right for ourselves. And for our kids."

"Yes," I said. "Agreed. We have epitomized the American dream." But at least now she let me make an armful of her, and so I pulled her to me. "Gloria is no Michelle Hooks, though. If she were, I'd feel a hundred percent better about it."

"She's turned out better than the rest of those Glancys have. And anyway, she's our best chance to get Michael back."

"We're never going to get Michael back," I said as we both slid under the comforter. "I think the best we can hope for is some sort of relationship that isn't characterized by exchanges of gunfire."

"I know," she said. "But wouldn't it be great if he really were missing us? Wouldn't that be nice?"

"Wouldn't it be lovely to think so?" I muttered.

"*The Sun Also Rises,*" she said, correctly, nuzzling my neck, and then Michelle and I set aside our discussion of the merits and demerits of Gloria Glancy to speak the infinitely more interesting language of love.

The next morning I thought I would check in with Phillip, and after feeding and watering the calves I headed for town, coffee, and eventually, his place. The boys at McBee's were in high spirits because of the moisture we'd gotten over the weekend and the sunny skies awaiting us now. It's amazing how a change of weather can put a smile on a farmer's face. After two cups of thick black coffee with them, I climbed into the truck and drove north. At Phillip's, I opened the gap, drove through, closed it behind me, and bounced down the well-rutted track to the trailer.

"Phillip," I called as I got out of the cab. No sense being shot as a trespasser when I came as a friend.

The door screeched open, and a tiny old lady shuffled out onto the top step. It was Ellen Smallfeet, Phillip's grandmother, an ancient woman who seemed to be grandmother or great-grandmother to most of the Southern Cheyenne in the state of Oklahoma. It was through her that Phillip and my neighbor Michael Graywolf were cousins, and I had known her since I was a baby—or known about her was maybe more accurate. Years ago she was reputed to be about a hundred and fifty and to have supernatural powers, but I had never seen her do anything more dramatic than scramble eggs for Michael and his family.

"Phillip is catching dinner," she said. "Down at the pond. I was just going to walk down and catch some with him."

And then I saw that she was carrying a rod and reel in her other hand. "Let me help you with that," I said.

"You're that John Tilden lives next door to my Michael," she said as I took the rod from her and gave her my other arm to hold onto as she stepped down slowly from step to step. "You married that teacher."

"Yes, ma'am," I said. "Used to be Michelle Hooks."

"Ah," she said, nodding. "I remember now. Michael says you are a good neighbor."

We followed a cow path into the cedars and I brushed a branch out of the way. "I didn't expect to see you out here," I said.

"I come out sometimes," she said. "Someone has to see Phillip eats, and he won't shoot at me. I'm his grandmother."

"Yes, ma'am," I said. "Where is this pond, anyway?"

"Right there."

We took a few more steps in the direction of her finger, and then through the cedars I could see the flickering of sunlight on water. A few more steps and we were past the encircling screen of trees and next to a small circular pond fed by a creek at the north end and drained on the south. Phillip was sitting with his back against a tree, and I recognized his level of comfort; that, I thought, was what I must look like when I fished at my favorite place.

He raised his free hand in silent greeting—noise scares the fish away—and inclined his head to indicate that we should sit next to him. I helped Mrs. Smallfeet to a sitting position and expected to bait her hook, but she simply reached out a hand to Phillip's coffee can, took out a big juicy nightcrawler, and double-hooked it without a wasted motion.

"Howdy," he said quietly. "Not much biting yet."

"They'll come," his grandmother said. "I've got the frying pan on the stove."

And sure enough, within a few minutes Mrs. Smallfeet's float bobbed under, she set the hook with a sure movement of the rod, and she began reeling in a good-sized green sunfish.

"Nice little sunny," Phillip said, nodding.

Ellen Smallfeet nodded back. Then, as she brought the fish to shore, she said, "Thank you for the gift of yourself, Little Brother. Your sacrifice will make us strong."

"She always thanks the fish," he told me. "Thanks trees, too, when we cut them down. It's more respectful, I guess."

Mrs. Smallfeet was pulling the hook out and preparing to put the sunny onto a stringer.

"How does she know it's a little brother?" I asked.

"It is because I say so," she said, without looking up at me. "That's why."

After they had caught half a dozen sunnies, crappie, and bluegill, Ellen Smallfeet handed me her rod and got slowly and laboriously to her feet. "Enough to cook," she said. "Come."

We went up to the trailer, Mrs. Smallfeet going up the steps as slow as geological time, and Phillip held the door open as we filed in.

The inside was not what I'd expected, at least not from the broken-down fences, piles of trash, and junk cars outside. The little trailer was sparsely furnished but clean, the sort of spartan living quarters a prisoner might get used to. We sat at a Formica table in the kitchen while Ellen Smallfeet cleaned the fish, dipped them in cornmeal, and plopped them sizzling into the hot oil in her skillet.

"Can I help you, Mrs. Smallfeet?" I had asked when she took out a cleaning knife, but she didn't answer and Phillip inclined his head to seat me at the table.

Lunch was fried fish, white bread, and some pear honey one of the cousins had made. We drank cold well water from plastic cups commemorating the Watonga Cheese Festival. Watonga had a cheese factory that made huge wheels of cheddar; people came from all across the state to buy them and came every fall to attend the Cheese Festival, complete with the requisite Cheese Festival Queen.

What's more, local girls actually competed to be that queen;

Lauren herself talked about entering the competition in a few years. Whenever we griped about running her to piano lessons, she'd say, "When I'm Queen of the Cheese Festival, you'll be glad you did."

"That will be our ticket to the good life," Michelle would agree, tousling her hair. I thought I'd rather have her be town tramp than Cheese Queen, but there's no accounting for taste.

We ate in silence. The food was good, and the pear honey was smooth and sweet, although Mrs. Smallfeet just smiled sadly when I commented on how good it was. "The old ways are vanishing," she said. "Young people don't learn to cook anymore. They all eat from those microwave ovens."

"It's a shame," I said.

"You have a microwave oven, Grandmother," Phillip said, and Ellen Smallfeet held a finger to her lips.

"You're not supposed to tell people that," she said. "It will spoil my—what do they call it?—mystique."

"So I shouldn't say anything about your CD player either?"

She took a swipe at him, but I don't think it hurt much.

"I'm going to play basketball," he told her. "Do you want to come watch me play?"

"It is good for you to get out of your trailer," she said. "But why basketball? Why don't you go to the powwow, dance with your own people?" She speared a morsel of fish, put it in her mouth, and chewed thoughtfully. "No offense," she said, turning to me.

"None taken," I said.

"I was good at it once," he said. "Basketball. Haven't been good at much else that wouldn't land me in jail. You ought to be excited."

"Excited," she said and sniffed. "I don't know. What is there to be excited about anymore?"

"Please come and see us play," I said. "It would be an honor."

"You were good once," she said to Phillip, and to me as well, "when you were young men. Those days are gone."

"We're not dead yet." He smiled to himself before saying, "While there is life, there is hope."

"Yes," she said, gesturing at him with her fork and nodding as vigorously as her neck would permit. "That is a good Cheyenne saying. You have heard me say it many times."

"I have," he said, and he shrugged. "Maybe there's something to it after all."

She sniffed, as if to say she didn't think it necessary to affirm that with words.

"I can drop your grandma back in town," I told Phillip after lunch. I didn't think she could hear me, but she turned from the sink, where her rubber-gloved arms were elbow deep in hot sudsy dishwater. "Someone will come after me if I don't show up tonight," she said. "But it might take awhile for them to get up their courage. They think Phillip will shoot them if they come here unannounced."

Phillip did not chuckle to show that this was a ridiculous idea. "Let John run you home, Grandmother," he said, then turned to me. "She'll walk it if I let her. She's a tough old bird."

Ellen Smallfeet cackled.

When she had dried the dishes and gathered her things, we all walked out to the porch. "Why don't you come to homecoming?" I asked Phillip. "A lot of people you know will be in town."

He shook his head. "More reason to stay here." But he shook my hand and gave me a small smile and thanked me for coming by. "I owed you a dinner."

"You didn't owe me anything. It was great to have you out to the house. You're welcome anytime."

"Good-bye, Grandmother," he said, turning to her. "You make sure John doesn't take you off to Mexico." She kissed his cheek, and then she stepped to my truck, opened the passenger door, and clambered up inside, refusing all offers of help.

"See you Sunday," I called as I got in the truck. Phillip inclined his head slightly—half of a nod—and pulled the trailer door shut behind him with a screech.

Mrs. Smallfeet didn't talk as we bounced across the rutted track taking us across the pasture or up to the road, nor did she talk until after I opened the gap, drove through, and closed it behind us. When I got back into the cab, she said, "Thank you for being a friend to Phillip. He has not always had good friends."

"I know," I said. "But I haven't been a good friend. How can I claim to be a good friend now, when I haven't been there when he really needed me?"

"Ah," she said. "How do you know that now is not the time of his greatest need?"

I pursed my lips and mulled that over for a bit. "I guess I don't." I turned onto the highway headed for town.

She furrowed her brow, tapped it once or twice, as if retrieving something from a mental vault: "'We should never be afraid to do right now what we should have done right a long time ago.'"

"Sounds like something I've been thinking about lately," I said. "Is that a Cheyenne saying?" I slowed down for the right turn onto

2nd Street, where Mrs. Smallfeet lived in a tiny composition-shingled house two blocks from Gloria, a house with a swing set and lots of outdoor toys for her many grandchildren.

"Martin Luther King," she said. We pulled up in front of her house and she opened the door to get out. "Indians cannot take credit for all wisdom, you know." She cackled again before she shut the door.

I thought about that all the way home: It's never too late to do the right thing, to make the right choice, to correct the mistakes of the past.

Or is it? Did this apply equally to the way I treated my children, to the job I performed, to the woman I married?

Or was she just a senile old parrot who could squawk historic phrases?

The phone rang as we were sitting down for dinner. I would have been happy to let the machine pick it up, but Lauren made a dash for it.

B. W. rolled his eyes. "It's probably just a salesman," he said.

"Hello," she said, her voice vivacious. Then the smile left her face, she dropped the phone to her side, and she held it toward me.

"It's a man," she said.

"Bill Cobb," the voice said.

"Bill," I said.

"Ah," he said. "John. Glad to find you at home." There was a momentary pause, as though Bill was looking for his next words. "Just thought I might have a word with you."

Then he sat silent again for a moment. "You can have several," I said into the silence. "Words," I explained helpfully when he made no reply.

"I have to go," he said, and then he did, and I stood there holding the phone for a moment with what must have been a quizzical look on my face.

"What did he want?" Michelle asked.

"I don't rightly know," I said. I replaced the receiver on its cradle.

"At least he wasn't selling something," B. W. said.

"No," I said. "He wasn't." I sat back down at the table. "Lauren, will you say grace?"

That night I dreamed I was at some kind of gathering on the farm; it was unquestionably our place, only it looked like it did back before my father added the extra bedrooms, a strange trip back to when this place had a screened-in side porch where I used to sleep covered with sweat on sweltering summer nights, a world remembered in the black and white of old photographs. A big get-together was taking place, lots of family—aunts, uncles, cousins—and friends talking, eating, laughing inside, but I was standing outside the big picture window looking in at them from the flowerbed.

There were Gloria and Michael, sitting together in my father's big recliner. Gloria looked up, saw me, and waved, but when she nudged Michael, he just frowned and kept his eyes to the ground. Why should things be any different in dreams?

There was B. W., wearing rolled-up jeans, a flannel shirt, a watch cap, and carrying an ax. *Hi Dad*, he said silently, and he waved.

I couldn't see Lauren. Maybe she was out on a date.

Into the living room shuffled my grandfather, sober and somber, a tall man I'd always thought made John Wayne look like a sissy. I never heard of him smiling, and now he simply looked sourly at me and waved me away from the window with one hand like a quarterback waving a receiver back farther. Maybe I was standing on something he had planted.

I stepped up onto the front porch and looked through the screen door. Just inside, where Michael had been, I saw my brother, Trent, standing at ease in his Marine dress uniform, the one they buried him in, his hat in the crook of his left elbow. Next to him were Bill and Samantha Cobb, talking quietly about something.

"Hey, Johnny," Trent said, turning to me with genuine surprise in his voice. "Long time no see."

"Hey," I said, and then something caught in my throat, and I could only raise a hand in acknowledgment. Even in my dream I realized that Trent was dead, as dead as my grandfather, but at that moment, I didn't care; I just wanted to open the door and throw my arms around him. Twenty-five years is a long time to miss your big brother.

Samantha looked up at me as I pulled at the door, rattling it, then she looked back to Bill and they continued their conversation, something about polls and early voting.

"It's locked, buddy," Trent said. "Hang on and I'll let you in."

The door swung wide, and for a crazy second it was like the world had swayed sideways—I had a sense of essential imbalance, of the earth teetering beneath me—and then I stepped inside and felt Trent's strong hand shaking mine, and I threw my left arm around his neck and felt the muscles bunched there beneath his collar and shoulder braid.

"Hey, buddy," he said, and his voice was soft in my ear. "How many cattle you running?"

"I don't want to talk about cattle," I said, taking him by his shoulders. "That's all you ever wrote about. Every letter home, you said everything was fine, you just wanted to know about things on the farm. Well, you weren't fine. You weren't!"

People turned to look in my direction, and hot tears burned at the corner of my eyes. "Hey, get a hold of yourself, Johnny," he said, pushing me back a step and stiffening to attention. "You're the man of the house now. You're going to have to act that way."

Then he saluted me, executed a crisp about-face, and disappeared into the dark interior of the house.

"Trent," I called after him. "Trent! Hey, man. Come back. I'll be strong. I'll be a man."

He was gone. My eyes were full of tears and my chest full of rocks, and I turned to Samantha and Bill, who were looking at me like I was an interesting species of insect. "I never got to say good-bye," I said. "That's all. I loved him and he died and I never got to say good-bye."

But they turned away from me and continued talking percentage points and constituencies; in fact, everyone in the room showed me their backs. The world became unstable beneath my feet again, and I reeled out of the house and out to the gloomy barn, banging into hay bales like a man on the deck of a boat in rough water. Finally I caught hold of a rope hanging from the rafters, and I climbed up it thinking, *Maybe I can see better from up here.*

But all I could see when I got to the top were the rafters and the underside of the tin roof. So I climbed back down. When I came outside, the sky had grown as dark as the interior of the barn, and big drops of rain were beginning to fall. Across the way, I saw the windmill, and the same dream logic that had impelled me to climb the rope sent me up the windmill, only the rain was making the metal wet and slippery, and lightning was flashing uncomfortably close by, and all of a sudden, somehow, I was naked. This dream was starting to feel ridiculous even to me, and I started to think maybe I should climb down from the windmill, and then people started coming out the side porch, the door closest to me, and the world was shaking again.

And then I woke up to Michelle sobbing quietly beside me.

"Michelle," I said. "Hey, sweetie," and she slid into my arms, and I felt her face, warm and flushed, and the wetness of her tears on my shoulder.

"It'll be okay," I said. "Everything will be fine." I didn't ask what she was crying about; although I should have, there were just so many possibilities. She was always emotional just before her period; in days past I'd known her to wail for half an hour about a speeding ticket, a student failing an exam, or a cross word from one of the kids.

There were plenty of serious things for her to cry about, too, regardless of her hormonal state: Michael, our grandchild, me.

"I know I wasn't your first choice," she murmured. "But you do love me a little, don't you, J. J.?"

So I guess that would be me.

No, she hadn't been my first choice; I wasn't even conscious that I had had a choice. Because really, if I'd had my choice—

I flashed to Samantha, our last dance at the reunion. Our last rainy night together, the pattering on the windows, her skin iridescent in the glow from the dashboard.

I thought that only a few seconds had passed since she asked— not enough to make a difference, I hoped.

I smiled at her, although I didn't know if she could see it in the dark.

"More than a little," I said. "You know I do, Shell."

And I held her until she returned to a troubled sleep. I had no desire to join her. I lay there, her head on my shoulder, listening to the farm stir to life with first light.

Fools

Since Michelle had to get to the football field early Friday evening to work the concession stand for homecoming, I got to play the major role in the Lauren First Date story. It was my job to take her to fetch Martin, and then to chauffeur them around town, which wasn't so bad, really, even if it was a preview of plenty of late-night worrying to come, because Lauren did look beautiful, even without the excess makeup Michelle had ordered her to take off. "You look like a twenty-dollar hooker," she said, chanting the time-honored refrain of parents of young women throughout the ages.

Maybe the reason we use the same tired accusations as our parents is because our kids make the same tired excuses. I knew "Everyone else is wearing their makeup like this," would be Lauren's reply before it came out. I left the room to avoid being caught in the loop.

Lauren had mostly gotten over her sulk by the time I got her into the truck.

"Don't embarrass me," she said as she checked her lips and hair in the dusty visor mirror.

"Do I ever?"

"Don't tell any jokes," she said. "Talk about sports. Or school."

"You look great," I told her. "Martin is lucky to be seen with you tonight. I think maybe we should talk about how lucky he is."

"God help me," she muttered and put the visor up as we bounced to the end of our driveway.

"Let's see. What else could we talk about? Is Martin a vegetarian?"

"God help me," she repeated. She rolled her eyes and looked across at me with tolerant affection.

"I'll be good," I promised, and I was. I shook Martin's hand firmly but without bone-crunching malice when he got in, drove quietly from the Amos place at the corner of Seventh and Laing, across from the fairgrounds, to the football stadium. Lauren's jacket sleeve rustled against mine—she, of course, had scooted into the middle to make room for Martin. Beneath it she wore one of those satiny Mo Betta Western shirts with a wild geometric design and a pair of tight-fitting Lee jeans. I figured if her mother had let her leave the house in this outfit it wasn't my place to send her back, but I did indeed have that thought.

As we passed my hideous gymnasium—bluish and greenish metal siding with a brick front—we saw that the stadium to the north was already filling up with people decked out in red and black. I could see Bobby Ray up on top of the red press box with the video camera he used to film the games for the coaches—perks of school board membership—and if I'd been able to stop and look closely I could have located Michelle dishing out coffee and cokes in paper cups from the concession stand in the northwest corner of the stadium, just off the west end zone.

When we stopped and Martin opened his door, I quickly outlined the ground rules: "Fifteen minutes after the game ends, you will be at this truck. We'll take you to Pizza Hut. You may sit with your friends. After we've eaten, you've played video games, Michelle and I have had a last cup of coffee, we will head for our respective homes. Understand?"

"Yes, sir," Martin said.

"Got it," Lauren said, sliding toward Martin and freedom. They disappeared toward the stadium at a dead run before I could say something like, "Synchronize your watches," as Lauren knew I probably would.

After I bought my ticket, I sauntered over to the concession stand, stopped almost every step of the way by people asking after the basketball team. Maybe with the football team a miserable failure, people would turn to basketball. Maybe basketball would become everyone's sport of choice. Maybe God would plant in the heavens a pillar of smoke by day and a pillar of fire by night to guide these record crowds toward the gymnasium.

In any case, I tried to sound hopeful about my kids, and when people asked enthusiastically about the benefit game at Christmas, I smiled and said we'd work hard to put on a good show. That seemed to satisfy them.

After tossing such mendacity about like chicken feed, it was pleasant to spend a short truthful moment with Michelle as she poured coffee into the big insulated mug I'd brought.

"Kids okay?"

"They were polite," I said, pulling out my wallet to replant the change she gave me. "To expect more would be pointless."

"True enough," she said. "Come back later?"

"Of course." I raised my mug after securing the lid. "I'll be back when it's time for a refill."

The size of the crowd surprised me, as homecoming crowds

always do. It's like Easter Sunday services—people you haven't seen all year apparently decide it's a good thing to show up and demonstrate where their loyalties lie. I pushed up toward the spot in the home bleachers where Oz and Michael Graywolf and a few others normally sit and couldn't even see them. The stands were full of strange people—strange in a familiar way, admittedly—but still people who normally weren't sitting in my seat.

I climbed up to the press box, thinking I might presume on school connections for a seat up there. Reporters from the *Watonga Republican* and the Geary paper shared the booth proper with the PA announcer, George Hoberecht. George looked up and waggled his triple chins at me. "Try the roof," he said. "Bobby Ray'd likely welcome the company."

I went up the ladder, one hand holding my coffee, rapped on the trapdoor to announce myself, pushed it open, and pulled myself up onto the roof. "You got room for an old friend?" I asked, aware that we had not acted much like old friends the last time we'd seen each other.

"If you don't mind sharing the roof with an idiot," he said, and gave me a rueful smile. Then he extended a hand and pulled me to my feet.

The roof of the press box was about twelve by fifteen, and there was a railing around it. Up here, you could feel the wind blowing in from Kansas. On the flagpole above us flapped the flags of the United States of America, the state of Oklahoma, and the Watonga Eagles.

The video camera pointed to the fifty-yard line from its tripod, and Bobby Ray was sitting on a folding chair sipping his own cup of coffee. "Good idea," he said as I took the lid off my mug, both of us sending mist into the air. "I always spill half of mine on the way up."

"I have my moments," I said, sipping and feeling the warm welcome bitterness spread out from my stomach.

"That you do," he said. There was a moment when he studied his shoe, then he inhaled deeply and looked up at me. "We still have practice this weekend?"

I exhaled fog. "How's Sunday afternoon for you?"

"Sunday afternoon is good for me. Any chance we'll get Bill up here for a practice?"

"Probably, now that the Texas elections are over," I said. "I should have asked him—" I stopped. I really hadn't had a chance to ask anything the last time he called.

Bobby Ray broke off mid-sip and leaned forward confidentially. "Bill better have supported good folks this time," he said. "'Cos I'd guess his chances of getting himself elected dogcatcher now are about as good as my chances of getting a big loan from First Watonga. Not that I care, mind you."

"Why do you say that?"

He eyed me curiously. "I've never cared for Bill. You know that."

"No," I said, rolling my eyes. "Not why don't you care. Why couldn't he get elected dogcatcher?"

Bobby Ray looked through the viewfinder and adjusted the focus. "He's lost the wholesome family man thing now. Grave political liability."

I set my mug down on the ground and straightened up to look Bobby Ray in the eyes. "Lost what?"

"When Samantha left him," Bobby Ray said, as though he were explaining something to an infant. The band was coming out onto the field, and I could hear the smart slap of their feet as they marched past on the asphalt track.

"What are you talking about?" I said. "Who left who?" I remembered Samantha's breathy "We need to talk," Bill's bizarre phone manners, and suddenly I felt a sledgehammer blow to the solar plexus.

"Whoa, partner," he said. He reached a tentative hand out as if to steady me, and I must have needed it, because I found myself leaning heavily against the railing. "I thought you knew. Marcie told me she ran into Michelle in the frozen food aisle at Homeland and told her all about it." Marcie was Bobby Ray's third and most recent wife, a more recent former head cheerleader, former secretary for Bobby Ray. He hadn't found another secretary as good, and he was still mad at her for quitting when he married her.

"Michelle didn't tell you that Samantha and Bill split up?"

"Must have slipped her mind," I said. At the edge of my hearing, I heard the crowd roar its approval at the conclusion of the national anthem. It sounded like the ocean in a big conch shell my dad brought home from Guam after the war.

"Why?" I finally said, and it must have been some time later, because Watonga had already kicked off and Bobby Ray was bent over the viewfinder of his camera.

"Get the wind at the end of each half, I guess."

"No." This was why I never liked talking to Bobby Ray. "Not why didn't we elect to receive, if that's what you're telling me. What happened to Bill and Sam?"

"I hear she had an affair." He shrugged without looking up. "I hear he had an affair. Who knows? Their parents aren't talking about it, and they aren't talking to each other, either."

The sledgehammer was gone, and in its place my stomach now felt as empty as if I were coming off a five-day fast. I took a gulp of coffee to try and counteract it, but this was one of the few things coffee couldn't make better. "So what's going on? Are they getting divorced? Where are the kids? Is she coming back here?"

Bobby Ray lifted his eye from the camera to look across at me. "You better hope not, old son."

And dimwitted as he could sometimes be, about this Bobby Ray was right. It was a strange feeling to hear that my first love had left her husband, and stranger still to think about running into her in the flesh.

"I hear Samantha's moved to Fort Worth with the kids," Bobby Ray said a few plays later, after Canton had punted and Watonga took over on their own thirty. "She's still selling real estate. Making good money, I guess."

"Uh-huh." Through the crowd milling in front of the stands I saw Michael Graywolf, and next to him, someone else I knew. "Look. There's Phillip."

"Really?" Bobby Ray couldn't take his eyes off a pass play, but the surprise was evident in his voice.

"Down below and to the right," I said, and he took a look as the referees conferred about what to do on the play they'd just whistled dead.

"That was interference, plain and simple," Bobby Ray said.

"Uh-huh," I said. "They're looking up this way."

"Well, I guess you better wave," Bobby Ray said. "Wouldn't want 'em to think we're unfriendly."

"No, we wouldn't," I said. I waved. Michael waved back and nudged Phillip, who looked up hesitantly. He nodded. Beside me, Bobby Ray nodded back.

"He's had a tough old row to hoe," Bobby Ray said, as close to an apology as he was ever going to get.

"That he has," I said, and took another sip. "I think I'll pop down and tell him howdy."

"You're welcome to come back up here if you like," Bobby Ray said, followed closely by a curse as a Canton Tiger blocked our punt and chased it toward our goal line. "We are just god-awful."

I understood his frustration. It's hard to be a fan for a team that loses, unless they do so in lovable fashion—like the Chicago Cubs. Our Watonga boys that year didn't make endearingly horrendous mistakes like running the wrong way for touchdowns. They just got beat by better teams week after week, and there's not much fun in that.

After climbing down and through the press box, I made my way into the bleachers to Michael and Phillip, and managed to get a few words in to both before we were swept apart by the tide of fans. I took a step in the direction of Michelle, then remembered that what I most wanted to talk to her about was not suitable for a public conversation. So I went back up on the roof after answering another round of questions about the varsity team, about the basketball fund-raiser, about my hopes for the season.

"God save us," I said when I got back up on the roof of the press box. "The worse the score gets, the more people want to know about basketball."

"You may have to sneak out the back before it's all over," Bobby Ray said. We had gone down two touchdowns in the short time I had been gone.

"What happened?"

"Converted on the blocked punt, then ran in an interception. Our guys would be better off just falling on the ball for the next three quarters."

And he was right. It might have made the score more respectable. After the final gun went off and we had lost by thirty-eight, I patted Bobby Ray on the back, told him I'd see him Sunday, and started out toward the truck.

Carla caught me on the sleeve as I passed the gate. "Run for your life," she told me. "These people are desperate for a winner."

"They've probably been asking my kids about our chances," I said. "I hope they lied."

"You hang in there," she said. "Looks like some more folks are waiting on you." She smiled and took off toward her Jeep, and I turned, ready to put on a false smile and give a big Chamber of Commerce handshake.

"Hurry up, Dad," Lauren called, for indeed it was my lovely daughter and her beau leaning against the truck. "Pizza Hut will be full."

Which it was. Had there been chandeliers, kids would have been swinging from them. Every booth was full to overflowing, angular adolescent knees were jutting out into public space, and the waiting line seemed to contain as many folks as were already stuffed into booths. "What do you want to do?" I asked. "McBee's? Hi-De-Ho?"

Lauren rolled her eyes. *As if.* "We'll stay here, Dad. You're welcome to go if you want."

Michelle arrived then, having parked her car down the highway in front of the Dodge dealership and walked over. "What a madhouse," she said, and smiled admiringly.

"We're staying," Lauren said.

Michelle looked across at me and saw my grimace, then checked her watch. "Okay. We'll be back for you at eleven thirty. And woe be unto you if we have to go looking for you." Then she hooked her arm through mine and led me out into the chilly air of the parking lot.

I looked across at her. "'Woe be unto you?'"

"That's right, cowboy." She gave my arm a tug. "Buy me a cup of coffee?"

I grunted assent. "How about McBee's?"

"I guess so. Who's driving?"

I shrugged, and she looked up at me and blinked. "Bad night? Did the kids act up?"

"Not now," I said. "When we're in the car."

We walked in silence, our footsteps crunching on gravel as we approached the car. I didn't open her door for her. The stars were dancing wildly in the cold night air, and I stood for a moment at the passenger door looking up and out into the inky darkness splashed with light. How peaceful it all looked up there.

"You're angry," she said after I got in and she started the car and I still didn't speak.

I held myself still and let my voice stay calm. "Why didn't you tell me about Bill and Sam?"

"Ah," she said. "That." She pulled onto the two-lane highway headed back into town. "Well," she said as she stopped at the four-way stop, "it's like this." Then she eased straight ahead instead of making the right turn toward McBee's. "Let's say that there's a convicted killer who escapes from prison, and you know he's coming back to get you. No. Hang on. That's not a good analogy. Strike that."

She kept her eyes straight ahead as she drove. She turned right, then right again, through the middle of town. When the silence seemed like it would never be broken, she tried again. "Okay. Let's say that your husband is an alcoholic, and you know a liquor store the size of a Super Wal-Mart is about to open up the next town over." She grimaced, wrinkling her nose, chanced a look at me. "No, that makes you sound like—well—not good. I don't mean that."

She took a deep breath, took another look across at me, and said quietly, "Okay. Let's suppose that you're a wife whose husband still misses the woman he lost when they were kids, a woman who has just split up with her husband and is headed back to town. She's rich and beautiful and smart and funny, and why wouldn't he still love her?" She took a deep breath. "But why should the wife have to be the one to break the news to him? Why should she be the one to watch his reaction?"

She turned right again, drove for a bit, stopped at the four-way stop again, this time headed west out of town. Finally she asked, "How did you react?"

"I was—surprised."

"I'll bet," she said. "I just didn't want to see that. Can you understand?"

"Better," I said. "Although you should know by now that you've got nothing to worry about. You could have told me."

"I don't know that," she said, and her voice was no longer calm and pleasant. "I don't know that at all." Her head jerked, and the car eased over slowly to the side of the road, stopping on the shoulder. She covered her eyes with her hands.

I leaned across toward her and tried to take her in my arms, but she pushed me away. "J. J., if you're going to leave me," she sobbed, "I don't want you to be nice about it. Don't lie to me and disappear. Just tell me. We'll get along fine. I won't make things hard for you. Just tell me, that's all."

"I'm not going to leave you, Shell," I said, and at that moment, I certainly didn't want to. "Get that out of your head." This time when I tried to gather her up she consented. I held her while she sobbed, her frame shuddering as she tried to hold it back, all the time telling her, "It's okay. It's okay. I'm not going to leave you."

And as I said it I was praying, *Please, please, let that be true.*

After awhile, my arm went numb, and I looked over her shoulder at the steamed-up windows, wondering if she believed me, wondering if I believed myself, wondering why I was wondering.

And at last, I realized that I was wondering because we had been sitting there for a very long time. I didn't want to say anything—there wasn't anything I could say to make things better—but I cleared my throat and asked, "Shell, what time is it?"

And since Michelle was a parent as well as a frightened human being, she instantly caught my meaning and checked her watch. "Well, that's not good," she said. "It's eleven thirty." She fumbled for the ignition, started the car, and pulled a highly illegal U-turn.

"Set the car clock back ten minutes," she said. "As long as we're still the parents in this family, time is what we say it is."

Lauren and Martin stood shivering outside the Pizza Hut when we pulled up. Michelle had blown her nose just before we turned into the parking lot, and I had brushed some wisps of hair off her flushed face and back behind her ears. When we pulled up, I opened my door while Michelle sat, motor running, and got out.

"You're late," Lauren said. "We've been standing out here for hours."

"She says we're late," I said.

"Not by my watch," Michelle said. "You hurry home."

"We will," I said. I smiled at her, but all I got in return before I shut the door was a pursing of the lips.

I gave Michelle a complete postdate debriefing in our truth-telling period as I got ready for bed: how Lauren had not held Martin's hand in the truck, how Lauren had not walked Martin up to the front porch, how their good-byes had been truck-borne and brief—"See ya."

By common consent we did not speak of our earlier conversation in the car, although naturally it filled the bedroom like air, invisible yet tangible whenever one of us moved.

I noticed that I was the only one making preparations for bed. "Are you staying up?" I asked around a mouthful of toothbrush.

"Of course I'm standing up," she said, so I spit and asked again.

"Oh," she said. "For awhile." She poked her head into the bathroom. "I'm not mad. Okay? I'm not mad."

"I'm not mad either," I said. I shivered as I slid between the cold sheets. "Don't stay up too late."

When she did come in, it was after two, and it was to whisper in my ear: "J. J., do you love me?"

"Of course I do," I must have muttered, and rolled over, but she had more to say.

"You know, J. J.," she whispered, "it hurt me the first time you went back to her, and I didn't really have a claim on you. And I was younger and more resilient then."

I grunted, because there was little I could say that I hadn't already said, and because I was really tired.

She nestled in next to me like a bird nudging a nest toward comfort. At last, she settled down, and as I dropped off, I heard her murmur, "Don't leave me, J. J."

"I won't leave you," I tried to say, but my eyes were heavy, my lips didn't seem to move, and the next thing I knew, it was morning.

I got up in the dim light, spent several hours taking care of my calves, filling troughs with feed for the older ones and moving unweaned babies onto the waiting udders of the milk cows standing around for that very purpose.

When I came in, the house was warm and smelled of sourdough biscuits, and I smiled, took off my boots and coveralls, and went into the kitchen. Lauren and Michelle were sitting cross-legged and facing each other in adjacent chairs at the table, and they were giggling like schoolgirls sharing secrets.

"Sorry," I said. "I'll just back out of here before I hear something I shouldn't. You never saw me."

"Oh, get in here," Lauren said. "I made biscuits."

I sat, split open several steaming biscuits, spread them with butter and blackberry jam, and ate slowly, savoring the mingling of hot and creamy and sour and chewy in each bite.

Meanwhile, decorum had returned to the table, and the girls sat primly, straight-faced, although their eyes occasionally darted to meet the other's. "I'm being left out of something," I said between biscuits, and Lauren simply said, "Yup," and they both donned identical wry grins. That was all I got.

Our senior citizen practice the next day began on a similarly lighthearted note, although for very different reasons. It is true that Bobby Ray was, for Bobby Ray, positively kind to Phillip, which was a good development, and since I'd invited a bunch of the varsity up to shoot while the gym was open I was able to orchestrate a scrimmage between old and young teams, a predress rehearsal of sorts. And Jimmy Bad Heart Bull was there in tennis shoes instead of the football cleats he'd occupied all fall, which was pleasant. I was starting to think that I'd only imagined him. I invited him to play with us old folks, since the first team I'd been running in practice all fall was present and had gotten used to playing with one another. B. W. led their offense and I led ours, such as it was—my team was so bad that really all you could do was laugh about it.

We hadn't been up and down the court a half-dozen times before Bobby Ray and Phillip were gasping, and when B. W. took an outlet pass from Micheal Wilkes at half-court and dashed past Jimmy, I knew we were in trouble. They had scored four times in a row—five, after B. W.'s layup—and we hadn't done anything. We were staring embarrassment in the face.

I tried to be patient, to find one of my guys when he was open, but my guys—except for Oz—stood around waiting for *me* to do something. Oz spent most of his time setting picks for me, which meant my chances of hitting him for an open shot were almost nil unless he rolled off and got open after setting his pick, which he had apparently forgotten how to do. No, when he set a pick he became a semipermanent organic wall; he was standing around like everyone else but was at least preserving the illusion that he was doing something useful.

Several times I passed to Bobby Ray, who had taken up occupancy to the right of the basket outside the three-point line, and every time he put up a shot. One was blocked spectacularly by Martel Sparks into the fourth row of the bleachers; one caromed back off the rim for a long rebound and another easy layup for B. W.; another missed the rim and the backboard, and I was a little surprised that it managed to hit the floor.

On defense we weren't much better. I had put us in a zone defense because I didn't think we could keep up with them man-to-man—a pretty easy prediction to make, since Phillip and I were our most fleet footed, and that wasn't saying much—but my kids were moving, cutting along the baseline, setting screens for each other like I'd taught them, and even in a zone we old men looked like stumblebums.

So we must have been down about 12-0 when I finally decided that, even though my role since childhood had always been assist man and not scorer, maybe I should take things in hand and see if I could fare any better than my cohorts, which is to say, not well at all.

At the time, it seemed to happen in a flash of motion and momentum, but when I related it to folks later I realized I could slow it down and run it back to see what I did wrong, what I might have done differently. I have had other such moments in life: on a sweltering summer day when I was fifteen, turning a tractor over on a steep side hill and jumping for my life into the hot sandy soil; on a Friday night, with the tangible scent of sweat seeping in from outside of the coach's office and of ersatz orange on our breaths from drinking Gatorade and Everclear, kissing Michelle Hooks just before we made Michael; on a muddy Sunday morning, stepping into the house with my boots thick with manure while down the hall I knew my sons were trying to hurt each other.

On this occasion, what happened was this: I thought I saw a passageway between B. W., who wasn't guarding me that closely, and Martel Sparks, who was hovering close to Bobby Ray. I was dribbling slowly with my left hand, my head up, seemingly scanning the floor for a pass, and not watching the opening I thought I could drive through.

I gave a slight head and shoulder fake left, shifted my dribble to the other hand, and tried to dart to the right around B. W. and up the center of the three-second lane. My strategy was textbook; since we weren't doing anything from the perimeter, we needed to penetrate, and I could either dish off when the defense collapsed or take the easy layup if it presented itself. My execution was not, however, textbook.

You see, I didn't exactly dart around B. W. He was too quick for me, had sidestepped to cut off the path to the basket, and I saw this almost as soon as I pushed off. So I went up for what I hoped would be a floating jump shot from inside the foul line. It was, and I had the pleasure of seeing the ball bank off the backboard and into the bucket before the not-so-pleasurable realization that B. W.'s new position was directly in my flight path.

I twisted my body to try to keep from running into him, bringing my left shoulder down and in. I was not so conscious of anything else after my left foot came down on the side of B. W.'s shoe and my ankle bent sideways at an angle it is not meant to assume, and I collapsed to the floor with a nest full of hornets buzzing about my foot and up my shin.

I gasped, felt my face contort.

"Are you okay, Dad?" B. W. asked, on one knee next to me. "Can you get up?"

I flexed my foot once experimentally, and let out another gasp of pain. "Help me up," I said.

"I'm sorry," he said. "I think that was a blocking foul." He held out a strong arm, and I pulled myself up, hopping on my right foot.

"I think it would have been a charge," I said, and I gingerly put my left foot lightly to the ground. Hornets. I hopped over to the sideline, letting my left foot touch ground as briefly as possible. I figured I had better not let it stiffen up on me, so I told everyone to take a short break, and I walked slowly up and down the sideline until the pain subsided to a throbbing.

"Somebody should take a look at that," Oz said when I walked back onto the court and we huddled briefly. "You could have a real bad sprain."

I waved him off through gritted teeth. "It's nothing. Remember what Coach Von used to say whenever one of us went down in practice?"

"Walk it off," came the simultaneous reply from Phillip, Bobby Ray, and Oz, and they raised their heads and looked at one another with happy recognition.

"Let's see some more movement," I said. "We need to screen Bobby Ray for some open shots." I looked meaningfully over at him and gave him a wry smile. "I know he's going to find the range eventually. We may have to double-screen Martel. He's tenacious today, for some reason. Phillip, you and Jimmy need to crash the boards on both ends. Work for position. You remember how."

"It's been a long time, Coach," Jimmy said.

"No kidding," Phillip said. "But we'll do our best."

And we made a game of it. Not if you were keeping score, of course; we were so far behind that all we really could have claimed was a moral victory, whatever that is. But we stayed roughly even with the varsity from that point on, and it felt good. Even without Bill in the middle, we hit some shots from outside, put some offensive rebounds in, and closed the sieve that had been our defense.

I myself didn't do much besides limp, and B. W. could have driven on me at any time, but he was generous, or maybe still feeling guilty; he was prone to that. When we decided to call a halt after an hour or so, I was grateful. I could see the swelling coming up and out of my high-topped Nikes and knew that when I took off that shoe I was not going to like what I saw.

"Dad, I really think you need to get that ankle looked at," B. W. said. "It looks like trouble."

"If I ice it down when we get home, it'll be fine," I lied. I didn't want to go to the emergency room; too much money, even with Michelle's insurance. "Could you run Phillip out to his place?"

"I'll walk," Phillip said. "Y'all shouldn't have to cart me around."

"Hey, it's freezing out there," B. W. said. "I don't mind."

"One of these days I'll get my old truck running," Phillip said, and B. W. was asking him what was wrong with it as I limped for the exit door.

"You sure you can get home okay?" Bobby Ray asked as we pushed out into the cold.

"Just need one foot to drive this truck," I said, and clapped him on the shoulder. "Thanks for asking. And good shooting."

"I did all right," he said. "Maybe we won't make fools of ourselves after all."

"Maybe," I said, hopping off like an idiot. I still had more than a few doubts on that score, at least where I was concerned.

Crutches

I don't know why we protest when doctors tell us what to do. If we make the mistake of entrusting our well-being to them, what can we expect but advice? I suppose it makes us feel better to complain; it doesn't seem to accomplish anything else. I left my doctor's office on crutches. It was a bad sprain, I should get plenty of rest, I should stay off it completely for at least five days, and it could take months before it felt completely trustworthy again. This was more answer than I wanted.

"But I've got to coach basketball," I protested. "I've got to go out and feed cattle. I've got to play point guard after Christmas."

"You've got to stay off that ankle," he ordered me, and rightfully so. After I removed my shoe on Sunday night I was in the worst agony of my entire life. My ankle was about the size of a softball—a red, throbbing softball. The pain was so overwhelming it made me sick to my stomach, and I couldn't stop myself from groaning. Michelle couldn't sleep with me lying there mooing, and anything that disturbed her sleep had to be momentous indeed. Then on Monday morning when I tried to get out of bed to feed the cattle, stepping on it was like setting off a three-alarm fire from my knee down.

Michelle ran in from wherever she had been when she heard

my plaintive noises and found me on the floor. She took me to the
doctor in Watonga, with the results I have already described. This
was a solution to my pain, but still left the cattle hungry. B. W.,
Michelle, and Lauren fed them Monday and Tuesday—Lauren
under protest—but it was apparent to me that with their busy lives
and anticattle convictions, I couldn't count on them to do it daily. I
would have to come up with another idea.

Meanwhile, I asked Carla to help with basketball practice when
on Monday it became evident that I couldn't stay on top of things
from the bleachers.

"Glad to," she said. And I was glad too; we could learn things
from her.

When I went out for practice Tuesday afternoon, I seated
myself gingerly in the fourth row, my ankle propped on the seat in
front of me. I figured I would be safe there from errant passes and
out-of-control bodies. Shortly before the kids started to arrive, the
outside door opened and Phillip walked in, wearing a jean jacket and
a T-shirt with Joe Camel on it. His hair was clean and gathered in a
ponytail; he was wearing his tennis shoes.

"Hey," he said, and walked across the court to sit next to me.
He looked down at my bare foot and swollen ankle. "That looks
awful."

"That's how it feels," I said. I sniffed discreetly and couldn't
pick up any trace of alcohol, which was heartening. "I've got some
Percodan. Helps some."

"Be careful with that stuff," he said solemnly. "It gets a hold
of you and doesn't let go." He shrugged off his jacket to reveal Joe
Camel in his full glory.

"You own any clothes that don't advertise cigarettes?"

He smiled a little. "Ralph Lauren and them guys don't hang out in my neighborhood."

"Sorry," I said. "I just don't want the kids getting the message that smoking's okay for them. What brings you up here?"

"You do. My grandmother heard you were bad off. I thought you might need some help with practice."

"Your grandmother?"

He shrugged. "She has her sources."

I was thinking mystic spirit guides, maybe animal totems. I raised an inquiring eyebrow.

"Someone told her at the beauty shop," he said.

"Well," I said. "Thanks. I'm glad you came. Carla Briggs—the girls' coach—is going to help out today, but you're welcome to stay if you want to."

He shifted uncomfortably and shot a glance at the door. "That lady coach? The one who was up here that Sunday?"

"That's the one."

He fidgeted some more, raised his first two fingers and thumb to his lips and tapped for a minute, then decided. "Well, I guess I better get going."

"Why?" I started to ask, but that's when a voice came from the gym doors.

"Hey, boys," Carla called. "I left my class watching a film so I could come over early." She crossed the court with her ground-eating stride, and I pushed myself slowly to my feet, not because I always rise in the presence of women, but because Phillip seemed to be towering over me, and I guessed that Carla would too.

"Carla, you remember Phillip One Horse," I said. "My old teammate. Phillip, Carla Briggs."

She held out her hand, and his rose from his side to take it. "Good to see you again," she said.

"Ma'am," he said, nodding. When his hand dropped back to his side, it patted his leg a few times. Then he nodded again and said, "Well, I'll let you two get to work."

"Phillip came up to see if I needed any help with practice."

"Why don't you hang around?" Carla asked. "Three heads are better than two."

"Nah, I'm in training," he said, and he looked down at his shirt and smiled. "Down to a pack a day. Next stop, the Atlanta Olympics."

"Wait a sec," I said. "Carla, will you get the balls? I've got a little business to talk over with Phillip."

She went off toward our offices, and Phillip and I sat back down for a moment. "What do you need?" Phillip asked, watching Carla disappear into the hallway before he turned his full attention back to me.

"I've got a bunch of calves I can't feed because of this thing," I said, grimacing at my ankle. "Could you come out morning and evening and give me a hand for a week or two? I can't pay much, but I could give you a couple head of cattle when we're done. And I heard you talking to B. W. about your Chevy the other day. I can't walk, but I'm still good with a wrench. Maybe I could help you get that thing running."

"Okay," he said. "But you know, John, you don't have to pay me. I'd help you for nothing."

I patted his shoulder. "Well, you're worth more to me than nothing. Do you still have a driver's license?"

"For all the good it does me."

I pulled my keys out of my pocket. "Why don't you take my truck. I'll catch a ride with Michelle. Until I'm up and around, you drive out in the morning, move the cattle around, fill the feed troughs. I'll show you what needs to be done. When the weather's good, I'll come home with you and we'll work on the Chevy. Then in the evening we'll feed cattle again, and you take the truck home."

I held out the keys in my upturned palm. He stood looking at them. "Go on," I said. "I'll see you about six or seven. Stay for dinner if you like."

He nodded, as much to himself as to me, and placed his palm under mine. I turned my hand and transferred the keys in a sort of handshake.

"Okay," he said. "I'll be there." He looked around quickly, turned, and, by the time Carla tugged the cart of basketballs to the side of the court, had vanished.

"Phillip has a kind face," Carla said when she was seated by me again. "Was he really in prison?"

"A long time ago," I said. "He's trying to put his life back together now."

"And you're trying to help."

I looked over at her. "Yeah," I said. "I guess I am."

"That's nice," she said, patting my shoulder. "Now let's talk about the agony I'm going to inflict on your kids today."

And thus was set my routine for the next few weeks: Phillip arrived early in the morning, and after he'd fed the calves per my instructions, we spent the day troubleshooting beneath the hood of his old pickup—I was convinced it needed a new carburetor, Phillip insisted it needed at the least a valve job—then Phillip would take me up to basketball practice, loiter a few minutes to say hello to Carla, and go on out to the farm to do my evening chores. He worked hard and did the job right. With a minimum of effort, he moved the unweaned calves in and out of the pens where the milk cows were tethered, talking softly to both cows and calves to keep them calm. Before he left at night, he filled buckets of feed so he could go immediately to work in the morning.

"I may fire you and keep Phillip," Michelle said one Wednesday night after he'd taken supper with us and headed home.

"I may fire myself," I said from the kitchen table, where I remained while dishes were taken up.

We went into the living room to work. Michelle had papers to grade and I wanted to get off a few letters, but before we had a chance to get too involved with either, Lauren called us to the phone.

"It's the police," she said, whispering the last word emphatically and handing the phone to Michelle, who naturally reached the kitchen more quickly than I did.

"Uh-huh," she said. "This is Michelle Tilden." Then I saw her jaw clench, her lip curl.

"Let him out," she said. "Now. Every word he told you is true." She listened for a moment and then yanked the phone away from her ear and thrust it at me. "Talk to this fascist," she said.

"Hello," I said. "This is John Tilden. What's wrong?"

"Like I was telling your wife," the voice of some Watonga good ol' boy said, "we got Phillip One Horse down here at the jail. Pulled him over driving your truck. He said you loaned the truck to him. That he was working for you. Any of that true?"

"My wife just told you it was," I said. I was headed rapidly toward teeth clenching. "Why did you pull him over?"

"Tail light was out," he said. "So we should let him go?" He seemed disappointed.

"No," I said. "You should apologize to him and then let him go." I hung up forcefully and looked across at Michelle. "Pigs."

"Fascists."

"Cool," Lauren breathed. "My parents are radicals."

I apologized to Phillip—more than once—when I saw him the next morning. He just shrugged, as though he had gotten used to such things. But when he had finished with the chores, as I hobbled up to the back porch, preparatory to heading out to Phillip's, he said, "Let's not work on the truck today. It's too cold."

"It's not any colder than it was yesterday." I looked closely at him but I couldn't read him. "Okay," I said. "Maybe tomorrow." After he'd driven off and I'd bummed Michelle's car to get up to practice—I thanked God again for B. W, who agreed to take his mom and little sister to school—I settled back to do some reading. I was just finishing up the last pages of *A River Runs Through It* when I heard the back door open and slam shut.

Maybe Phillip, I thought. Maybe he changed his mind. I started down the hallway to see.

The door to Michael's room was open, and I could hear the noise of wire hangers jangling in the closet. I crutched my way silently to the doorway and inside to see my eldest standing in front of his closet, looking down at the Watonga letter jacket in his hands. It was my old jacket from high school, but when he'd been a kid, he asked me for it, and wore it until he quit basketball.

"Hi," I said, pleased that my voice didn't fail me.

Michael jumped, but didn't turn around. "You're supposed to be in town guzzling coffee with your buddies. The truck was gone."

"Yeah," I said. "Sorry about that. I hurt my ankle playing basketball. The guy who's helping me has the truck."

He pulled on the letter jacket. "Maybe you should take up something more suited to your age. Bingo or something." He threw a few more things in a duffel bag and then brushed past me, stepping around my crutches.

I followed him out into the hall. "I hear you're going to be a father."

His back went straight, and he stopped short of the door. "Yeah," he said. "I guess you disapprove. I guess you think we're messing up our lives the same way you did." He spat out the last words as though they were bitter, then hoisted his duffel and threw the door open.

"No, Michael, I'm happy for you. Really."

He paused for a moment on the threshold, and his head turned the fraction it needed to allow his eyes to shift back toward me. He stood there for a moment, met my eyes, and then shook his head and pulled the door shut behind him.

I watched as he got into his truck and drove away. He did not look up again. I turned and went into Lauren's room, sat down on the edge of her bed, set my crutches down on the floor, and stared at her wallpaper, a pattern of lavender ponies.

She had outgrown ponies.

Kids outgrow everything.

After awhile, I reached down to get my crutches and snagged one of Lauren's magazines from under the bed in the process. *Cosmopolitan.* One of those bodacious supermodels was on the cover with most of her breasts exposed.

Well, I'm only human. I looked.

And then I glanced over the rest of the cover, read the promised contents of the magazine.

Are you having your best sex?

How to have an affair with an older man.

Living and loving for the next century.

"God help us," I said. I slid the magazine back where I'd found it.

Michelle and I would have to talk to Lauren, all right, starting with why she was reading magazines like this.

The last football game of the season was the next night, and I hadn't planned to go because of my ankle, but when Phillip asked about it Friday morning, I told him I might, just to be encouraging. He had also asked if Carla went to football games, which I allowed she generally did. The chill I'd detected the day before was gone; in fact, he apologized for being so touchy. "I'm used to the Watonga cops being suspicious of me," he explained. "I was just afraid I might have embarrassed you. I wouldn't want that."

"We weren't embarrassed," I said. "Michelle and I were furious that they treated you that way."

"Tell her thanks," he said. "She's a good woman." He climbed into the truck—which was cleaner, by the way, than I ever kept it myself—and said, "Want to come out and give me a hand this afternoon?"

"Let me grab my coat," I said.

That afternoon we agreed that the problem with the truck wasn't carburetor or valves.

"Gas line," he said.

"Gasket," I offered.

Ellen Smallfeet fixed lunch for us. It was simple and good: fried fish, canned green beans, fresh-baked bread—and she sat and visited with us for a bit before cleaning up.

"I saw your son at the Pizza Hut the other night," Phillip said, watching for my reaction. "Your older son. He brought us our food."

I nodded, and then when the silence became tangible, I asked, "How did he look?"

"A little tired," Phillip said. "Like he's not sleeping so good. But he made a couple jokes. Us Indians love a good sense of humor, you know."

"Tired, huh? He used to sleep all day long."

"He told me he took a day job at some welding place. Working in a big tin building without any heat."

"Well," I said. "That explains the letter jacket. It's the warmest coat he's got."

"What explains what?" he asked, so I told him about the day before.

"Sorry," he said, his dark eyes solemn. "You miss him?"

"Oh yeah," I said. "I wish I could do it all over. Everything. I said some things to him that I really shouldn't have."

"Words are like arrows," Ellen Smallfeet called from the sink without turning around. "Once sent they cannot be called back."

"That advice doesn't help me much now, Mrs. Smallfeet," I said, in what I hoped was a proper tone of deference.

She turned around and covered her mouth with her fingers, looking for all the world like a wrinkled, giggling three-year-old. "Sorry," she said. "When one reaches my age, it is sometimes difficult to turn off the wisdom."

"I forgive you," I said. "Thanks for lunch."

"We'll take you into town in a bit, Grandmother," Phillip said. "We've got to go to the parts store and order a new fuel filter."

"Head gasket," I said.

"I'll be ready," she said, settling into one of Phillip's chairs, her hands crossed primly in her lap. "Whenever you are."

We dropped her off and then stopped by the parts place. We ordered both parts.

Phillip took me back to my house, where I faced a more challenging task. Michelle and I sat down with Lauren as she was reading for school. Michelle looked at me and cleared her throat.

"Ah," I began, raising my eyes to take in the hairless pectorals of one of Lauren's poster boys. "Your mother and I were thinking it might be a good time to talk to you about, ah, boys. And girls." I could feel a warm flush creeping up my neck. "Sex. You know. Would you, ah, like to talk about that?"

"Uh, no," Lauren said, not looking up from her science book.

"Just checking," Michelle said, although she said it with substantial relief. "You sure you don't have any questions you want to ask us?"

Lauren gave a little exhalation of exasperation, tilted her head slightly to one side, and rolled her eyes. "If we talk about sex, you're just going to get embarrassed," she said, and looking up at me said,

"Especially you, Dad. And besides, I know everything I need to know." She met our gaze. "Secondhand, of course."

"Of course," I said.

"Well," Michelle said. "I'm glad we had this little talk. Aren't you, John?"

"Oh yes," I said. "Very glad."

"Me, too," Lauren said, turning the page. "Could I finish doing my homework now?"

"Sure," Michelle said.

"Absolutely," I said.

Back in the hallway, we exchanged relieved high fives, and I hopped back to the kitchen table. "Hey," I said, shuffling through the afternoon mail. "Would it be okay if we invite Phillip for Thanksgiving dinner? Indians do celebrate Thanksgiving, right?"

"Well, if Phillip's going to be here, why don't we invite Carla?"

Her tone was innocent enough, but I asked anyway. "What are you thinking?"

She looked away as she talked, and her voice took on a nonchalant tone. "I was just thinking that since Carla and I have talked once or twice about Phillip, and you said Phillip had asked about Carla, that maybe we should give them a chance to get to know each other better."

I shook my head. "He's not ready for something like that," I said. "You'll embarrass him."

"Not at all." She raised her hand—I swear on this Bible. "I know how sensitive he is. We'll invite some other folks so it won't be so obvious."

It didn't feel right, but I couldn't think of a reason not to. "Okay," I said. "I'll ask him tonight."

Shortly thereafter Phillip finished chores and knocked on the back door, and Michelle invited him into the kitchen for a cup of coffee. When she had him comfortable, she asked him, "Do Indians celebrate Thanksgiving?"

"Sure," he said, taking a sip. "We're a thankful people. It's Columbus Day Indians are not so crazy about."

"I thought maybe because of the Pilgrims ..." Michelle began, and shrugged.

Phillip smiled. "I think there are worse things than remembering that Indians are necessary for people's survival."

"Good point," I said. "You want to come for Thanksgiving dinner? We're having some other folks out. You wouldn't be any burden at all."

"I don't know," he said. "What kind of people?"

"Well," I said, "some people from school. Michelle's parents. The Graywolfs. Not a big group. And they're nice."

He sipped his coffee thoughtfully.

"John does most of the cooking, so the food is good," Michelle added. "He bastes a mean turkey."

"All right," he said, setting his cup down. "Thanks."

"Our first games are next weekend," I said. "You can help keep me calm."

"Good luck," Michelle said, bending to pull the meat loaf out of the oven. "He's been tossing and turning for weeks." She smiled sweetly at me. "I'm sure it's because of basketball."

The smile I gave in return was somewhere between sickly and ghastly. It was true that I had lost a lot of sleep. With my bad ankle, it was almost impossible to get comfortable; I was forever kicking something and yelping with pain, and I was in so much pain that I couldn't even tolerate the weight of a sheet on my foot.

But it was also true that I couldn't seem to stop thinking about Samantha, wondering what she was doing, where our talk might lead. I couldn't stop imagining her, also alone in bed, also, maybe, thinking about me.

"Things should calm down when I establish some kind of pattern," I said, shaking those images out of my head.

"Do you need any help with the varsity this week?" Phillip asked. "I can come up if you need me. I think we've gotten as far with the car as we can without that new gas line."

"Head gasket," I said. "You're always welcome," I said. "Carla and I could probably use you. We're getting ready for that tournament in Calumet."

"Maybe I'll do that," he said, and Michelle and I exchanged a quick confirming glance as he left.

After Watonga had lost its final football game in the same dismal fashion in which it had lost most of the others, Michelle, Lauren, and I stopped in at the Four Corners convenience store to return *Black Beauty* and maybe check out something romantic. "Something with sinuous bodies coiled around each other," Michelle whispered in my ear, her arm around my waist while I hopped, crutchless, toward the store. Maybe she was hoping to revive my libido; I had not showed much interest in her lately. Or maybe she wanted to live vicariously. I didn't ask.

"What are you talking about?" Lauren asked, holding the door open for us.

"Nothing," I said. "Go away."

Gloria was behind the counter, so while Michelle sifted through what videos remained late on a Friday night, I went over to talk. "How are you feeling?"

She looked a little pale, but her smile in return was genuine. "Awful," she said. "Is being pregnant like this for everyone?"

"Well, I don't know about everyone," I said, leaning on the counter and inclining my head toward Michelle, who was holding a video in each hand as though she were weighing them, "but she was sick as a dog every time."

"Michael says—" she began and then broke off, her smile dying at something in my face. "I'm sorry." She fumbled for something on the counter before looking back up at me. "He said he ran into you the other day."

"I don't think he expected to," I said, my voice even.

"No. He didn't."

"If he'd known I was going to be there, he wouldn't have come." Now it was less even.

She hesitated, then repeated, "No. I don't think he would have."

I sighed. "Please tell him to take care of himself," I said. "Make sure he gets some rest. He's not going to be much good to you or the baby if he doesn't."

She put her fingers gently on my forearm—fingernails still dabbed with black—and nodded. "I know. He's trying to save money for the hospital. For the baby. I tell him not to work so hard."

"Is this the sexiest thing you've got left?" Michelle asked, holding up a cover where somebody was kissing Meg Ryan.

"I think so," Gloria said. "Everything else has been picked through. There was a carload of Millers from down Greenfield way, and those Carson brothers from north of town. Between them, they pretty much cleaned us out of naked bodies."

"You must learn a lot more about people than you'd care to," Michelle said, offering the tape and a five.

She considered for a moment as she rang it up. "No," she decided. "I don't think I'll ever know enough about people." She handed the tape back across the counter with our change. "Have a good time. I'll tell Michael you asked after him."

After we got Lauren into bed, Michelle plugged the tape into the player in our bedroom and she got into bed and snuggled close. I lay stiffly, my leg hanging off the bed.

"What's wrong?" she asked about halfway through, turning off the sound with the remote.

"Nothing," I said, and patted her reassuringly on the hip. It was one of those body-switching stories, which might have been interesting if I cared about any of the bodies. It was hard to feign interest in the far-fetched problems of Meg Ryan and Alec Baldwin when I had so many real-life worries.

We watched a little longer. It wasn't happening. At last she turned off the movie and said, "Do you know what I think, John?"

"What?"

She paused for a moment, then just came right out and said it. "I think nobody ever gets the life they want. Not completely. Not you. Not me. Not the kids. Not our parents. They get the life they're dealt. And the test is what we do with it." She looked to see if I was hearing her. I was. "And we've done something good, haven't we?"

"Yes," I said. "We have." And that should have been enough.

So why wasn't it?

Later that night, I was still awake thinking, and I rolled silently from the bed and limped to the door.

"J. J.?" she groaned.

"It's okay," I said. "I'm okay. I'm just going to get something to eat."

"Yeah?"

"Yeah."

I could see her stretch and then settle back into the pillow, nestling in the sheets and quilts. "Okay. I love you."

"I know," I said.

I closed the door behind me and hobbled off to write a few letters. They wouldn't come, though. Instead, I jotted down some random things: the names of people in my life, past and present; my plans for the future, which written down seemed a scanty set of things to keep me occupied in the second half of my life; the phrase, underlined twice, "What am I going to do?"

I crumpled up all my pages, threw them into the fireplace, where they blazed and died, dropped my head to the desk, and let it rest there, my forehead against the cool, smooth surface. I thought about praying for guidance or help or some such thing, but if prayer is indeed answered, then the only response I've ever gotten has for twenty years been, "Hang in there."

I thought a touch more about prayer in church that Sunday morning. I generally do a heap of thinking during the sermon, since our young pastor, Tommy Heiliger, never has an original thing to say, and thus I can pretty much tune him out and not worry about missing anything I haven't been hearing since I was seven years old.

I don't mean to be critical—he's a good kid, and it takes a special kind of person to pastor a church full of farmers.

We sang a hymn—

My hope is built on nothing less
Than Jesus' blood and righteousness.
I dare not trust the sweetest frame,
But wholly lean on Jesus' name.
On Christ the solid rock I stand.
All other ground is sinking sand.
All other ground is sinking sand—

And then his sermon was about how we Christians must associate only with right thoughts and right-thinking people, which was to say other Baptists, preferably the ones sitting to our left and right.

"To pull somebody up out of the quicksand, you've got to stand on solid ground," Tommy was saying, to which a couple of people said "Amen." "You can't help somebody to safety if you get down in the quicksand with 'em. That just guarantees you're going to sink too."

It seemed to me like he was advocating a return into the ark—close up the doors, I'm safe, who cares about the world outside—although admittedly I am not much of an expert on theology. There were things I believed and rituals I practiced, but as the years rolled by I seemed to be absolutely sure about less and less. And as I sat there with the sermon buzzing about my ears, it began to seem to me that maybe on top of everything else, I was suffering a full-scale crisis of belief.

At last the organ began to play softly, which meant the sermon was winding down and we were launching into the invitation, so I checked the program and turned to the invitation hymn. We stood up and started into "I Surrender All," and after two verses, we stopped singing, the choir continued humming softly, and Brother Tommy began to talk.

"There's someone out there today who's unhappy. Who feels the weight of the world on his shoulders. Who needs to just surrender himself and his problems and let God take over. Who needs to come forward this morning and publicly confess Jesus Christ as his Lord and Savior, or rededicate his life to his Lord." And for a moment I was tempted to step out from my pew and come forward, really I was, although I didn't think I was lost.

I just didn't feel found.

But I didn't leave the pew. Tommy's call was not for me. My life was living proof that everything was not as it was meant to be. I could never believe what he wanted me to believe. Maybe I lacked faith, maybe I lacked understanding, but ultimately, one thing was even more important: I lacked peace.

And no matter how ardently I had asked for it and no matter who I had asked for it, I had never gotten it. I'd also asked for strength, and I was just about out of that. I was at the end of my frayed rope, and God, whoever and wherever He was, wasn't going to magically change my life and make me happy just for taking a stroll down the aisle on Sunday morning. He wasn't going to heal my broken spirit just because I walked into His office and asked for it. I was starting to wonder, in fact, if I had any use for a Physician who prescribed nothing but twenty years of "Hang in there." But what else was I going to do? Take up Buddhism? Worship flying saucers?

I was in Oklahoma, after all.

He had me good, and He knew it, and I knew He knew it.

So I stayed right where I was, and after church, I ate roast beef at my in-laws' house and listened to them praise that very same sermon, and after lunch, I went outside and walked and walked in circles around the block.

The only place I could go after that was home, and that is where I went, no wiser, and even less peaceful.

November 19, 1994

Miss Candace Tilden
1425 E. Fifth
Albuquerque, NM 87106

Dear Candy,

Have you ever heard that old Chinese greeting/curse, "May you live in interesting times"? I am living in times that have become way too interesting for my liking. What would you do if you had the opportunity to do something you've always wondered if you should have done in the first place? What if you knew that your chance at happiness would be tempered by the unhappiness you would create by such a decision?

I am still wrestling with the problems I mentioned obliquely last time. I remember what you wrote once when I was asking these questions (because, let's face it, these are just about the only questions I ever ask). You said that what could have been is the greatest enemy of what is. Wise words. I hope I can live up to them, to you, to everyone.

I dreamed about Trent the other night. I wish you'd known him, because I'm not sure I'll ever be able to talk about him in a way that will be valuable to you. I idolized him, you see, and that's a lot of freight for anyone to carry, alive or dead. I know I probably wouldn't have done that if he were still around, because we disagreed on a lot of things. But that's one of the advantages of being dead, I guess—it freezes you beyond disapproval and disagreement. He was my brother, and I loved him, and he died, and that's all that will ever matter, I guess.

Do take good care of yourself. I want the privilege of continuing to disagree with you, especially about bringing Arturo home to the folks. I still think Christmas would be a good time. Come out here. I'll protect you both. I am still spry enough to wrestle a shotgun out of Dad's hands, you know.

And please, if it doesn't sound too Southern Baptist of me, say a prayer for me. I'm a mess. I want to do what is right. I've wanted that all my life, but I am so tired of doing what is right for everyone else and wondering if it will ever be right for me.

I am too tired and too emotional. Don't worry about me. All will be fine once basketball starts and I become too busy to think.

But do come for Christmas. I miss you and covet your presence, Baby Sis.

Love,
John

P.S. You are going to be a great-aunt. Really! More about this as it happens.

November 19, 1994

Mr. and Mrs. John Tilden
7743 Sunny Acres
Scottsboro, AZ 85372

Dear Mom and Dad,

It will hardly seem like Thanksgiving without you, although we are looking forward to your presence at Christmas, our celebration of Christ's nativity and Bill Cobb's generosity. In his mind, there may be no difference, although there should actually be other things on his mind these days. I hear that Sam and Bill have separated, and she's taken the girls and moved to Fort Worth. I never thought that would happen, not in a million years. I hope everything will work out for everyone.

Basketball begins next week. We will do all right this year, although I only just now got one of my starters back from our rotten football team. They might just as well have let me have him all fall. Now I have to ease him into the rotation, and he's about as cold as you would expect someone to be who hasn't been at practice for months. He can just about hit the backboard from directly underneath it.

Phillip One Horse has been helping me out around the place. Yes (he says, hearing their jaws drop from across a continent), Phillip. The boy on my team who went to prison. I had a little accident that's kind of made it hard for me to get around, and he's been a huge help. You'd like him now, Dad. He takes his work seriously, and he doesn't talk much. I've gotten to know him again because of this stupid benefit game, and I guess that's one positive result. He's got a good soul, as Candy would say, despite all the knocks he's gotten—and given.

As for the rest of this reunion stuff, Michelle is being run ragged trying to keep track of who is coming, when they will be in town, who we can expect for each event, and so on. The only good thing I can say about the reunion is that in a month or so it will be over.

Oh—maybe the biggest news, although I guess I've put off telling you as long as I can. Michael and his girlfriend are expecting, so you folks are going to be great-grandparents sooner than any of us expected. I talked to Michael briefly the other day. Very briefly. No breakthroughs there, and I don't know what it will take. You might call and give your good wishes to him and Gloria, if you feel comfortable doing that. I don't want to dictate your moral stance or anything, but I remember you as forgiving even in disapproval. You were—and are—good parents, and I am grateful for your example, even though I haven't always been able to live up to it. I hope you will still love me in the event that I fall short.

Hope you are well. I think of you often. B. W. and Lauren are fine and look forward to seeing you soon. As do I.

Your son,
John

November 19, 1994

Ms. Samantha Mathis Cobb
6503 Trail Lake Drive
Fort Worth, TX 76133

Dear Sam,

I'm not sure just what to say in this letter. I'm not sure, in fact, that I should even be writing it, much less sending it. I guess what I wanted to say is that I am sorry for you and the kids, that I hope you are well, and that my thoughts and prayers are with you. If I say much more than that, I start to get myself in trouble, so perhaps I had better stop there. But I can't just stop there. So here goes:

Your separation from Bill was such a surprise that I can't really say yet what I think about it. It was like a kick in the gut from an angry cow, and I haven't had a chance to draw a good breath.

That said, I don't think I can stop without clearing some things up first, or trying to. Some time back, the last time we talked on the phone, you told me we needed to talk about something. Well, we haven't. Was this the something that you wanted to talk about? If so, why did you want to talk to me about it? And what did you expect me to think, to do, to feel about it?

When I see you next, maybe you can give me the answers to these and other questions, because they are bouncing around in my head and interfering with my day-to-day business. That's another thing that I shouldn't tell you, I guess, but it's the simple truth, like the fact that I both dread and cannot wait to see you at Christmas.

It is late, and I really must stop before I say something that will get both of us into trouble. Take care of yourself and the girls. I'll see you soon.

John

Wild Turkey

If you'd asked me which Cobb I'd have preferred to see first, Samantha or Bill, I would have said Sam, no question, even with the not-so-vague unease I was feeling about the roads less traveled. Our whole lives, Bill Cobb and I had never been more than barely civil to each other—or maybe I should say that I had never been more than barely civil to Bill, although he was so dense and good-natured that it never seemed to make any difference in the way we got along. I'm guessing it would be a strain on even the best of friends when both of them have loved the same woman and only one can have her, and Bill and I were never the best of friends.

I would have preferred Samantha, but it was Bill who pulled up at my front door on the Tuesday morning before Thanksgiving. We'd had a couple of days of bad ice storms and were currently in the middle of a morning fog so dense I could barely see the outlines of the barn not twenty yards away. Our phone and electricity had both gone out on Sunday night, and although the electricity had come back on after we'd spent a night curled up in the living room in front of the fireplace, the phone was still defunct.

So when the ghostly form of a white Range Rover, headlights on, appeared almost magically in the driveway as I sat at the table drinking a cup of coffee, the unexpectedness of it gave me a hearty thump in the chest. I didn't recognize the vehicle, although I knew what it was. I can assure you that no one in my immediate acquaintance owned a Range Rover.

That was itself a big clue, though, and as it pulled up close to the house, I was pretty sure that I had solved the mystery. When the driver had to lower his head to get out of the Range Rover, I was sure of it—Big Bill Cobb, as tall as ever, a little wearier, to judge by his sagging shoulders.

I hopped to the front door by the time he knocked.

"Morning, Bill," I said, and opened the door to him. "What brings you out this way?" I held out my hand, and he shook it once, perfunctorily, the grip clammy. He looked down at my foot, raised off the floor while I balanced, wobbly, on the other. Then without a question, he began.

"Your phone was out, and I'm in town for the week. Thought I'd come up to spend some time with the folks at Thanksgiving. Samantha's got the girls for the holiday. Don't know if she'll be coming up here or not." He wet his lips, took a deep breath, slid his eyes over to see how I was reacting. "I guess you've heard all about that."

I hopped back into the kitchen, and after a momentary pause, he followed me. "Only a little," I said. "I'm sorry."

"It's all for the best, I suppose," he said, although he did not sound like he believed that. I indicated a chair at the table, but he shook his head. "I can't stay. I just wanted to ask if we might be able to get the guys together before Sunday. And your phone is out."

"Yes," I said. "Yes, it is."

We looked across the table at each other. The defunct phone might be our only point of agreement.

Then the back door opened, and Phillip, finished with the morning feeding, stepped into the washroom and shed his boots. "Well," I said, "here's at least one guy we can ask."

Phillip stopped stock still in the doorway of the kitchen when he saw Bill. He hadn't had the benefit—if that's what it was—of the Range Rover appearing out of the mist, and I doubt he had seen Bill face-to-face since Bill went off to college.

"Phillip." Bill nodded. "Good to see you." This sentiment did not travel from his mouth to the rest of his face. We were certainly a superficial group; I wondered for a moment what we might be able to say to each other with complete sincerity.

"Hello, Bill," Phillip said. "Welcome home."

That wasn't it, exactly, although Phillip's heart was in the right place. Bill gave him another of those nonsmiles. "I was hoping maybe we could get together for an extra practice this week. Would you be up for something like that?"

"I'd have to check with my social secretary," Phillip said. "But I'll bet we could arrange something."

"What about after varsity practice today?" I asked. "I'd rather do that than tomorrow afternoon."

"Call the other guys—" Bill began, before remembering my defunct phone. "Okay, I'll get in touch with Oz and Bobby Ray and see what they think. I'd just like to get out on the court, run a little. I've been shooting some. At home." He broke off abruptly and turned away.

"I'm sorry," Phillip said. "I hope all that will work out."

"Thanks," Bill said gruffly. He was, if anything, even less happy about accepting sympathy from Phillip than he was from me. "I'll see you guys in town. I've picked up some uniforms and some warm-ups. Let's plan on this afternoon and hope everyone can be there."

"Okay," I said. "Thanks for driving out." I ushered him to the front door. We did not speak again as the door closed.

Only when the taillights disappeared into the fog did Phillip turn to me and say, "That was weird."

"Tell me about it."

"I think he had something more on his mind than basketball."

"Lots of things besides basketball," I said. "Whatever, I'm glad he's gone. It spooked me." And it had, his somber appearance out of the fog like an apparition in a bad dream.

Phillip looked down at the carpet. "When I saw who it was, I thought he might be one of those unbalanced ex-husbands come out to do you harm."

"Hey," I said, holding up my hands. "I haven't had any special influence in that household for twenty years."

"Right." His eyes flicked to mine and away again. "So what are you thinking he was thinking?"

I hopped back into the kitchen. "About what?"

Phillip sat down with me at the table, and this time he turned and looked me full in the eye. "About you and Samantha," he said.

"Has the whole world totally lost its mind? What do I have to do with them splitting up?"

"I can't speak for the whole world," he said. "All I can speak for is me. I remember how things used to be. And I wondered how you feel about her now." He spoke with sincerity, and my face burned, and I turned away from him. "Maybe I shouldn't ask. I don't mean to put my foot in where it doesn't belong. But you've been good to me. I don't want to see anything bad happen to you."

I tried to lighten the mood. "What is your grandmother saying?"

He laughed. "My grandmother? She says the spirits are telling her something big is in the wind. It could be you. It could be a winning night at bingo." He stood up, got ready to go, but before he did, he let his hand drop for a moment to my shoulder, a strong, solid presence. "You don't need my advice. But you've got a good family here. Take care of them."

"I know," I said. "I'm trying. I'm doing the best I can."

"Okay," he said. "Nobody can ask for more than that." He paused at the door. "You want to run with me out to the house?"

"Why, that gasket come in?"

"Yeah, for all the good it'll do. But I thought I'd humor you and help you put it on."

I pushed myself upright and gathered my crutches from their leaning place in the corner. "You're a good man, Phillip," I said.

"Oh, I don't know about that," he said, helping me pull on my jacket and gloves.

Maybe he didn't know.

But I did.

We didn't have much success with the truck that afternoon. My mind was on other things, including the icy wind that whistled across the plains, made a brief detour around Phillip's trailer, and then flowed directly down the back of my neck. When it came time to go to practice, I was more than ready.

"It'll be done when it's done," Phillip said when I apologized for our slow progress.

"It's just that we're not going to get much done on it the rest of the week," I explained as I hoisted myself into the passenger seat. "Thanksgiving, then the basketball tournament Friday and Saturday. And I was hoping to see this thing fired to life along about now."

He laughed. "I don't want to rule it out completely," he said. "But that thing has been out of commission almost as long as I have."

He dropped me off and headed out to the house to do chores early so he could come back and shoot with the other guys after practice, which I was running on my own. Carla had volunteered to stay on and help, but I had started to feel unnecessary, never a good feeling at the best of times.

I ran a hard practice, maybe to compensate for not being able to do anything physical myself: fast-break drills, rim to rim, the rebounder kicking the ball out to midcourt; full-court presses; half-court traps. I had them hustling and puffing, and their pace for their final laps was noticeably slower than usual, their arms dangling uselessly, feet dragging. It was a good practice, though, and maybe would help compensate some for the turkey, gravy, and pie they would consume over the next few days.

Oz and Bobby Ray were the first to get dressed and join me on the court after the boys were finished. I was standing with a ball at the free throw line, my crutches planted in my armpits.

"How's our star player?" Bobby Ray asked, clapping me on the shoulder so hard I had to pinwheel my arms to keep from falling flat on my face.

"I haven't seen him yet," I said, surrendering the ball to someone who could do something useful with it and making my way to the sideline.

"Bill said he came out and talked to you. How does he look?" Oz asked quietly as Bobby Ray banked in a set shot from about eighteen feet.

"Mentally? Physically? Emotionally?"

"Is there a difference?"

"No," I said. "He looked pretty bad." The crutches and I winced our way over to the bleachers, and I sat down with a sigh of pleasure on the hard wood.

"It's understandable," Oz said. "In his place I'd feel the same." He picked up a ball from the cart next to me and dribbled out to join Bobby Ray and Phillip, who had wandered in and was now being greeted by Bobby Ray and Oz with varied degrees of enthusiasm.

B. W., in street clothes and tennis shoes, his hair freshly shampooed and toweled, emerged from the locker room and took a seat next to me in the stands. "I'll hang around to drive you home," he said, leaning back on his elbows on the bench behind him. "We haven't had much time to talk lately."

"No kidding," I said. "But Phillip said he'd be glad to bring me out. You don't have to hang around and watch these old guys just for my sake."

"It's okay," he said. "Hey, I can stand in for you again if it'd help."

"It would," I said. "That would give me a better sense of where these guys are."

Bill was the last one to arrive, dressed in new Nike Air Jordans and a satiny warm-up suit, his arms full of boxes, which he set down on the bleachers in front of me.

"Gather 'round, gather 'round," he called out in a hearty Santa

Claus voice. "Got warm-ups and game uniforms for everyone." Then he proceeded to call out names and pass out correspondingly labeled boxes.

"Thanks," Oz said when he opened his box and ran his finger across the sheen of his warm-up.

"These are beautiful," Bobby Ray said, and his face lit up. As he held up his jersey to his chest, I saw that it was an exact replica of the home jerseys we had worn in the state championships in 1975.

"Had them custom-made from a photo," Bill said. "Naturally, they don't make them like this anymore. Jerseys are different and everybody is wearing those big baggy shorts."

"Those big baggy shorts would look a lot better on me nowadays than the ones we used to wear," I said, but I was clearly outdone, outvoted, outuniformed. I don't know what I'd thought we would wear for our big game; I don't know why it didn't occur to me that Bill would have thought about it. "Thanks," I finally said. The jersey seemed like it would fit all right when I held it up to my chest, so at least Bill hadn't been so carried away by his nostalgia kick that he'd ordered the same sizes we'd worn in high school.

To his credit, when he skinned off his warm-ups, Bill wasn't dressed in some sort of designer basketball ensemble. He was wearing a pair of old drawstring shorts and a T-shirt proclaiming "Bush for Governor."

He looked good, especially compared to the rest of us. He had been lifting weights, judging from his bulky shoulders and upper arms, although like most guys who lift, he had concentrated on his upper body to the detriment of his legs, which were fit but skinny. I suppose I shouldn't have been so critical—the man was in a whole lot better shape than I was. It was just a symptom, I guess, of how much I had allowed myself to dislike him over the years.

It's almost impossible to play basketball with someone you don't like. Maybe some people can separate the person and the player, but I never could. Coach always used to get on me about feeding Bobby Ray when Bill was open under the basket, but I'll be honest: Then, and now, I didn't want him to have the ball, didn't want him to score, didn't want him to look good. He already looked good enough.

I was glad B. W. was out there now instead of me; at least he could pass off to Bill without feeling a twinge of anything.

Mostly they shot around, rebounded each other's misses. Bill worked down in the low post, shooting turnaround jump shots and hook shots, and he shot well enough, although he seemed a little stiff.

Why did I still feel an inner warmth when he muffed a hook shot or misjudged a rebound? Sam had left him, which might have made me happy, even if I couldn't have her. But if anything, I should have commiserated with him; more than anyone, I knew what it felt like to love her and then lose her.

"Instruct us, Coach," Bobby Ray called over after they'd shot for twenty minutes or so. I called out an offense, and B. W. pointed out positions—and in a few words reminded Bill what his role was. The kid was not just a better player than I was, he was also a better coach, and for a brief moment, I was seized by a burning resentment that smoldered in my gut before turning into something like pride. So talented, so smart—

I hoped he was making the right decision about spending his life out among the trees.

The rest of the practice was uneventful. Bill meshed all right with the offensive setup we'd been running, although I noticed that he didn't speak to Phillip and was reminded that there was another of our old tensions come back to visit us twenty years on.

After practice, I hobbled out to B. W.'s truck, him following close to make sure I didn't get knocked over by the gusting wind or slip on the ice patching the parking lot.

"Thanks," I said after I'd clambered inside the cab and pulled my crutches in after me like a turtle retracting his limbs.

"Jeez, it's cold," he said as he slammed his door and shivered, his shoulders jerking involuntarily toward his neck.

"Sneak preview of Montana," I said. "It's not too late to reconsider."

"Dad," he said, turning and giving me the disapproving look I deserved.

The truck started on the third try. We'd have to work on this one before much longer—certainly before I trusted him to drive it north to Montana.

"How do you feel about playing this weekend?" I asked. "Think we'll do okay?"

B. W. made the face he used to make when we gave him medicine. "I'm not really excited about it," he said. Then he shrugged. "But maybe it'll be fun."

"Thanks for sticking with it," I said. "I don't know what we'd do without you."

B. W. inclined his head slightly toward me as if to say, *Yeah, you would be in a mess of trouble.* He drove across the road where we should have turned left toward the highway, and I must have raised an eyebrow, because he looked at me and then cleared his throat.

"I thought we might just drive around a little," he said. "It's too cold to sit down by the pond and talk in your secret place."

"Used to be secret," I corrected. "I hear they published its location in the *Daily Oklahoman.*"

We drove for a bit, the radio playing low, the tune unrecognizable although I could feel the bass, which buzzed the cones of the cheap speakers I had helped B. W. install in the doors. We seemed to be drifting aimlessly around the west side of town, past tiny houses with particle or wood siding. The affluent families in this part of town had aluminum or even vinyl siding.

Phillip's grandmother lived in this part of town.

Gloria—and now Michael—also lived in this part of town. Michelle was still pushing me to visit them. I hadn't knocked on the door since my last abortive try, although on a couple of occasions I had coasted past on my way home like an adolescent cruising neighborhoods to see if Michael might be outside doing lawn work.

Of course, these were forlorn hopes. I knew my son. First, he would not willingly do lawn work in any season; second, if he were outside for some reason and I pulled up, he still would have nothing to say to me.

We passed ever-shabbier houses, their wooden siding peeling or unpainted, approaching the end of 8th Street. "Dad, what's wrong?" B. W. asked, and he threw the truck into park. "You seem—distant— lately. Lauren has noticed it too. Are you mad at me? Are you upset about Michael?"

"Family meeting," I muttered. We sat for a moment in

silence before I looked over at him. "I hadn't realized it was that noticeable."

"Well, you're not exactly Robert De Niro," he said. "You can't pretend you're feeling something you're not. You're just not that good an actor."

"No," I said. "I guess I'm not." I shifted uncomfortably and looked out the window. We were parked in front of the shell of a burned-out house. Boards were nailed diagonally across the smoke-darkened windows. I could understand the impulse to try and protect what is yours; I could understand the impulse to try and keep people out; what I could not understand was why you would nail up your windows after your house had burned down.

"I've got a lot on my mind," I said.

"So it's more than just me and Michael," B. W. said. He seemed relieved. "That's what Lauren thought."

I nodded. "It's more than you two. It's more than Lauren. It's more than your mom. But it's also all of you."

"Lauren is afraid you're going to leave us," B. W. said, and his voice caught, and I could tell that Lauren was not the only person who feared that possibility. I didn't ask what made them think that, didn't try to plead innocence.

I wondered suddenly how much they knew about me and my sad history, how much they had always known.

"I don't think I could do that," I said finally, and I looked across to catch his gaze. My equivocal wording didn't go unnoticed, but it was as close to a promise as I could make. "I don't want to."

"Then don't," he said, and he tried to be gruff but couldn't quite manage it. "Please don't," he amended.

We sat, both of us looking down at our respective floor mats. There was too much here, too many years, too many lost opportunities. How could I even begin to explain?

"Your mother's going to wonder about us," I said. He nodded, and throwing the truck in gear he executed a U-turn that took us through the burned-out house's yard and into the opposite ditch before putting us in the direction of home.

"How was your day?" Michelle asked me that night after we'd fed the kids. We were rinsing dishes, and I was standing at the sink without my crutches with only a little discomfort and only a few grimaces of disapproval from family members who noticed. The kitchen was beginning to fill with wonderful smells from the pumpkin and peach pies Michelle had put in the oven earlier.

"Not bad," I said. "Practice was not quite a total disaster. My old men were panting like Frank."

"What was it like being with Bill?" She bent to put bowls in the dishwasher. I took a moment to see what she might be asking, but it seemed like a straight enough question.

"I didn't like it," I said. "He took over, the way he always does. He bought warm-ups and jerseys for the team. And those old-fashioned shorts we used to wear. Like I want my flabby middle-aged butt hanging out for the town to see."

"John," she scolded, and looked around to see if the kids could hear, although I knew they couldn't or I wouldn't have said it. "How is he doing?"

"Not so well. He put on a good front. But it was probably a mistake to come up here over the holiday."

"That's what I was telling Samantha," she said, again bending to load the washer, although that was a little like shooting someone with a .357 Magnum then politely turning your head so as not to embarrass your victim by seeing the gaping hole.

"Urhmn," I volunteered.

"I ran into her in the store," she said. "We got to talking. She said it wasn't much fun being home. Said she was really feeling judged. Said her folks were determined to get them back together. That they were supposed to have Thanksgiving dinner with Bill and his family so that the girls could be with both their parents."

"Uh-huh," I said.

"I told her she ought to come out and have dinner with us," she said. "Said that since we were having such a big group already she'd be welcome." And this time she didn't load the washer but ran warm water over her hands before wiping them dry with the dishtowel.

What I wanted to ask was "Are you crazy?" but of course, to state things quite so baldly was not our way. "Uhmm," I said.

"She's bringing candied yams," Michelle said. "And a pecan pie."

"I like pecan pie," I said, and pulled the stopper out to let the rinse water drain.

"That's what I told her."

"How was school today?" I asked.

"Wonderful, wonderful," she said, and her enthusiasm pushed for a moment past other thoughts and spread across her face. "*Othello* with my seniors, *Gatsby* with Mrs. Edmondson's juniors. She was out sick again."

"What part of *Gatsby?*"

"The big garden party. All the strange names of the party guests.

And Gatsby alone in the house while everybody enjoys themselves at his expense."

"Not the shirts?" I knew that was always her favorite part, that and the ending.

"Not yet," she said, and she placed the back of her hand against her forehead in a highly dramatic way prior to declaiming, "'I'm just crying because I've never seen such beautiful shirts.'"

"Is she crying about shirts?" Lauren asked, popping into the kitchen and sniffing the wondrously spiced air. "Mom, have you popped your cork?"

"It's *literature,* my dear," I said, pronouncing the second "t" in a way I fancied was British and high-toned. "Perhaps someday you'll understand."

She looked at me intently. "I don't think I'll ever understand crying over shirts."

B. W. entered at the end of this exchange. "If someone took your favorite Mo Betta shirt I bet you'd be bawling your eyes out," he said. He nudged her away from the refrigerator door with his hip and opened it, although you could see that his attention was not on the food in the fridge but rather somewhere else.

"Didn't I just feed you two?" I asked.

"I want something sweet," Lauren said, and B. W. said, "I'm still hungry."

"There's more cookies," Michelle said. "Everything else is for Thanksgiving. Hands off the pies."

Their faces fell—hope springs eternal—but they settled, if you can call it that, for a handful of Michelle's carob chip health cookies, baked with applesauce instead of butter and still pretty good.

"I hope it was okay to invite Samantha," Michelle said after the kids had left. "You don't mind, do you?"

"No," I said, and filled my mouth with cookie.

"I thought it would be good to spend a little time with her," she said on her way out. She didn't say how she thought it would be good or for whom, and although I sat there for awhile longer, I still didn't have a clue.

I spent Wednesday making noodles from scratch, boiling chickens to go along with them, and getting things ready for Michelle to make her stuffing when she got home. Our bird was a good-sized tom I had shot the previous fall over on the Old Place; he had spent the year filling the top of one of our freezers, and to be honest, I was going to be glad to see him out of there, even though I hadn't been able to replace him this fall. I took him out in the morning and stuck him in the sink to thaw all day.

Very early on Thanksgiving morning we wrestled the turkey—stuffed full of bread crumbs, diced apples, walnuts, sage, and other things in Michelle's secret recipe—into a pan and then into the oven, where it would spend the rest of its useful life in metal-walled safety before emerging golden brown to be dissected for the joy of holiday eaters. I drained the chicken broth from the chickens and began to cook my egg noodles in it while I picked morsels of meat from the bones to add to the huge pot later. Potatoes boiled in another large pot, ready for mashing; flowerets of broccoli and cauliflower steamed in a third. Although the world outside was cold and dark and dead, the kitchen was filled with light and steam and wonderful smells. It was almost enough to make me forget that my wife had invited Samantha Mathis Cobb to my house for Thanksgiving dinner, that a dozen people would be watching every move we made and listening intently to every word that passed between us.

As if a houseful of people weren't pressure enough.

I still wasn't sleeping much, and when I slept I was having dreams that struck me as portentous, although they were also simply painful. In the one I had had just before waking, I found myself sitting in a corner office, looking out onto some mythical sky-scrapered city— Metropolis, maybe. My desk was big, the size of an old Buick, bare mahogany except for the picture of Samantha in the corner, her lips pursed, an inscription reading,

To the only man
I've ever loved,
Sam

It was the pounding that finally got my attention. Outside my office door stood my kids—Michael, B. W., Lauren—banging their fists on a thick wall of glass. I realized it was the final scene from *The Graduate*, when Elaine is getting ready to marry that schmuck and instead makes another bad decision—to run away with Benjamin.

They were pounding on the glass, and from the shapes of their mouths, what they were shouting was "Dad!"

I wanted to let them in. And I wanted to hide under my desk.

What I did, at last, was wake up.

I believe in dreams. I don't know that they're necessarily signs, although I am open to that possibility. But I definitely think that they're windows to the soul, a direct line to the unconscious, and it didn't take a whole lot of thought to see that this *Graduate* dream was about choice, about making a painful decision that would hurt someone.

But what about Elaine's last words to her mother, who told her, "It's too late!"?

She said, "Not for me."

And then she ran from one disaster to another.

I knew it wasn't too late for me—but when every choice is going to hurt someone, when every choice is going to end in regret, what are you supposed to do?

Gradually the kids followed the smells into the kitchen for breakfast, noses twitching like rabbits as they got down bowls and cereal, poured milk. B. W. and Lauren even joined me for a cup of coffee while Michelle broke out the silver and inspected my parents' old china for smudges and spots.

"What time are Grandpa and Grandma getting here?" Lauren asked. I deferred to Michelle, since they were her parents.

"When they get around to it, I guess," she said. "Most likely whenever your grandma decides that she's happy with her lemon meringue."

"I hope she makes chocolate, too," B. W. said. "I don't like lemon."

"She knows that," Lauren said. "She always brings both." Then she turned to me and announced, "I'm not eating any turkey. Mrs. Anderson told us that they're raised on huge farms under inhumane conditions and that they pollute the water something awful."

"I shot this one over on the Old Place," I protested. "It's a free-range turkey. It ate bugs or berries or whatever turkeys eat. It lived a happy life. You saw me bring it home. Remember, you asked me what I thought I was doing, shooting another of God's creatures?"

"I don't care," she said. "It's a protest."

"More for me," B. W. said.

"Just as long as you save room for pie," Michelle said.

The Hooks, Michelle's mom and dad, were, as always, our first arrivals. They pulled up in front of the house just past ten o'clock. I wasn't completely dressed yet, but the kids ran outside to help them with their precious Thanksgiving cargo. Michelle was pulling on one of her favorite T-shirts, a sort of orange, and then buttoned an embroidered vest over it, while I pulled on a clean pair of Wranglers, my dress boots, and a denim shirt.

Carla arrived at eleven thirty with a squash casserole. Michael Graywolf, his wife, and three kids arrived at eleven forty-five bearing fresh-baked rolls and a sugar-cured ham. Oz and Caroline and their four boys, hellions all, showed up around noon, each boy carrying something appropriate to his size and level of trustworthiness: relish plate, green beans, homemade fudge, strawberry cake.

The table and cabinets had begun to resemble the all-you-can-eat bar that is Thanksgiving, the kids' tables had been set up in the living room, and we were beginning to think about eating when it happened. A dark blue Buick Century pulled to a stop in front of the house, and Samantha and her two girls got out, although they loitered hesitantly near it.

"Go let them in," Michelle told me, and I wandered to the front door, feeling every eye on me.

"Come in," I called, sounding much heartier than I felt. "Come in!"

"Hello," Samantha said with a wan smile as she leaned forward for a chaste hug. "I hope you don't mind our coming."

"Not at all," I said, relieving her of what I presumed was candied yams.

"You look great," she said.

No—she looked great, like a model, perfectly made up, every hair in place. It was the kind of face that probably doesn't stay that way without a nip or tuck here and there, the kind of hair that doesn't stay that color without an assist from the hairdresser, but who could argue with the results? The dream about the two of us in my truck flashed into my head, and it took a moment of mental wrestling to body-slam it to the mat.

The silence behind us was thunderous. "I'm glad you could join us," I said, and turned toward the kitchen with my burden. Michelle came forward to steer the girls over to the other kids and make introductions and then conducted Samantha back to where we were.

"Everything smells so good," Sam said, nodding at the faces she knew.

"As soon as Phillip gets here, we'll say grace," I said.

"Phillip One Horse?" Her voice could have expressed either surprise or disapproval. I opted for the first.

"My cousin is becoming a social butterfly," Michael Graywolf said. "First he agrees to play basketball and make a spectacle of himself. Now he's coming to Thanksgiving dinners."

"Why don't you all just go in and watch football until we're ready," Michelle said. "It won't be long now."

And it wasn't—maybe ten or fifteen minutes until Lauren came into the kitchen to tell us, "Phillip's coming!"

"I'm glad," I said. "Everybody's getting hungry."

"I'm glad too," she said, and ran out the back door to meet him. Shortly thereafter, she slipped quietly back into the kitchen and pulled me into the back hall.

"Something's wrong with Phillip," Lauren said. "He hasn't gotten out of the truck. When I waved at him, he just stared at me."

"I'll go check on him," I said. "Don't worry. He's not used to being around a lot of people, you know. Probably just getting his courage up."

Which he was, although not in the way I had hoped. As I stepped carefully out the back door, I could see him raise a bottle to his lips and take a long pull.

I got in the passenger side and shut the door quietly behind me. The cab smelled of whiskey.

It was cold in the truck—the heater wasn't on, and Phillip was wearing only a windbreaker, a promotional jacket with a Winston logo.

"I can't do it," Phillip said, his eyes on the hand holding the bottle. "I'm sorry, John. I'm going home. I just can't come in." Then he caught my gaze and brought the bottle up so I could see the label. "Wild Turkey. Ha. Happy Thanksgiving."

"Phillip," I said, "we're all happy to see you. You don't have to be so nervous."

"Your family doesn't make me nervous," he said. "But there's other people in there. I see all the cars. So many people." He took another swig, shorter than the last.

"You know them all," I said. "Or most of them. I'll stick close to you. There's nothing to be nervous about. And that—" I gestured at the bottle in his lap—"doesn't help."

"Nothing to be nervous about? If I know them, then they know me." He gestured at himself. "They know all about me. They know about all I done. Did. Everybody knows."

"That's over and done with," I said. "You've got a chance to put all that behind you now."

He laughed, and it was not a pretty sound. "It'll never be behind me," he said. "Not as long as I live. I'm trapped in this life and there's no way out. The most I can do is make it hurt a little less." He tilted the bottle for another swallow, and my cheeks flushed with anger.

"That's an easy way out, Phillip. Do you think you're the only person who feels trapped? The only person who hurts? The only person who's ever made mistakes? The only person who wants to escape?" I yanked the bottle from his surprised grasp and raised it to my lips before he could do a thing, the unaccustomed taste burning as it went down. I took a long drink and fought the roiling of my stomach, the watering of my eyes, before handing him the bottle back. "Maybe I'll climb inside that bottle with you, Phillip," I said. "How would that make you feel?"

"Stop," he said. His eyes were wide.

"How'd it feel, watching me just now? How would you like to see me throw my life away, to hurt my family and friends, everyone who ever cared about me? It would be so easy to do. Easy as taking a drink."

"Stop," he said, and now he was pleading. "John, don't talk like that." He capped the bottle, and it dropped to the floor with a muffled thump. "I'm sorry. So sorry. I'll just go now."

"I want you to stay," I said. "Please. Phillip, you can do this." I dropped my head, and then I raised it.

I had figured it out—why this mattered so much to me. Why I couldn't just let him give up. "Phillip, I need you to do this. To show me it can be done."

He realized it too, and there was a moment when I saw the fear in his eyes. Then he took a deep breath, nodded slowly, as much to himself as to me.

He leaned over in front of me, rummaged unsteadily on the dashboard, and found an antiquated roll of butterscotch Life Savers. "For your breath," he said, taking one and offering me the roll.

"All right," I said. "Come on. Let's go in and wash up."

I led Phillip inside, we got cleaned up, and then Michelle invited everybody into the dining room for the prayer.

"Dad," she said, turning to Mr. Hooks, "will you say grace?"

And there followed a rendition of the long and rambling prayer my father-in-law delivered every Thanksgiving while we stood, feet tapping, stomachs growling, as he thanked God for the beasts of the field and the birds of the air, for our families and friends and all the people in all the world, for the wonderful lives we lived, for car phones and fax machines and satellite TV. It was a prayer that could have been a four-part TV miniseries.

"Amen," we all said at the end, although that hardly seemed proportional to all the praying. "Amen," Phillip said, a little more loudly than necessary, I thought, but no one else seemed to notice, and I marked it up to being hypersensitive.

B. W. and the kids filed past the food first and were exiled to the kids' tables in the living room, all except for Lauren, who pleaded with her mom to stay with the adults. At the main table, so many leaves in that it looked like the flight deck of an aircraft carrier, Michelle, Lauren, and I were joined by the Hooks, the Graywolfs, the Osbournes, Samantha, Phillip, and Carla. Lauren seated herself next to Phillip, and Michelle maneuvered things so that Carla was on his other side. Samantha was directly across the table from me.

Phillip talked shyly with Carla, his head rising only occasionally to meet her gaze. She asked him questions about basketball, talked about her team. I had not suspected she had it in her to be something other than brusque and abrasive, but there is plenty in the world that I don't know.

Instead of looking across the table at Samantha or joining one of the conversations orbiting the table, I took a big bite of dark turkey, tender and juicy, and followed it with a bite of Michelle's stuffing, a riot of spice, savor, and tang. I began to reconsider some of my recent feelings about life. My stomach even acted like it was willing to be friends.

Then Samantha leaned forward to talk to me, and a vista appeared that suggested someone may have paid for a little improvement on God's original creation, and I guess maybe that distraction and the huge swig of Wild Turkey I'd taken on a practically empty stomach kept me from following the turn that the conversation around me was taking until it was too late.

"So what have you been doing with yourself, Phillip?" Mr. Hooks asked.

Phillip looked across the table at him, and I was pretty certain he was weaving.

"Since I got out of prison, you mean?" he asked, and his voice was again just a little too loud, and I could see a stirring around the table, heads rising from plates throughout the house.

"Phillip helps Dad around the farm," my dear Lauren said, launching herself into the silence like a solitary skater onto a frozen pond.

"I keep a few cattle," Phillip said. "I fish. I hunt."

"Sounds like a good life," Michael Graywolf said, trying, I think, to inject a little congeniality back into the conversation.

"I think," Phillip said. "I think too much." Then he stopped, laughed a disturbing laugh. "I think too much and I drink too much."

That's when I knew that our Thanksgiving dinner was doomed. The Hooks dropped a collective jaw as they realized that Phillip was toasted; Sam shook her head and rolled her eyes; Michelle and Lauren looked stricken.

I tried to think about what I might say to redirect conversation, tried to imagine that I was a talented conversationalist, and all I came up with was an innocuous remark about the Dallas Cowboys. And desperate as I was, I said it, although no one seemed to even hear.

"Well, what if I do drink too much?" Phillip was saying into his plate. "Maybe you would too. John said he might. Maybe all of you would." He shoved his chair back from the table and stood, his voice rising with the rest of him. "Maybe all of you would. What do you know about me? What do you know about my life?"

And then, in that complete and utter silence, not a fork clanking on a plate, not an ice cube clinking in a glass of iced tea, he looked up and saw the faces turned toward his. As he looked from person to person, an expression of growing awareness spread across his own face. By the time he looked at me, his eyes were full of such pain that I could barely stand to meet his gaze. I read pain and anger and shame there before he looked away, mumbled, "I'm sorry," stepped away from the table, and clomped out of the room and out the back door.

Michelle, Carla, and I all half rose to follow him. "I'll go," I said. "It'll be okay." The Hooks returned to their meals, since whatever had just happened had been planned since before the creation and therefore was not worth puzzling over, which was their way of looking at the world in general, and a soothing way of looking it must be. A slow murmur of conversation began at the other side of the table and spread slowly, like fire in a damp meadow.

I got up, stepped to the kitchen window, and saw Phillip standing outside in the cold without his jacket, his head down, his shoulders slumped. Maybe he was crying.

I headed for the back door, and as I pulled It open, I heard my truck start up.

By the time I was out the back door—slowed as I was, I probably was not the ideal candidate to chase Phillip down, although it's also true that I knew him best of all those gathered for dinner—the truck had started down the driveway, and where it had previously stood was the bottle of Wild Turkey, empty.

I kicked at it with my good foot, and it spun like a bottle in a teenager's game. It pointed at the house when it was done, at the house where I was going to have to return and face Samantha's enhanced cleavage and my in-laws and a million questions, not one of which I was the least bit qualified to answer.

I was mad—mad at Phillip, mad at life, mad at myself, mad at the empty bottle.

If he was going to take off like that, he might at least have left a little behind for me.

Shame

The phone rang that evening. I was in the kitchen, making a cold meal of Thanksgiving leftovers while the rest of my family watched football in the other room.

"Hello," I said through a mouthful of mashed potatoes.

"John Tilden?" came the voice.

"Speaking."

"Is Phillip One Horse still working for you?"

I instantly straightened in my chair and choked down the last of my potatoes. "Yes, he is," I said. "Why do you ask?"

"Can you think of any reason that he would leave your truck sitting in front of the police station with the keys under the floor mat?"

Yes, I could. I smiled sadly. "I'd guess he wanted to leave it someplace where he knew it would be safe," I said. "We'll be in to pick it up later, if that's okay."

"This is not a parking garage," the voice said, as though I'd made the mistake of assuming that it was.

"I know," I said. "Thanks for your help." I hung up the phone and shook my head.

"Idiots," I said, before lifting my spoon again. "Complete and total idiots."

"Who is?" Michelle asked.

"Game over?" I filled my mouth with potatoes and swished them around between my teeth before hissing again: "Idiots!"

"Commercial break," she said, coming over to put her hands on my shoulders. "Was that my parents?"

I snorted, which was almost enough to send mashed potatoes out my nose and did send me into a choking fit, which Michelle abetted in some way by pounding me between the shoulder blades. When at last I could speak and caught my breath, I said, "Phillip. He left the truck at the police station."

She turned this information over in her head. "How did he get home?"

I shrugged, let out a long sigh. "Walked, I guess."

"In this cold? Do you think he got home?"

Our eyes met.

"We should check," I said. "If he's still out there, he could freeze to death."

"I'll get my coat," she said. Thirty seconds later we were on our way down the driveway in Michelle's car.

We drove in silence until we got to the blacktop and the tires hummed beneath us. "Do you think he's okay?" she asked finally, when the silence became oppressive.

"Why did you invite Samantha today?" I asked at the same time. Our questions got fouled on each other in midair like neighboring tree branches. Neither one was answered.

We drove on through the darkness, through the blowing snow occasionally obscuring the road, until we reached the highway and turned toward town. "Should we pick up the truck first?" She turned to me. "We should make sure that Phillip got home safe, right?"

"Right," I said. "Let's start at the station and then head toward his house to make sure we don't miss him."

We followed the street back to the highway, around the airport, driving slowly to make sure there was no one lying in the ditches we passed, and then we made the turn toward Phillip's. At last we came to his gate, which was open; two forlorn cows had wandered out into the road. Michelle threw the car into park and jumped out.

"Git," she told the cattle, waving her hands in the general direction of the gap. "Go on. Shoo." They slowly turned, made their leisurely way back inside the fence, and began walking across the snow-covered pasture.

"Nice job," I said, as she climbed back in and we headed down toward the trailer.

"Farmer's wife," she said, and gave me the first big smile I'd seen in hours. "I know plenty of useful things." She took off down the track, bouncing my foot around painfully before I was able to induce her to use a little more caution.

As we came over the rise, there was a light on in the back of the trailer where Phillip's bedroom was, but none showing anywhere else. It was dark as dark could be. Michelle pulled up between piles of bottles, wrinkled her nose fastidiously, and came around to help me up and out of the car.

We made our slippery way up to the front door. I banged with my fist, the noise resounding in the clear, cold air. "Phillip," I called.

"Phillip," Michelle joined in. "Are you okay?"

The lone light went off.

"Phillip," I called. "We just want to make sure you're all right. Phillip, please!" I tried the door. Locked. I rattled it in the frame, but it stayed put.

"Phillip," Michelle called. "It's us." She made a face. "We should have brought him some dinner." I saw that she had his windbreaker folded over her arm; he'd walked back without even that feeble protection.

"Phillip," I called again, but I did not pound on the door. I knew he wasn't going to open it.

"Well," Michelle said, stamping her feet on the top step to keep warm, "at least we know he got in. Let's give him a chance to cool off." She winced. "I mean, warm up."

She laid his jacket gently in front of the door.

"I know," I said. "But still—"

"Come on," she said. She took my arm and led me carefully down the ice-encrusted steps. "We can't do anything for him until he's ready to let us."

"I don't want to believe that," I said, petulant as a three-year-old. I stood at the front of the truck and looked up at the trailer. Still no lights.

"I don't either," she said, opening her door. "But it doesn't do any good to try and help somebody do something unless he wants to do it." She sighed, a long cloud of her warm breath making the night air visible. "Let's go home."

Early the next morning, I made my way back to Phillip's. The gap was open again, although I couldn't see any cattle in the road, and it was imperfectly opened at that, the post dropped right next to the fence as though it had been opened just far enough for someone to squeeze through. I hobbled over to open it enough for the truck to pass without shredding my tires on the barbed-wire strands, then made the bumpy way down to the trailer.

I honked once or twice, experimentally, and slowly got out of the truck, half expecting to see a rifle barrel emerge from the door. When I tried the knob, I found it locked again, but I noted footprints coming down off the porch and heading off in the direction of the road.

"I hope he's wearing a good coat," I muttered and then climbed shivering back into my heated cab. "I hope he *has* a good coat." I drove slowly back to town, scanning for him all along the way, but I saw not a trace. On a hunch, I drove to Ellen Smallfeet's home and made my way to the front door, where I knocked twice, respectfully.

After a period of time familiar to me from my own convalescence, Mrs. Smallfeet cracked the door. When she saw it was me, she threw it wide and invited me in for breakfast.

"Have you seen Phillip?" I asked as she seated me at the table. "I've been trying to track him down, but I haven't had any luck."

She shook her head. "He's gone off again," she said. It was not a question.

"How do you know? Have you talked to him?" I slowed myself down. "I just want to talk to him."

"He does not want to talk to anyone," Mrs. Smallfeet said, pouring me a cup of coffee. "When he is like this, he wants to be alone and try to forget his life."

I took a sip—it was good coffee, strong and fresh.

"Can't you do something? Can't you talk to him?"

She shuffled back over to the stove and began to load a plate with scrambled eggs and bacon. My cardiologist would be grateful.

When she said nothing, I tried a new tack. "Will you go over with me, then? To Phillip's?"

"What for?" she asked as she placed the plate in front of me and produced a fork out of thin air. "So I can freeze on the porch with you while he hides in the back bedroom?"

"He'll open the door if you're there." I took a bite.

She shook her head slowly. "Phillip is my grandson. I love him and he loves me, but he will not do what I tell him. Family should do anything for each other, but this is not always so. You know this."

"Yes," I said, remembering Michael disappearing out my back door. "I do."

"I would like to save him," she said. "But I do not have that power." She looked at her hands, wrinkled and spotted with age. "Before we can be saved, we must choose it ourselves."

"What can I do—" I began, but she rose and placed those aged fingers, dry and slight as a bundle of twigs, across my lips.

"You are not listening," she said. "I have heard about what happened. So I know that Phillip has shamed himself in front of people he loves. Shamed himself." And she looked at me with intensity, with the unblinking gaze of a bird of prey. "Ask yourself, John Tilden, how it must feel to do something which you know you should not do. Ask yourself how it must feel to be eaten up with shame, and you will understand."

This was not just a message about Phillip. "I do understand," I said. "We must all do the best that we can, even if sometimes we fall short."

"Do not fall short," she insisted. "Remember your friend, my grandson. I believe he is looking for an example."

"I will remember," I said. I let out a breath. *An example.* Would I ever get to stop doing the right thing?

I twirled my fork through the eggs, then pushed myself back from the table. "Thank you," I said.

"What for? You did not even finish your eggs."

"For your wisdom, and for your care for me."

"I hear many things," she said. "The wind talks to me." And as she said it, the wind howled around the eaves of her tiny particle-board house, and she grinned from ear to ear.

I think we both knew that her best sources were the women at the beauty parlor.

Our tournament game that night in the ancient gymnasium in Calumet was against Hinton. They had decent speed, some height, and they brought much louder fans than we did; maybe more importantly, they knew each other well. Their starters had played together for three years, and they passed the ball to where their teammates would be, an extrasensory awareness that we would not have for some time yet, assuming we ever got it.

We lost by seven, and the margin was that small only because Bird Burke threw off a game-long torpor and arced in four three-pointers in the last three minutes. It was one of our few bright spots. Jimmy Bad Heart Bull played like a football player, like his namesake instead of the antelope we so desperately needed.

"Basketball is a game of agility and endurance," I reminded him when I pulled him off the court to sit after bulldozing his way to three first-half fouls in only four minutes of play. The sideline lecture is the coach's classroom, his last chance to instruct—that is, if the player will listen to you and not watch the action on the court or lose himself to the voice inside his head instead of yours. "Jimmy? Look at me. You understand what I'm saying?"

"Yessir," he said, and he nodded to himself. He wanted to be an antelope, but he had spent so many months being conditioned to knock people on their cans that it was difficult to adopt another way of life.

B. W. alone played with grace and intelligence, and he made excellent decisions, although his teammates did not always justify his faith in them. He finished with eleven points and eight assists. I thought he had every right to hold his head up, but he was not doing this when I found him in the locker room, shoulders slumped, naked except for the towel around his middle.

"That was loads of fun, wasn't it," I said, patting him on a humid shoulder.

"Loads of fun," he agreed, slowly letting out a long stream of air. He looked up at me. "We were awful, Dad. They weren't even that good, but I never felt like we had a chance to beat them."

"They didn't have great players," I said. "But they played better together. Give it a chance. We'll get better."

He looked up at me, misery written on his features. "You think so?"

"Things'll get better," I said, because a coach can never tell his players otherwise. "Keep hope alive."

He smiled. B. W. was, like his mother, a big fan of the Reverend Jesse Jackson.

"I said I'd stick," he said. "And I will. That's all I know how to do."

You and me both, I thought. *No matter how much it hurts.* "I'm proud of you," I said. "I couldn't have asked for a better game from a point guard."

"Really?" A corner of his mouth crept surreptitiously upward.

I nodded. "Really. I didn't see a single bad decision. Keep up the good work."

On the dark bus ride home, though, I had the opportunity to imagine the worst, and it wasn't difficult to imagine, because already I could see the possible shape of the season: Unless something changed, we could not win. I leaned my head against the window, felt both the cold of the outdoors and the moisture condensed on the inside of the pane, heard it rattle with our slow, steady progress back to town. My stomach knotted up on itself as I thought about a season of games like tonight, of fans yelling abuse, of scoreboards in every gym of every rival proclaiming our utter and humiliating defeat.

To be a good coach, you have to strike the right balance between caring too much and not caring enough. If you care too much, you're on the expressway to Ulcer City. Nothing in coaching is ever really under your control: If your players perform well, your decisions look good; if they don't perform to your expectations, you're a dunce, an idiot, a chowderhead, no matter how brilliant your plans may have been on the chalkboard.

And if you care too little, it won't hurt so much, but the kids will know it. The fans will know it. You can't motivate other people if you don't believe—at least a little—in the dream.

I could already read my boys, an unremarkable group of high school players: steady and dull, or brilliant and inconsistent.

It is a sad thing to see the possible future one game into a season, but such is the curse of vision.

And it's a sadder thing still for a man's vision to be directed not to curing the sick or working for peace or even to building a better mousetrap but to pursuing a boy's game.

"Things'll get better," Michelle said when I tried to tell her all this that night, because, of course, a wife can never tell her husband otherwise. "Oh, Carl Vanderkirk called from the *Republican*." Carl was the sports editor as well as the news editor, the obituary editor, the society editor, and the entertainment editor. In fact, he was responsible for every word in the paper except the jokes that a local insurance man had been running in his weekly ads since before I was born—knock-knock jokes and riddles and endless variations on the dumb-blonde joke, which was his stock-in-trade.

"Tell Carl we sucked," B. W. said. "Tell him we were awful. Tell him we should have stayed home and baked cookies."

"You're not supposed to say *sucked*," Lauren said, sleepy in her nightgown but trying valiantly to stay awake long enough to get the news. "It's vulgar."

"Why don't you go save the world and leave my vocabulary alone," B. W. said as he poured himself a tall glass of milk and drank it down, his Adam's apple glugging.

"Why don't you—" Lauren began, but then she saw my face.

"Why don't you both be still," I said. "Let me get my clichés in order." I tapped my forehead meaningfully a couple of times, then picked up the phone and dialed Carl's number.

"How'd you do?" he asked, once I'd identified myself. "Tell me everything."

"Lost sixty-seven to sixty," I said. "Our top scorer was Larry Burke. He had sixteen points."

"Give me a meaningful quote, pithy yet succinct."

I spoke without thinking. "They outplayed, -pointed, and -talented us."

He was *tsking* before I even finished my sentence. "John, that's way too negative this early in the season. We're trying to keep people interested in basketball. We want them to come to the games, cheer your players, buy my papers."

"Okay," I said. "Hold onto that one for later." I thought for a bit while Carl crunched away at an apple or something on his end of the line. "Okay. There were some fine individual performances tonight. What I'm looking forward to is the boys coming together as a team. Then we'll really accomplish some things."

"Good," he said. "That'll fly."

I gave him the individual stats. Everybody wanted to read about their kids, grandkids, or neighbor kids.

"Got it. If you don't see me at the game tomorrow, call me when it's over."

"Sure thing, Carl," I said. "Good night."

And so went my life, or at least my basketball routine, into and through the month of December: interminable bumpy rides down country highways on a cold, rattling school bus, suiting up in chilly visiting dressing rooms filled with the ancient smell of sweaty boys who by now had grown old, the repetitive chants of the cheerleaders, the groans of disappointment from our loyal supporters, the occasional bright spot—a steal and breakaway layup by Micheal Wilkes, the beautiful trajectory of a three-pointer when the other team left Bird unguarded, a no-look pass from B. W. to a waiting Jimmy under the basket, and even a couple of notches in the win column.

The rest of my December routine? Feeding cattle in the cold

pre-dawn, breaking ice in the stock tanks so they could drink, climbing onto the tractor to haul huge round bales of hay the height of a man over from the Old Place, coffee in town every morning, Lauren playing on the seventh-grade girls' team two nights a week, church twice on Sunday and once on Wednesday night, almost daily trips by Phillip's trailer, where I watched bottles with shiny new labels accumulating in a pile of their own just off the steps until the day when I arrived to find a shiny new padlock on the gate and could no longer keep tabs.

"We should have expected it," Bobby Ray, a man not completely unacquainted with the bottle, said one morning at coffee. "The man's an alcoholic. An ex-con. He couldn't ever be trusted." He didn't look at me as he said this. I was willing to trust Phillip more than Bobby Ray most of the time. "I'm just glad he pulled this now, and not the night before the game or something." He set his empty cup down on the table with a thud. "You remember that time he got drunk before the Thomas game?"

"I remember," I said. "I was supposed to be watching after him. And I also remember that after Coach Von suspended him, he still came back and helped us win state." I looked around the room and then back at Bobby Ray. "We gave up on him before. I'm not going to make that mistake again."

"Well then," he said, rising dispiritedly and dispensing some change onto the table for his coffee and tip, "you're a better man than I am."

Maybe. But deep down I figured I was just bad in different ways.

Shortly afterward on a cold and foggy night, I found myself

with my head full of thoughts. I had stayed up trying to write letters beside the dying fire, but I couldn't seem to be honest with anyone, and I couldn't see the point of writing otherwise. I had consigned three letters to my sister to the fire and written and rewritten a letter to Samantha in my head until my head throbbed. I had been at it so long that even Michelle yawned, gave me a peck on top of the head, and went to bed.

After my fourth bad letter to my sister, I went into the kitchen, put the teapot on the burner, lighted it. I could hear the water begin to boil.

Then the phone rang, loud as a church bell in the quiet night.

I plucked the receiver off the cradle before the first ring was finished, held it for a second listening to the house's reaction, my heart pounding.

Nothing.

"Hello," I said.

"I would have hung up if anyone else had answered," Samantha said, her voice low and happy. "Why haven't you called me, Johnny? Or written? I haven't heard from you since Thanksgiving."

"I was trying to write you a letter tonight," I said. "But it's not going so well." The teapot was starting to breathe steam, and I turned off the flame before the pot began to whistle.

"Still, what have you been doing all this time?"

"I've been thinking." I put my teabag in a cup, poured the water.

"So have I," she said. "I love the way you feel for other people. That empathy is a real gift. In my business, it would help you sell a lot of real estate. It's a good thing, being able to understand other people's needs and desires." She seemed to become unnecessarily breathy on "desires," like a Hollywood vamp, but I didn't mind.

"Needs and desires," I repeated.

"We all have them, Johnny," she said.

I dipped the teabag once, twice, lowered it to the side of the saucer.

"You know," she said, "I told you once that I thought you could do anything you set your mind to."

"I remember," I said, stirring in sugar. "But it was more than once."

"I still believe it," she went on as though she hadn't heard me. She paused for a moment, and the only sound was my spoon, clinking quietly as I stirred. "Do you imagine that coaching and farming are going to be enough to make you happy? That they're the most fitting use of your gifts?"

I thought I heard a noise from deep within the house—movement.

Or the house shifting.

Nothing.

"Are you still coming up for the dance?" I asked.

"Of course I am," she said. "People will talk. But people are talking now."

"Yes," I said. "I guess they are."

"I never miss a chance to dance," she said. There was a longer pause, and I could feel her sadness in it. "Do you know that in all the years we were married, Bill never once asked me to dance?"

"Well," I said. "He *was* raised Baptist."

"I didn't expect you to take his side," she said, although I could tell she was smiling.

"Believe me," I said. "I'm not." I had the vision of our last dance in my head again, the smell of her perfume, the proximity of her body making me dizzy.

I must have been remembering things longer than I thought, because her voice, when it came, had a tinge of impatience to it. "So what's going to happen next?"

I took a deep breath. "I'm still thinking," I said.

"I know," she said, and I could hear her take her own deep breath. "Well, so am I, honey. So am I."

There was a gentle click, then the buzz of disconnection, and I gently replaced the phone on its receiver, as though I were tucking her into bed.

I walked out into the driveway and turned in a slow circle there.

It was a still night, a little mist mixed in with the fog, and there was not a sound to be heard through the thick moist air. The cottonwoods and windmill stood like ghosts in the light shining from the pole, ethereal, gray-white, translucent. The world felt close and closed in, like I was the only creature on a dead planet.

I listened intently, my hearing growing more and more acute in the silence as I concentrated. But I couldn't hear anything—nothing but my breath blowing out in a solid cloud to join the rest of the fog surrounding me.

I couldn't hear anything, but I desperately wanted to.

I stood looking, listening, hoping, for something.

"I guess I'm asking for a sign," I said at last, looking toward the sky I could not see. "For help. Maybe I haven't done that often enough." I listened intently, turning my head slowly back and forth. Even the sound of my own voice seemed to vanish the moment it left my lips. "If You could just let me know that this is where I'm supposed to be, I'll stay put. Haven't I always?"

The universe seemed to hold its breath, and I couldn't tell at that moment if it was the loneliest I'd ever felt or the most aware. And then I did hear something, an unexpected noise out of the nothingness.

I swung around, and then it came again: a chicken or chickens clucking in their shack just back of the herb garden.

In the moment before I recognized the noise, I could have sworn it was somebody chuckling.

During the night, the weather broke, and the next day dawned sunny and bright. The thermometer outside the back window, which had been content to loiter in the forties, made a slow ascent throughout the morning into the sixties, which is where it was when the phone rang midmorning and my neighbor Michael Graywolf announced that a fence was down between us and that a dozen of his cattle had made a break for it and were now wandering aimlessly across my hills.

I wasn't surprised by this news; this is what cattle do. Cows are senseless creatures who do not understand the concept of home.

"Well, let's go get 'em," I said. "Ride on over when you've a mind to." I went out to the barn and saddled up Patches, a black-and-white pinto who held the distinction of being the world's oldest living cowhorse, rubbed my hand over his silken muzzle, and marveled at how the world had changed since the first time I rode him as a young married man, riding the hills, counting cattle, and listening as my dad carried on a running monologue in his low and gentle voice about how to run a farm.

Michael rode down my driveway about eleven on his dun horse, Pancho. He was wearing that same wide-brimmed black felt hat he said made him look like Stevie Ray Vaughan. I grabbed a Wheeler Brothers Feed cap from the hat rack, pushed it down on my head, and sauntered out to meet him.

"Johnny," he said, raising his right hand.

"Howdy," I said, returning the gesture. "This'd be a lot more fun if we were tracking some cattle rustlers back to their hideouts. Any chance of that?"

Michael and I used to play cowboys and Indians together when we were kids, each of us wanting to be what we were not. I had a plastic feather headdress and a tomahawk with a plastic head, and Michael had a great black cowboy hat and matching cap guns. Thirty years earlier, we chased each other across those selfsame hills on foot and on horseback.

He shook his head sadly. "Sorry, man. I'd say we're talking bovine stupidity here, pure and simple."

I slid up onto Patches, and we rode back to the first gap behind my house and then through it into the big pasture. Frank made his snuffling, meandering hound dog way in front, alongside, behind us. The sun was bright, the wind calm, and we faced the unusual spectacle of sweat in late December as we rode toward the pond, which was where we both suspected we would go if we were cows on the run. Patches moved sure-footedly down the side of a hill almost too washed out to drive down in the pickup; B. W. and I would have to come back here and dump a couple loads of dirt to make it navigable.

At the top of a rise, we paused for a moment and looked around.

To our left, the Canadian River Valley; to our right, my winter wheat, sprouting green across hundreds of acres; ahead of us, the dense cedars that surrounded and masked the pond.

"We looking for some of those white-faced critters you like so much?" I asked, the first words either of us had spoken in some ten minutes.

Michael nodded, and we made our slow way down the twin pickup tracks leading to the pond. Pebbles rolled from beneath the horses' feet, dry grass rustled, and a jet soared soundlessly overhead on its way from Oklahoma City to somewhere else as the water came in sight, the sun reflecting madly off it like someone had given the world a liberal dusting of diamonds.

"When do your folks get in?" Michael asked as he followed the plane northwest across the sky.

"Day after tomorrow," I said. "They'll be here ten days, fly back the second."

"You going down to the City to get them?"

I nodded, then said, "Yup," since he was still looking up.

Michael pulled back on the reins, shifted slightly in his saddle to face me better. "You know, we appreciate what you've tried to do with Phillip. Everybody from my grandmother on down. Don't feel bad. Nobody's ever been able to help him."

I looked out over the pond, dancing lights and blue water, and didn't say anything. I spotted the first of Michael's black-and-white heifers off in the trees and gave Patches a light jab in the flanks with my boot heels. We apprehended the culprits, white cow faces mooning up at us as they chewed contentedly on whatever species of dry ragweed they had discovered. Michael took the rear, I took the flank and rode down strays, and we pushed them slowly back up the hill, across the pasture, past the house, and down the road to Michael's, a task of some hours. Michael and I rode in easy silence and copious sweat, and I again pondered the fate that had given me a job that left me with hours on end for reflection.

When I got in, my legs were sore and bowed like barrel staves from an afternoon holding onto Patches. Michelle was home from school and cleaning house with a frenzy, she and the vacuum cleaner doing a dance that I momentarily mistook for the Hokey Pokey.

"I want everything to be nice for your folks," she announced over the roar. "I thought I'd just tidy up a little."

"Isn't that why we had kids?" I yelled back.

"Lauren's at a Christmas party. And you and B. W. have to get ready for the game."

"Oh yeah," I said, pulled off my cap, and wiped the sweat off my forehead with the back of my hand one last time prior to getting cleaned up.

It was a home game against Woodward, and I'd been dreading it for two weeks because it promised to be a bloodbath: Woodward had flown through their season thus far undefeated. They'd been to the semis at state the year previous, and although they'd lost two fine players off that team, they still had three starters with state tournament experience. The only Watonga person on the court who had gone to a state tournament was, unfortunately, me.

I sat my team down before the game—which would be the last except for Bill's game after the holidays—and talked with them about tradition and making new traditions, about individual achievement and teamwork, about home crowds and parents and friends—pretty much every inspirational phrase I could throw at them besides the Gipper and the Great God Almighty.

Then I sat down myself, looked around at them. "Except for that thing against the old folks after Christmas, this is our last game of the year. It is the last game that matters. So here's how it's gonna go." I picked up my clipboard. "Martel and Tyrel—you're both in the game at the beginning. I want you to run their legs off. Jimmy, I'm going to bring you in off the bench when I see the other guys sucking wind and then you're going to haul down every rebound in sight."

I'd made Tyrel Sparks very happy; he and his brother slapped skin in every conceivable congratulatory fashion. Jimmy, for his part, nodded staunchly at me, although I knew that he would rather start than ride lumber.

"Everybody gather round," I said, and they formed a shaggy-sided circle, inserted their hands like spokes toward the center, and I prayed the same prayer I always prayed before a game: "Lord, watch over every player tonight so that no one gets hurt. Be with us out there on the court. Help us to play our best and give You the glory for it. Amen."

They said "Amen," and we ran out onto the court and got a good look at the crowd, mostly ours, and a big one, despite the distractions of the holiday season. My boys ran their pregame drills, shot free throws, and then the starters shot while the reserves rebounded for them. I waved at Lauren, Michelle, Carla Briggs, and the Hooks up in the stands. Bobby Ray joined me on the bench as he sometimes did so he could tell me how he thought I ought to be handling game situations, and then the PA announcer read off our lineups. The teams arrayed themselves around the half-court circle for the tip, and

Martel directed it to Bird Burke, who promptly had it stolen from his hands in a blur of motion by Woodward's small forward, who took it in for an easy layup.

Behind me, Bobby Ray cursed loudly and violently.

"Ixnay on the ussingcay," I said, inclining my head toward Jimmy and the others on the bench. "Jimmy," I called back, my eyes on the action, "your hook has looked good this week. How're you feeling down in the post?"

"I feel strong," he said. "My shot's not falling like I want, but it's coming back."

I turned to him and blinked. That was quite an outburst, coming from Jimmy. "Well, I want you to shoot that hook tonight. You hit a couple shots, and they'll collapse on you whenever you get the ball. That'll open up a lot of other things for us."

"Yessir," he said.

Behind us, the crowd was yelling—I could pick out individual parents calling encouragement and instructions. Off to my left stood the cheerleaders shouting and stamping—"Let's go! Let's fight! Let's win tonight!" When B. W. was fouled running the break and stepped to the line, there was a cheer from the other cheerleaders (a breech of etiquette, by the way, to cheer when someone was shooting free throws)—"Rebound that basketball," *stomp clap stomp clap clap*, "Rebound that basketball"—and our cheerleaders were jumping and kicking and doing joyful cheerleader things when he made his first shot, providing even greater histrionics when he made the second.

It occurred to me that life would be so much more exciting if we had cheerleaders off the court as well. Wouldn't it be wonderful to know that whenever you did something right, people were going to jump up and down and call out your name?

With every defensive rebound, every inbound pass, my kids pushed it up the floor quickly, just like I wanted. A gratifying number of times, I looked up to find B. W. dribbling hard up the center of the court, the Sparks brothers on either side of him, just like I'd diagrammed it. When they didn't have an out-and-out fast break, they'd kick it back out and work it around. This was my team of scorers, not my best defensive team, and I was willing to concede Woodward some points, even let them build up a lead.

I knew Bob Tryon's philosophy on the other bench. I'd played against him in high school. He was a thinking player then and a thinking coach now, and his offensive approach was slow and methodical: Move the ball around, look for the open man inside or the open shot outside. I thought that if I pushed the pace, I might get Woodward playing outside their game plan, get their kids itching to show they could run with mine.

I knew that no one else had a point guard like mine to run the break, so I was willing to take the risk that they'd score some points off of us.

At the end of the first quarter, we were down eleven points, but the pace of the game had shifted.

"The best-laid plans," I said, looking over at the Woodward sideline, where Bob was making emphatic gestures, his palms to the floor—*slow down.*

"What?" Bobby Ray said, then looked and nodded. "It's working."

"We'll see. We're losing." I put Jimmy Bad Heart Bull and Ramiro Garza into the game at the start of the second quarter to rebound and give the Sparks brothers a breather and Albert Heap of Birds in for a short stint while B. W. came off the court and gulped air like water. The Sparks and B. W. had run at a furious pace, but it was starting to pay off. The Woodward players weren't getting as high off the ground; they were starting to leave some of their jump shots a little short—sure signs they were getting tired—and I quickly rotated B. W. and Martel back into the game to take advantage.

By halftime we had pulled back within five, and it might have been two if they hadn't sunk a long three-pointer at the buzzer. Back in the locker room I closed the door as they seated themselves facing me, and when I turned around, I felt a smile spread slowly across my face.

"You're finally playing like a team," I told them. "Our sprinters are wearing them down, our grunters are pulling down rebounds, and right now Bob Tryon is yelling at his team, telling them to remember what they did to get this far undefeated. Great job!"

I left them to sit so I could get a little air of my own and evaluate my plans for the second half—mostly more of the same unless Bob changed his plans, which he was almost sure to do, being the smart coach that he was.

There were things he could get his team to do to try and counter that pace—but what if I pushed even harder? Before halftime was over, I pulled the boys back together and sketched a few diagrams as a reminder as I talked, the ancient chalk occasionally screeching on the blackboard. "Same starters in the second half. We're going to push the pace even more, continue taking them off their game, make them play ours. We're going into the backcourt to press and trap on the inbounds, make them hurry their passes." Smiles spread across their tired faces.

"Martel, Tyrel, I want to see you use that quickness on defense for a change. Trap and release, trap and release." They nodded.

I turned to the others. "In half-court defense, I want Micheal to release when they shoot and B. W. to move to half-court—you get a head start like that, we can push it down court even faster. Jimmy, you're in for Bird to start. Keep fighting under the basket. I'm going to depend on you to get those rebounds." Then I stepped away from the blackboard and toward them, got down on one knee. "We're going to press them even harder than the first half and see if we can take them down for the count. You've done everything right so far. Come on. Let's take these guys."

It is an oft-repeated but nonetheless valid truism that any given team can beat any other given team on any given night given certain conditions, so let me stress that what happened on that given night was not a result of my brilliant coaching. It was a result of a lot of things, almost none of them having anything to do with me other than the fact that I fathered a brilliant point guard named Brian Wilson Tilden.

B. W. threw baseball passes, lobbed the ball up for Martel to take to the basket, bounced, backhanded, and flipped the ball behind his back, and when he saw that the Woodward boys were laying way off him to play his passing lanes, he started taking it directly to the basket, scoring nineteen points in the half. Our backcourt press was executed just the way I diagrammed it, with the Sparks brothers closing in so quickly on the inbounds pass that they must have caused half a dozen turnovers. And under our basket, Jimmy pulled down rebound after rebound, elevating over the panting Woodward five and even putting in a few buckets of his own.

It was one of those games you dream about as a coach: The ball always bounced in the right direction, shots that caromed up off the rim came back down through the center of the hoop, calls that could have been decided either way went ours. The last two minutes of the game—normally the most nerve-racking—were actually almost uneventful. Sure, Woodward, down by twelve, tried to foul us to stop the clock, then come down and shoot threes, but we made all our free throws, and their three-pointers looked like rockets launched by hair-brained Lithuanian scientists from backyard workshops.

When B. W. tossed the ball toward the rafters as the final buzzer went off, I walked across the court savoring an eighteen-point win over one of the top teams in the state, and accepted Bob Tryon's congratulations. I could truthfully say to him, "Everything just went our way, and next time you'd kick our butts."

I couldn't say that to anyone else, though, because no one would have heard me. Our fans were berserk; if there had been goalposts, they would have been twisted metal. I couldn't tell you when Watonga had last won this big a basketball game, but I could certainly say that it hadn't happened on my watch or in the memory of most of those in attendance. The cheerleaders were still jumping up and down and doing backflips, throwing their hands high and doing that sprinkling thing with their fingers; the crowd was swarming around my players and raising their index fingers toward the ceiling while our high school principal was yelling, "No street shoes on the gym floor"; and Michelle and Carla mobbed me, almost knocking me off my feet.

"Congratulations," Michelle was shouting before she jumped into my arms and wrapped her legs around me; Carla was pounding me violently on the back; Lauren stood behind her clinging mother and shouted "Nice job" through Dr. Pepper-flavored lip gloss.

"Decorum," I said to Michelle. "Don't give your seniors the wrong impression."

She was laughing and squeezing and sliding back down onto the floor, and Carla was still pounding me and had been joined by Bobby Ray, judging by the violence being done to my shoulder blades, and then the ocean of players and fans and cheerleaders and our poor principal still shouting "No street shoes," swept over us and I felt myself pulled out of Michelle's arms and lofted atop the surface of this human sea, full of swirls and eddies, where I saw B. W. and Martel Sparks and Jimmy Bad Heart Bull similarly walking—or at least sitting—on water. I waved across the roiling sea of heads and arms, and they waved back, and if I could ever have stopped time and lived continuously in one moment, I think that instant would have been a serious contender.

But at some point even the greatest of heroes has to put his feet back on the ground and take his own faltering steps, to live and breathe and love and make mistakes like any ordinary human, and after the crowd had carried us around the gym a few times, I found myself slipping from shoulders and hands tired of bearing my weight.

At last, I made contact with my poor scuffed floor.

B. W., deservedly, was the last of us to come to earth, and although the hoarse shouts of "Yeah!" and the jumping up and down continued for some minutes, I made my way under the stands, shaking with the weight of celebration, and back to the locker room.

The boys had played a great game, and they deserved every credit for their win, so I left them a message to that effect on the blackboard, added "Have a Merry Christmas," underlined "Merry" twice, sighed, and hit the showers.

My own holiday was about to begin.

Domino Buddies

When I picked my folks up at the airport in Oklahoma City the next afternoon, Dad and Mom wobbled slowly off the plane and up the ramp toward me, younger and fitter specimens of humanity striding briskly past them and into the arms of loved ones. I realized for the first time that this might be the last trip both my parents would make back home, that they would die, not eventually but soon, and that I would then be exposed to the world as the pretender I had always known that I was. As long as I had my folks to hide behind, I guess I thought I could avoid the full responsibility of being an authority figure; as long as you're a kid to someone, somewhere, I think it's okay if you're still not completely grown up, but that day of reckoning was approaching, coming toward me, in fact, a whole lot faster than my parents were.

But at last, they reached me. Dad shook my hand, his grip as frail and skeletal as tumbleweed.

"Good to see you, John," he said, and he smiled.

I smiled back and gave him a reluctantly accepted hug.

I could feel every rib in his back.

"Johnny!" my mother squawked. She threw her arms around my neck, and I breathed in the rosewater and must of her skin, an old woman's sachet.

"Hey folks," I said. "Good to see you. Merry Christmas!"

"My Lord, what a pilot," my mother said, as though with her half-dozen flights she constituted an aerial authority equivalent perhaps to the FAA. "Bumpy trip. I thought Poppa was going to be sick."

"I have the constitution of an ox," he muttered. "Airplanes don't make me sick."

"Now. Poppa, remember how the last time we came home, you spent half the flight to Phoenix in the lavatory," she said, and my father rolled his eyes so that I could see. I ushered them slowly from the waiting area and up the long walkway from the terminal back into the airport proper.

"We'll grab your bags and off we'll go," I said. "I'm parked downstairs close to baggage pickup."

My dad put his hand on my arm and held me back for a moment. "How does the wheat look?"

For a second, I remembered my horrifying dream—Trent and his questions about the farm. Then I realized, what else do farmers—or ex-farmers—talk about?

"It's real pretty," I said. "We've had nice weather and some rain. It's real green and about six inches high."

Mom shook her head sadly and told the ceiling, "My husband will be asking about wheat with his last breath."

"And your son'll be telling me," Dad said, giving my arm a bony squeeze and letting out a wheezing cackle.

We passed the security checkpoint where people were lined up to subject themselves and their baggage to inspection on the way in. A burly cowboy with silver-tipped lizard boots set the scanner beeping, and a blush spread across his already rosy face when the black woman at the scanner directed him to take his boots off and try it again.

"The airport in Phoenix is much nicer than this," Mom said as we crept toward the exit at a roaming cow's pace. "Where are those carts to haul people around?"

"It's not that big an airport," I said. "This is Oklahoma City, not New York City, in case you forgot while you were gone."

When their baggage was collected and loaded in the truck bed and we had pulled out of short-term parking, I headed off down Meridian Avenue toward the highway. As we passed Chili's, I asked, "Did you eat on the plane?"

"Breakfast on the flight to Dallas. Nothing on the flight up. But I think we're okay. Are you hungry, Poppa?"

"I want a hamburger," he said. "A big one. With cheese and tomato and pickle. And bacon."

She looked daggers at him. "Poppa, you know you're not supposed to eat fried foods," she said, and Dad contritely folded up his desires and put them away.

I wondered at what point life would begin to encroach that strongly on me, at what point my fight with those extra ten pounds would be transformed into an epic battle with cosmic forces determined to do me in. And moreover, I began to wonder as I pulled onto the interstate and headed west, at what point do the things you give up to stay alive start to outweigh the pleasures of being alive?

"Do you miss hamburgers, Dad?" I asked, and he raised his right hand as if I'd called upon him to testify.

"I miss everything," he said, "but at least I still have my family and my church and my TV shows."

I chuckled. "You still watching *Unsolved Mysteries?*"

"Sure thing." And that affirmative response launched him into an involved—in fact, to judge by the incredible degree of complexity, I'd also have to add, *confused*—account of a long-missing young woman, a single mother who had disappeared seven years ago on a night out. Last seen getting into a car with some men she had known since high school. No evidence of foul play. No evidence of anything.

"Left her little girl all alone in the world," he said, and his voice quavered a little as he went on. "She's all growed up now, but she hasn't never forgot her mother. Hasn't never stopped wondering what happened to her. The TV people were talking to her, and she told them, 'I remember.' She told them, 'It won't never get behind me.'"

"Like to made me cry." My mom sighed with something close to pleasure. "Lord have mercy."

"So did they catch them?" I asked.

"Who?" my dad asked.

"The people who made off with her mom?" For they had to have caught somebody, there had to be some point to such a story as this, some kind of justice.

"Look at those boats," my dad said, looking out his window. We were passing the back lot of Boyd Chevrolet, where Mr. Boyd always lined up enormous dump trucks and speed boats and tractor trailers along the highway frontage to show that he was not just any car and pickup Chevrolet dealer, but rather a purveyor of all forms of modern conveyance. "You been fishing lately?"

"Not in the last week or two," I said, and I gave up on solving the unsolved mystery. "If the weather holds, I'll take you down to the pond while you're here. You want to come with us, Mom?"

"Lord, no," she said. "You boys are welcome to that. These days, only fish I want to see are on my plate looking up at me. I'll stay around the house and help Michelle."

"The Hooks are coming out for Christmas dinner," I said. "They were with us Thanksgiving. When's Candace supposed to get in?"

"Said she'd get on the road tomorrow," Dad growled. "I worry about her, young girl driving all those miles by herself. The roads aren't safe these days."

"Amen," Mom said.

Unlike them, I knew that when Candy arrived she wouldn't be alone; she'd told me in her last letter that she wanted to introduce the family to Arturo all at once to lessen the surprise for us (to say nothing of the shock for him), and this looked like her best opportunity, although it added yet another complication to a holiday season already so full of them that I felt that if I had to accommodate anything else, I might just split open like a wet paper sack.

"How are the kids enjoying school?" Mom wanted to know.

"Not as much as Michelle does, and not half as much as they ought to be," I said. "They don't know how good they have it. I'd give anything to be learning things instead of watching calves chew."

"None of us know how good we have it," Mom said. "You know, you should go back to school yourself. It's not too late for you."

I felt a pain shoot through my chest, and I had to clench my teeth for a moment before answering. "That train left the station a long time ago, Mom."

"It's not too late," Mom repeated. "You're still smart as a whip. All the books you read—"

"Smart isn't everything," I said. "I'm almost forty years old, as you probably remember. And there's the money—"

"We could help you with the money," Mom said. "Couldn't we, Poppa?"

He looked at her as though she were dangerously insane. "How many kids can one man have in college at the same time?" he asked, but this negative impulse was followed by a grudging nod. "I suppose there's no point us having money if we can't use it on a good cause."

"A lost cause," I said, although the idea of going off to school curled up the corners of my mouth. I saw myself walking down a hallway and into a college classroom, felt the hard seat of the desk beneath me, heard my name called: "John Jacob Tilden?"

But the me I saw responding was a me with an unlined face, bushy sideburns cut level with my earlobes, a head full of brown hair.

A me I hadn't been for twenty years.

Yes, a lost cause.

"Why didn't you offer to send me to college before now?" I said, trying hard to keep the bitterness out of my voice and mostly succeeding, although I could not keep it out of my throat, my mouth, my stomach.

"You never asked," Dad said. "Only thing you've ever asked of us was if you could make a place for yourself and your new family on the farm. I always thought Trent would be the farmer." He shook his head and then looked out the window away from us. "I miss that boy."

"Lord, Lord," my mother seconded.

"It won't ever get behind us," I said, so quietly I don't think they even heard me over the road noise.

"Well, the Lord has His reasons," Mom said, wiping her eyes, although it sounded as though she might be willing to be talked out of that opinion. "All things work for good to them that love the Lord."

"Amen," Dad said, a long sigh falling away to nothing. "God is good."

The highway whined underneath our feet, and we rounded a long gradual curve heading down into the Canadian River Valley. Ahead, a red Dodge Daytona, just pulled over by a highway patrol cruiser, lights flashing, eased to a stop and the driver's side window began to roll down.

"How fast you going?" Mom wanted to know as we approached the blinking lights.

"Speed limit," I said. "A little over."

"He's already got one on the hook, Momma," Dad said. "He won't worry about us."

In the rearview I could see the tall black patrolman walking up to the car and a slender female arm offer up a license and registration. That arm, unaccountably, made me think of Samantha. I saw her arm reaching out to me for a hug when she arrived at our place at Thanksgiving, felt my own heart stand still and the world around us collectively hold its breath as we met for a minimal contact, side-to-side embrace. But I could feel the pressure of her hand on the top of my shoulder long after I'd said hello to her kids, long after she'd deposited her load of pie on the cabinet, and even now, I could feel her touch like a burn that stays tender long after a fool sets his hand on something he shouldn't have.

"I hope you faithful folks have been praying for me," I said. "This reunion could be the death of me yet."

"Oh, don't be silly," Mom said. "Everything will work out."

And as far as they were concerned—even if they had known what they did not know—everything would. The world had an order, preordained, and the mind behind that order was a generous and kindly one. End of story.

While there had once been a time I was willing to believe such a thing, I had done so entirely on faith, not on evidence, although I guess that's what we all must do in the long run if we're going to believe in anything. Peace of mind depends on how much faith we can muster and how steadfastly we can hold on to it, and that might explain why lately, I had almost no peace of mind.

We got off Interstate 40 at the Geary/Watonga exit, passed the Cherokee Trading Post—which was not an actual Cherokee trading post, of course, but a Texaco station, restaurant, gift shop, and KOA campground.

"Okay," I said at last. "I'll trust you on that."

"Oh, don't trust us," Mom said. "Trust God."

"Okay," I said to stop the conversation. I had forgotten how present God tended to be in every conversation with my folks.

After creeping through the dying town of Geary, where Officer Gary Monday sat vigilant in his police cruiser just off Main Street, we drove on into almost-dying Watonga instead of straight out to the farm so the folks could judge for themselves how the town had fared since their last trip home. We drove past the Homeland, for several years now the only grocery store in town, past the bowling alley and the Anthony's store on Main, and as we were passing the barbershop on Main, Dad made a sort of hooting noise and told me, "Pull over there," pointing toward a parking space next to two old

men shuffling up the sidewalk in striped gray overalls and white felt
Resistol hats.

When I stopped and shut off the engine, Dad opened his door
and slowly lowered himself to the pavement. One of the men raised
a hand in greeting, and his partner nodded.

"Should we get out?" I asked. "Just to be sociable?"

"This won't take long," Mom said. "Domino buddies." And she
sniffed at this frivolity; although she herself was inclined to play a
game or two of dominoes when family came together, she didn't much
hold with a man leaving his family behind and pushing dominoes
around with a group of men who were probably bad influences. I
guess she figured she had gotten Dad off to Arizona just in time to
prevent both his physical and moral collapse.

Dad got back into the truck, and the two men passed on into
the barbershop. As the second man reached the door, he turned and
raised a hand again, then stepped inside.

"Me and that old boy was raised up together," Dad told me. "But
we growed apart."

We drove back to the main highway and headed toward home,
past the Sonic and Kentucky Fried Chicken, past the liquor store
Phillip and friends robbed three owners and half a lifetime ago.

Thinking about the way my own life worked, I realized that while
for me it was half a lifetime ago and didn't matter in the slightest, for
Phillip it was an everyday thing. It still looked back from the mirror
at him every morning.

It was his life.

I had to try harder to reach him.

"But how?" I asked Michelle that night after we'd gotten my folks stowed in B. W.'s room, and gotten him set up on the couch (he'd refused to stay the night in Michael's room, which more and more looked like it was going to be preserved as some sort of museum kept in loving memory of our poor lost boy, drawers forever full of dingy white socks and frayed Jockey briefs, walls forever plastered with posters of Aerosmith, Van Halen, Nirvana, Iron Maiden, dresser covered with the toiletries that he'd left behind, mostly unopened bottles of Brut from Michelle's parents every Christmas and a half-full bottle of Drakkar Noir, the cologne he'd decided he liked when Mindy Stallings told him she liked it on him and had stopped liking when he stopped liking Mindy Stallings).

"Well," Michelle said, pulling on one of her warm socks, "you just have to be persistent. Don't give up."

"I am persistent. I've always been persistent. What good does it do? He won't talk to me." I raised my hands palm up in front of me. "No one will talk to me. Phillip doesn't have a phone. Michael does, but he won't answer it. And I'm not much good on the phone anyway. I can't imagine what the other person is doing. If they're paying attention to me or watching the Cowboys or making faces about how much they hate talking to me."

"Oh, I'm sure they'd be doing that." Michelle pulled on her other fluffy sock.

"Well, anyway, my point is that it doesn't matter how persistent I am if I can't even talk to anyone."

"Write a letter," she said, now properly clad. She flexed her red-toed feet, purred in satisfaction.

"Write a letter," I repeated.

"You know. Paper. Envelope. Stamp."

"I'm familiar with the concept," I said. "I just hadn't thought about it. It seems so—remote. You write letters to people—"

"—you don't see everyday." She nodded and took my hand in hers. "So. Write a letter."

I sighed. "All right," I said.

She rose, rolled her shoulders. "I've got to go to sleep. I'm tired out from talking with your folks. They can never seem to remember that I already love Jesus."

She climbed in between the sheets. I pulled the comforter over her, arranged it around her ears, and sat down at her side after she had snuggled into the mattress and found a comfortable spot.

"They're old," I said.

"Hmm?"

"My parents. They're old."

"They sure are," she said.

"It scares me."

She turned her head toward me and opened her eyes. "Scares you? Why?"

I shook my head. It seemed like another thing, on top of all the others. Why even talk about it?

"J. J.?"

I shook my head again, but with resignation; it was bedtime, so I had to speak the truth. "I'm afraid that they're going to die, Shell. I mean, now I know they're going to. And I don't know what I'm going to do when that happens."

She sat up and gathered me into her arms, pulled my head down onto her breast, stroked my hair. "I'll be right here," she said. "You know that. I'll always be right here—if you want me to be."

"I know," I said. Did everything have to come out into the open this baldly, this late at night, when truth telling was the law? How had we stumbled into this particular darkened corridor?

She squeezed my hand. "What else do you know?"

I shook my head and sighed. As long as we were telling the truth, there was something else. "Why on earth did you invite Samantha here for Thanksgiving? You've never liked her."

"Of course I've never liked her," she said. "Why should I? Do you like Bill?"

"I loathe him," I said. "I'd like to see him trampled by cattle. You haven't answered my question."

"Do you really want to know?" She fluffed her pillow, preparing, perhaps, for my saying no.

"I do." I did not say, "Tell the truth," for that would have been superfluous. I simply anticipated the blow, felt my stomach contract in preparation.

"Because," she said after a long pause in which I knew she'd been trying to think of the gentlest way to say what she had to say, "twenty years is plenty long enough for a man to mope after what might have been. It's time to make yourself understand that. Time to be here with us instead of somewhere else. Because part of you has always been somewhere else, no matter how I tugged and snatched and fought. With Samantha, or at least somewhere off down a road you didn't take."

"Don't cry," I said, for she was crying and smacking her pillow with her fist now instead of fluffing it.

"I think I've earned a cry or two, John Tilden," she said. "Don't tell me not to cry," but she did quit smacking her pillow and rested her head on it, and I held her hand and stroked her head, and shortly afterward, she was asleep.

"Amazing," I said, and shook my head. The sleep of the righteous.

I wandered down the hallway and back to the study to check on my writing supplies, maybe write a letter or two.

I was up late, but Dad wanted to go out early and look over the farm he had known so well, so after I'd fed and watered the calves and we'd had a good breakfast of egg substitute, turkey sausage, and real coffee, hot and black as night, we climbed into the truck. As we pulled around the house, Frank jumped in back and up onto the wheel well, his head hanging over the sidewall of the bed, his tongue lolling. We drove down our long driveway, an eighth of a mile to the road, then on around the section line to the Old Place.

I stopped at the gap, opened it, drove the truck through, closed it behind us before driving on. Normally the passenger gets out to open the gate, but for the first time, Dad didn't clamber out without speaking. He didn't offer, and I didn't ask.

We bounced down through the pasture, toward the old barn, Dad holding onto the armrest with white-knuckle force.

"Take a right," Dad said when we reached a pasture intersection—a place where two pickup tracks intersected, although the path we turned onto was much less used and had all but disappeared. It went to the foundation of the old house, the place where Dad's parents first lived when they got married and where Dad himself lived until he and Mom got married and built the place where we now lived. There was nothing left of the old house but the concrete foundation, atop a low rise and surrounded by dark green cedar trees, although once there were no trees here and you could have seen all the way down the valley to Whirlwind Creek.

After my grandparents died but long before I was born, Dad tore the house down and used the boards to add on to the barn at the Home Place. That's all there was to that house, boards. No plumbing, no wiring. He often told moral character-building stories to me when I was a kid about how he grew up toting buckets of water from the cistern down back of the house, about cold baths with rough lye soap stinging his skin, about lonely late-night trips to the outhouse in pitch darkness.

Now the foundation of the old house was almost hidden by the cedars clustered close by, and I resolved to cut down more than a few of them for firewood next winter.

I pulled up as close to the foundation as I could, and we climbed out.

"You know, John, memory is a funny thing," my dad said after walking up the concrete steps and onto the floor of what would have been the front bedroom. "I always thought this place was bigger."

"I've always thought of it as really small," I admitted, stepping past him to what must have been the kitchen. "I always wondered how you did it."

"It was a hard life." He looked around, pointing at this corner and that as if placing furniture. "But we were happy."

What did he see when he came up here among the aromatic cedars?

I didn't know. He'd shown me pictures, told me his stories, but there were other things on my mind, impediments in the way of my understanding. "Dad?" I asked finally.

"Uhm," he said, still seeing what had been.

"Have you had a good life?"

It stirred him out of his reverie. He looked at me owlishly, his head tilted to the side as if to better regard this improbable question. "Of course I have," he said at last. His tone indicated that there was no doubt in his mind.

Maybe there wasn't.

"Is there anything you regret?"

He knelt to pick up a petrified bit of branch on the floor and turned away from me. "Of course there is."

I stepped across the space between us, space that suddenly seemed to have dwindled. "You've had regrets?"

"Of course I have." Again the owl look. "What person with a thinking brain in his head goes through life without regret?" He shook his head. I would have given anything to know what he was thinking. "Things don't always happen the way we want them to. Whenever you step through a crossroads, you leave three paths behind."

I stooped down next to him to pick up my own twig from the foundation, turned it this way and that in my hands. "You never told me any of this," I said. "Why didn't we ever talk like this before?"

He rose to his feet to regard me. "Son, what earthly good would it have done?"

I stood up. "It would have made a difference to me," I said, a little more forcefully than I wanted. I shook the twig once or twice before I let it drop. "It would have made a difference."

He turned his head to the side and regarded me with bright eyes. "You talk to your own young ones about your fears and sorrows?"

"No," I admitted. "I want to protect them as long as I can from all the heartbreak out there."

"No different for me," he said gruffly and turned to toss his twig off into the cedar forest. "Anyway, your mother says there's a reason for everything that happens. Providence in the fall of a sparrow, she says."

"Do you believe that?"

He fixed me with his gaze. "Don't you?"

"I'm trying to," I said.

"No different for me," he said, and he turned away. "Take me on around the section line."

"Yes, sir," I said, and I watched his slowly departing back for a moment with a warm glow of love lighting my chest that I hadn't felt for a long time, if indeed I had ever felt it for him in that way.

Then I scurried on to catch up to him so he wouldn't turn and scowl at me for making him wait.

"Your trouble," he told me between bounces, as we drove back uphill across the pasture, "is you think too much."

"I've been told that," I said. "I wish that were my only trouble."

"You've done well for yourself," he went on. "Raised good kids. Honored your parents. Found a useful place for yourself. Provided for your family. Done just fine."

"I could dispute most of that," I said, bouncing so high off the seat that I almost banged the ceiling. "But the most important thing, it seems to me, is that even if I've done everything you say, I didn't always want to. Mostly didn't want to."

He smiled. "Got done all the same, though, didn't it?"

"The Lord loves a cheerful giver," I quoted. We pulled up to the gap.

"The Lord loves everyone," Dad said, and folded his hands into his lap.

End of story.

And it was; the rest of the morning we talked about cattle, about a part I couldn't buy for the combine and would probably have to weld up myself, about the price of wheat. The moment, whatever it was, wherever it came from, was gone, but I would always treasure the memory. It was the longest and most genuine talk we had ever had, and on the way home, I stole an occasional glance at my father, who now seemed like an altogether different person from the man I had set out with earlier that morning, the man I had loved and feared for forty years.

We were raised up together; we grew apart.

But maybe, toward the end of his life, we grew back together again.

At least, it gave me comfort to think so.

December 23, 1994

Phillip One Horse
RR 1, Box 127
Watonga, OK 73047

Dear Phillip,

*I hope you'll know that all of what follows—all of it, good
and bad—is written with the greatest affection and respect for
you. I also hope you'll think of me as a good enough friend that
I should tell you how I feel. So here goes:*

*When I think of all the people I've known and all the lives
I've come in contact with on this earth, it is you and yours that
frustrates me most. You're one of the kindest, warmest, and most
intelligent people I've ever met, but something in you seems to
want to pull the past along behind you like a trailer, to make
it pop up like a peacock's tail when most everybody else is ready
and willing to forget about it and accept you for the wonderful
person you are.*

*Now maybe you're thinking I've got no call to talk about
the past, and maybe you're right to think so, because I am still
wrestling the past like a man in a gator pit, but it's also true
that sometimes we can help people—or at least give unasked-
for advice—about the very problems that paralyze us. So take
these words, for whatever good they might do: I am proud to be
your friend, and I don't care about anything that might have
happened in the past. I understand that you're distressed about
your behavior at Thanksgiving. Please don't be. It's forgotten.
Scout's honor.*

Please know that my family and I worry about you, that we miss you, that we care what happens to you, even if you don't.

That's all I wanted to say, I guess. I won't ask you to come to the reunion or to come play basketball with us, although few things would give me more pleasure than to see you meet the past on even terms. I won't even ask you to let us know that you're okay, although it would clear some worries from my table, which is currently packed to the breaking point with apprehension.

Just know that our Christmas wish for you is peace, and that if I can ever be of help to you in anything in this life, you have only to ask.

Your friend,
John

December 23, 1994

Michael Tilden
122 E. 2nd St.
Watonga, OK 73047

Dear Son,

I keep thinking that I'm going to run into you in town—I'm sure we both frequent the Homeland, the Four Corners, the KFC—but your disappearance has been complete, and if we didn't see Gloria every few days, I'd believe you'd dropped completely off the face of the planet. Your mother misses you a lot. And she's so excited about the baby—I wish you could include her in your lives, at least a little.

It's a particularly hurtful time to be missing you. Christmas won't be complete without our oldest boy in attendance to play Santa and pass out the gifts, but I'm adjusting to the idea that we won't see you, just as I'm adjusting to the idea that you don't want to see us. What I can't adjust to is the void you've left in our hearts, a hole that the wind whistles through on lonesome nights. Your room sits unused and mostly untouched. I think Candace's boyfriend, if he shows, will occupy it for the holidays, but I'd boot him out into the snow (assuming we have snow) in a second if I thought you might be coming home.

I know that this is not going to happen. So I will close with my best wishes to Gloria, who is a good girl. I know I am not supposed to approve of her, that you may have even chosen her at first to make me mad, but I can't help myself. And she's the mother of my first grandchild, which counts for quite a bit, once

I got over the initial shock of becoming an old man. So take good care of her. Or continue to, I should say, for I hear good reports about you.

And also take care of yourself.

Your family is well, at least for the moment. I am trying my best to make sure it stays that way, but I am a weak and thoughtless person, which I'm sure you already know. If you ever do think of me, try to forgive me for all the things I said, and the things I should have said, but didn't.

Your loving father,
John Tilden

December 23, 1994

Dear Sam,

Since I'm writing other difficult letters tonight, I finish with a short note to tell you I have to talk with you, and soon. You have been on my mind lately in ways I don't understand. I don't know what you've been thinking since the last time we really talked, or even what you're wanting in your life from here on out, but I know that one way or another, I have to settle things with you once and for all. Michelle says it's time for me to make a choice, and she's a wise woman—the past has been on my mind for so long that it's impossible for me to live in the here and now.

My heart is pounding as I write this, and I keep thinking, Do I really dare to say this? To send it? To let you read it?

But I do dare.

I think it's high time for me to earn some peace, whatever that means.

Love,
John

The Harold Angels

Christmas morning dawned cold and damp. A front had moved in during the night to spit a light dusting of sleet and frothy snow, more sooty-looking than pristine white. Bing Crosby would not have recognized it as a prototypical white Christmas; it looked more like a huge flight of birds had passed over in the night and done its collective business on lawn, trees, and cars. The household rose gradually and in stages. First up were my parents, the habits of years long past still ingrained in them: brew the coffee, set the bacon (or, these days, bacon substitute) sizzling and the eggs (or egg-like substance) frying, and have a seat at the table to savor a warm meal and a steaming black cup of coffee. B. W. was next, drawn by the smell of coffee, then me, having spent the night staring at the ceiling, dreading this Christmas like Herod, but finally unwilling to lie in bed one more instant.

Next came Lauren and Michelle, appearing simultaneously like twins in the doorway, identical frowzy hair and dropped-jaw yawns. In that moment it would have been hard to say which I loved more, since each seemed so much the other, just at different stages of life. And some time later, after the table had been cleared and the dishes washed and preparations for dinner embarked upon, from their various wings of the house came Arturo and Candy, who had arrived past midnight after crossing New Mexico and the Texas Panhandle to arrive safely in the Sooner State. "God must love flat land, He made so much of it," Candy had said as she was hauling in her bag.

But I get ahead of myself, for much transpired before my sleepy sister made her way to the table. Shortly after I joined them at the table, mug of coffee warm in my hand, Dad was asking questions.

"Whose truck's that out back?"

"Arturo's," B. W. said, his mouth so full of biscuits and jelly that even knowing the answer, I could barely understand him.

"Who?" Mom asked, wrinkling her brow.

"Candy's friend," I said. "They got in last night about midnight."

"Girlfriend?" Dad asked.

I looked over at Mom, who leaned forward to hear better, and then back at my dad, who had paused in his chewing to hear me better. "No, sir. Boyfriend, I guess you'd say."

"Boyfriend," he said. He did not resume chewing.

"Who on earth?" Mom said. "Have we met him? Has she talked about him before? How long's she been seeing him?"

"One question at a time, Momma," Dad said, resuming his thoughtful mastication, although he, too, now leaned forward for answers. I am not much in the habit of pausing for prayer before I speak, but I did breathe a silent plea to the powers that be that my parents, wonderful Christians and closet racists that they had always been, would react with the first of those natures to this happy news.

"The boy's name is Arturo," I said. Dad and Mom shared a glance. "He's a PhD student in geology at the university in Albuquerque. I couldn't say how long she's been seeing him, but I'm sure she'd be glad to tell you when she gets up."

"Ar-tu-ro?" my dad drawled, making it into three separate and distasteful words. "What kind of name is that?"

"Nice boy?" Mom asked. "Is he religious?"

"He's Catholic," I said. "Candy says he's regular about it."

"How is it you know so much about this boy and we know so little?" Dad demanded.

"Whoa," I said. Maybe a man quicker on his feet than I might have parried that question in such a way that he wouldn't have to answer it, but I couldn't conceive of anything to speak at that moment but the truth. "She didn't know how you'd feel about it," I said. "She thought that maybe you wouldn't like him because he's Hispanic."

"Lordy," Mom said. "Hispanic." It was not, I imagined, a word she had ever spoken before.

"You know," B. W. said, casting about for a phrase more familiar to them. "Mexican American."

"His name is Arturo Ramirez," I said. "His father's a doctor in El Paso."

"I've always liked Mexicans," Dad said. "Used to have a harvest crew working for me every summer right out there in that field." He pointed, in case somebody didn't know where it was. "They were good little workers. I treated them good. Ask your momma."

"Well, I hope you'll like Arturo," I said. "He's smart, and a hard worker. Just don't talk to him about your field hands."

"Why not?" Dad asked. His jaw took a stubborn set.

"Just ... just don't, Dad. Please. Be nice to him, shake his hand, treat him like he was a deacon in your church."

"Well, I like this," Dad sniffed, and got up to bring the pot of coffee over to the table. "Getting so a man has to listen to his children to be told what to do," he went on, along with saying some other things so far under his breath that I could neither discern nor take offense at them.

"Does it look serious? I mean is she serious about him?" my mom asked, and I inclined my head once, slowly and emphatically. She sighed. "Well, the Lord moves in mysterious ways. Do you like him, John?"

"I like him," B. W. said, although nobody had asked him.

"Arturo's a good man," I said. "He treats her well. But what I think isn't important. She thinks he hung the moon, and that should be all that matters."

"Getting so a man has to ask his kids for news about each other," my dad muttered.

It did not look like a promising beginning. I had told Candy more than once that she should tell them what was happening before it got this far along, but, maybe rightly, almost no one ever does anything I advise.

Later, when I heard noises in bathrooms and knew that our midnight travelers would join us soon, I took a moment to look around the table and try to make things come out all right: "Candy's friend is going to be joining us now, and I know she's been nervous about how we're going to treat him. So make him feel welcome, you hear?" I looked at my kids while I delivered this rather hackneyed speech, although I was really speaking for my parents' benefit. "Make him feel welcome. He's a guest in our home, and he's come a long way to be with us for Christmas."

Then they came out, and Candy put her hand on Arturo's broad shoulder and introduced him. "Everybody, this is Arturo Ramirez. Daddy, Momma, this is the man I'm going to marry."

"Holy cow," Lauren said.

"Congratulations, you two," Michelle said, launching herself to her feet and throwing her arms around them to set a good example.

Dad stood up to shake Arturo's hand, and my mom, God love her, gave Arturo a hug, which he returned with a huge silly grin spreading across his face.

"Well, son, this is a surprise," Dad said. "You two hungry for breakfast?"

"Yes, sir," Arturo said. "We haven't eaten a decent meal since we left Albuquerque."

"Well then, you've come to the right place," my mom said, and she scurried off into the kitchen to locate currently unused pots and pans and rustle up a good farm breakfast for young people untroubled by cholesterol readings.

While Michelle asked questions about their drive and Dad watched Arturo, maybe to see if he would betray some sort of dangerous Mexican genetic trait, the kids filtered into the living room, where presents currently lay piled and wrapped beneath our old but still serviceable artificial fir. In years long past, of course, we could have never made it through a long and leisurely breakfast on Christmas morning. As recently as Lauren's tenth Christmas morning we had been led—dragged, practically—into the living room to sanction the handing out of presents by the ceremonial Santa—who always had been Michael, complaining about the indignity—and the ripping and tearing of gaily-colored wrapping paper and the throwing open of boxes and the raising of a paean to conspicuous consumption and planned obsolescence.

"Lauren," Michelle called into the other room as Candy and Arturo finished their food, "will you find the Santa hat and boots?"

"They're over by the fireplace," Lauren called back. "Next to the stockings. Where they always are." This last phrase was delivered with considerably less volume but still with the intention of audibility.

"Well, put them on," Michelle said. "You're Santa this year."

"Really?" she said, and after that, a murmured "cool."

We all rose from the table and relocated to the living room: Dad in his old recliner, Mom, Michelle, and B. W. on the sofa, Candy and Arturo on the floor in front of me, and despite my protests to them about the privileged status of guests, just me on the love seat, although Lauren would join me after performing her Santa duties.

At present, she stood in front of the tree, the red-and-white Santa hat perched jauntily on her head, white fluffy ball hanging behind her left shoulder, and the tops of the boots resting midway up her smaller-than-Michael calves. "How do I do this?" she asked.

"You're Santa," B. W. said. "Do it anyway you like."

"Okay," she said. "I'm going to give all the presents to myself."

"Hey." Michelle laughed, shaking her finger. "Greedy Santa. Bad Santa. We didn't raise you to be this kind of Santa."

Lauren waved her hands in front of her, palms toward us, and giggled. "I just wanted to see if you were paying attention." And then one by one she tugged the presents out from under the tree and delivered them to their intended. When the presents were piled up on and around us, we paused for a moment, as was our practice, to remind ourselves what we celebrated. Dad said a long and quavery prayer thanking God for sending His only begotten Son to be born on earth in a lowly manger so that He could grow to manhood and die for our sins. Then we sang a few carols: "O Little Town of Bethlehem," "The First Noel," and the first verse and enough of the second of "Hark, the Herald Angels Sing" to convince us we only knew the first verse.

"When I was little," Lauren said, perched next to me on the love seat amidst her haul, still wearing her hat and boots, "I thought that was the angels' name."

"What?" B. W. asked.

"Harold," she said, and giggled. "The Harold Angels."

"Herald, you idiot," B. W. said, rolling his eyes in a brotherly fashion. "Like a bringer of news. Glad tidings."

"Any tidings," Arturo said.

"Don't call your sister an idiot," I told B. W. "It's Christmas."

And then we opened our gifts, pausing after each to thank the person or persons responsible before tearing into the next one. As always, Michelle had handled most of the gift buying, being much better at it than I, but there was one gift I waited for with anticipation to be opened—a Noah's Ark charm bracelet I had picked out for Lauren at the Cracker Barrel store in Oklahoma City. With her recent interest in saving the earth and its inhabitants, she had adopted the Ark as a useful symbol, and when she opened the small box, saw the bracelet and let out a squeal, I felt a warm feeling well up into my chest.

"Mom," she said, putting it on (with a little help from me on the catch), "thanks! It's beautiful."

"Thank your dad," she said. "He found that for you."

And Lauren leaned over, threw her arms around my neck, and gave me the kind of head-crushing hug she used to unleash when she was a little girl and not a young lady.

"Thank you," she whispered. "I love it."

"I'm glad," I whispered back. "When you look at it, think of me."

"I don't need anything to remind me of you," she said. "I've got you." Then she sat back and went to work on the next package.

My presents were mostly utilitarian, as they had been for decades: white socks, new boxers, insulated coveralls for outdoor work. Michelle did get me a pair of Nike Air Jordans, gleaming and new, to wear for the game, and a new Western shirt to wear to the dance. I had wrestled as always about what to get her, this year more than ever. What I had wrapped and put under the tree was one of those sweeping crinkly skirts she liked with wild horses on it, and a boxed set of Kinks music. She held this last present up and whooped—"This has 'Come Dancing' on it!"—and then looked closer at the box and frowned. "J. J., I'll have to take this back. You got CDs."

"I know," I said, motioning her to follow me. And I led her back to the study. On the shelf where our trusty AM-FM/cassette/eight track turntable unit had rested, a new compact stereo system now held court.

"John," she said, smiling but with a tinge of concern, "how much did this cost?"

"Your music is really important to you," I said, without answering her.

She threw her arms around me. "It's a wonderful gift," she breathed in my ear. "Thank you."

"You're welcome," I said.

"Maybe next year we'll have a baby here," Michelle said, looking into my eyes. "Wouldn't that be great?"

I could see that she thought so. "That would be really nice," I said.

"Oh, J. J.," she said, taking hold of my forearms. "I'll be a good grandma."

"Mom," Lauren called from the other room, "B. W.'s throwing paper at me."

We looked at each other, and familiar grins spread across our faces.

"After you," I said, bowing a little at the waist the way I'd always heard courtly gentlemen were supposed to, and we made our way back to our family and the remains of gift giving.

Michelle's folks arrived shortly after, bearing gifts and cooked vegetables. Our parents got up to welcome each other, cordially if not warmly. They had not been friends before Michelle and I created Michael in the coach's office, and there wasn't much in that particular situation to bring them closer together; if anything, each set of parents had blamed the other set for not raising a better, more responsible child, so it was not until the grandkids came along that they'd found anything that could be described as common ground.

Michelle's dad pulled me aside into a corner of the dining room after he'd set down his burden, and not for a fatherly embrace. "John, I hope that Phillip One Horse isn't coming for dinner today," he said, one hand massaging my shoulder in a way I particularly disliked.

"No, sir," I said. "I haven't been able to get in touch with him since Thanksgiving."

"Well," he said, nodding, "I think we all know where he's crawled off to. Or into."

"Daddy," Michelle said, for she had seen the unusual tête-à-tête developing from her post in the kitchen and come over to investigate. "Phillip is a good person. He made a mistake, and we've forgiven him. I think you could do the same."

Mr. Hooks raised one hand dismissively in another way I didn't like. "Everybody knows what that boy's like. Forgiveness is for people who are trying to change their sinful ways, not those who are wallowing in their bad habits."

"Forgiveness is for everyone," Michelle said, to an "amen" from my mother, passing by and hearing only the last of the conversation.

Again that wave, and I realized suddenly why I disliked the gesture so much: It was Bill Cobb's dismissive wave, to a T.

"I'm sorry you dislike him so much," I said, straining for civility and to keep my feelings off my face. "He won't be here today."

The memory of Phillip's presence the last time we'd similarly gathered (and Michael's absence from every gathering in recent months) cast a pall over dinner, and it was a quiet meal despite the excellent stuffing Michelle had fixed and the goose I'd been up basting when Arturo and Candace arrived. It was especially quiet after Mrs. Hooks announced that they had to leave shortly after dinner to drop by Michael and Gloria's. She turned to Mom and Dad. "I hope you'll run by with us and see them. They asked about you specifically."

"Oh," Mom said. "Well. Poppa and I have talked about that, and I think we'll just take them out to eat later this week."

"You're not going to the house?" I asked. I wasn't sure I was understanding them.

"Why not?" Candace asked.

"Well," Dad said, clearing his throat, "we don't see how we can go visit him and that woman and not look like we condone what he's doing." He cleared his throat. "I mean, living in sin and all."

Michelle and I shared a distressed look. "Dad," I said, "I'd give years of my life for the invitation you're turning down."

He turned to me. "Son, you know how sorry I am for the way things have been between you. And I know that maybe such things don't matter much to you, but it seems to me that some things are right and some things are wrong, and you can't close your eyes to them."

"I don't see it that way," I said.

"They asked for you," Mrs. Hooks said again. "And it is Christmas."

"The apostle Paul says that marriage is a sacred part of the Christian life," my mother said. "If a man and woman are going to love each other and live with each other, it should only be within the bonds of holy matrimony." The Hooks nodded reluctantly; this was true.

"I don't like Paul," I said, setting my fork down conspicuously, as though I refused to eat another bite until the Bible was changed to my satisfaction. "I've never liked him."

My mother furrowed her brow, set down her own fork, and looked across the table at me the way she used to do when I was in high school and we disagreed, which was most of the time. "John, it doesn't matter if you like Paul. It isn't Paul talking. It's God. Those are God's words about how we're supposed to live."

"Okay," I said. "Fine." I was pretty sure it *was* Paul talking, but you couldn't have that argument with my mother. I picked up my fork, put a big bite of juicy goose into my mouth, and resolved not to say another word for the rest of the day, a determination I was able to keep for the most part. After pie we—minus the Hooks, who were going back into Watonga to spend the afternoon with my oldest son—retired to the living room for football and afternoon naps, and I fell asleep on the couch to the sounds of play-by-play and my dad sawing logs across the room in his old recliner.

When I woke up, the afternoon was well advanced, and after clearing the table later that evening of a supper of leftovers and more pie—mincemeat and peach this time instead of pumpkin and pecan, my choices at lunch—we played cards. All eight of us were in the dining room, although only six of us played—Lauren and my mom sat out, Lauren because she said she didn't feel like being chained to the table, and my mom from some vague moral conviction that made her feel uneasy whenever she picked up a deck of cards. Since Arturo had never played Spades, we taught him the basics of the game and then turned him loose. He played with good humor and some intelligence, quickly picking up the strategies. Dad tried to draw him out, to make him talk about himself, either to gather more information or to distract him from his game.

"When are you going to see your family?" he asked.

Arturo laid the five of hearts on Candy's eight of hearts. "They're coming through Albuquerque on their way back from skiing in Colorado. I have to get back to my research, so we'll have to leave here the 27th. Then my folks should visit us on the 29th."

"Have they met Candace?"

"Yes, sir. They're crazy about her. My momma pulled me aside the first time I brought her home and told me I better grab her up while I could." He took Candy's free hand in his and squeezed. "And so I did."

"When do you aim to get married?"

"Well, sir, with your permission," and here he inclined his head, gave my father a sort of bow, "we've talked about getting married when I graduate in June."

My mother let out a little sound—half gasp, half coo.

"Not much time," my dad reflected.

"No, sir. But we're thinking of a small wedding, only family, out in Albuquerque."

"Catholic wedding?"

Arturo and Candy shared a quick glance. "Yes, sir."

"We didn't raise Candace that way." Dad's face was impassive.

"You raised me to listen for God's call," Candy said. "You did a good job raising me. It doesn't matter where I serve God."

"I've known some good Catholic Christians," my mom said. She did not see that description as redundant or offensive; Arturo just smiled at her. Candy had briefed him well.

"Our children will be able to choose when they're older how they wish to worship God," Arturo said. "But we believe a family should worship God together."

"Raise up a child in the way he is to go, and when he is old, he will not depart from it," my mom said, but I don't know whether it was meant as argument or concurrence, and neither, apparently, did anyone else, for it simply hung in the air like Wile E. Coyote off the edge of a cartoon cliff before plummeting out of sight.

After we played cards for a couple of hours and Dad announced he had to go to bed, we broke off in our separate directions. B. W. and Arturo had taken a shine to each other, and Candace rolled her eyes as the two set off—without her—for the living room and still more football. On his way out of the room, Dad stopped by my chair and laid his hand on my shoulder like a hawk's claws. "Any young man who's going back to his work at Christmastime must plan to make his mark on the world."

"Yes, sir," I said, nodding. "I think that's a fair reading."

"Do you like him, Johnny?"

"Yes, sir, I do. Do you?"

He made a sour face that eased into a sour grin when he saw the way Candy was hanging on his answer. "No father likes the man who's replacing him. But I suppose he'll do."

"She loves him," I said quietly.

He nodded. "Seems to, all right. Well, good night, Son. Candace. Merry Christmas."

"Merry Christmas, Dad. Mom. I'll see you in the morning."

"I'm going fishing in the morning," he announced.

"You want company?"

He shook his head. "I'd just as soon go by myself."

"I'll see that B. W. leaves you his truck," I said.

That left just me and Candy at the table while Dad made his slow way out.

"He looks terrible," she said after a decent interval had passed. "I'm really worried about him."

"How's he been feeling?"

"Who can say? He won't tell me. I know he's been to the

doctor quite a bit, and I know that the bathroom is piled high with prescription bottles, but I don't know what they're all for."

"Does it scare you?"

"A little. But I guess what's supposed to happen will happen."

"Huh," I said. "That's the second time somebody has said that to me this week."

"It's just what I believe." She leaned across the table and whispered, "Do you think he liked Arturo?"

I patted her hand. "I think he likes him as much as he can. Don't worry. Everything's going to be beautiful for you."

"I like the sound of that," she said, and smiled big until she got a good look at me. "John," she said, biting her lip, "is everything going to be beautiful for you?"

She had no right to have eyes so direct, so full of trust. After a deep breath I shook my head. "I don't know, honey. I miss Michael. That whole thing is a bad situation, and I've done everything wrong there." I took in a deep breath, let it out. "And I'm not sure what the future holds. Not sure at all. I just know that I can't go on the way I have for—well, something has to change. Either me or the circumstances." I squeezed her hand to reassure her. "Maybe it'll be me." Then I stood up, walked over to look out at the snow-filled fields. "Things'll happen the way they're supposed to happen, I guess. At least, that's what I hear."

"That's three," she said. "You're a good brother, John. And a good father. And a good husband. You deserve the best. You deserve a beautiful life."

"Oh, sweetie," I said. "Good brother, maybe. That's about the best I could say for myself. But thank you for always thinking the best of me."

"What else could I think?" she asked.

There was no answer to that. She was mistaken, of course, wrong as anything, but to dispute with your kid sister about such a thing on such a joyful evening is also wrong as anything, so I decided to make for bed and, maybe, peaceful sleep.

"I love you," I said, hugging her and filling my nostrils with the wonderful fruit and herb smells of her hair. "Thank you for coming."

She kissed my cheek and threw an arm around my neck to inhibit my exit. "Thanks for inviting us. And for welcoming Arturo. He's the world to me."

"And should be," I said. "See you in the morning. We'll see if Dad remembers he wants to go fishing."

He did. After breakfast, Dad had me dig up my gear and asked if he could wear my new coveralls down to the pond, after which he proceeded out to the truck and disappeared from our sight.

"What do you have planned for the day?" Michelle asked, coming up behind me at the table, massaging my shoulders with her strong fingers, and making me feel better than I had any right to feel. If her dad had massaged my shoulders this way, I would have felt much better disposed toward him.

"Thought I'd deliver some mail before my practice with the geezers," I said.

"Mail?" Her fingers paused for a moment in their wonderful work.

"Remember when you suggested I write people I didn't get to see anymore?"

"Ah," she said. "Special delivery. Well, will you let me know how things turn out?"

"Of course I will," I said. I ducked my head so I didn't have to look her in the eye.

"I think Candy and Lauren and I are going into Oklahoma City to catch the sales and maybe check on some of the final details for the dance."

"Ah, yes," I sighed. "The dance."

"And tomorrow we're going to finish getting everything decorated. I can't believe we're actually going to pull this thing off."

"Who's the we doing the decorating?"

She finished up with my shoulders and walked over to the sink with my plate. "Me and a couple of other folks. Oh, I invited Samantha to help. Turns out her folks have gone off on that cruise they've been talking about all these years and left her alone in the house, this of all Christmases. I thought she might like a little distraction since the girls are over at Bill's folks until New Year's."

I was looking down at the table, at the place my plate used to occupy. It seemed safest. "I'm sure the dance is going to be great."

"Well," she said, "we're off. Be careful."

"Careful?"

"At practice." She bent over to kiss my brow. "I love you. Be careful."

"You said that twice," I said.

"Oh," she said, "okay," and she was gone.

I got my things together as soon as they pulled out of sight: my practice stuff, my letters, my jacket. On the drive into town I was listening to the Gospel According to Saint Bruce—Springsteen, that is. Michelle always said that if Bruce couldn't teach you something, you weren't listening, and I was listening, although nothing struck me right away except that *Darkness on the Edge of Town* was a pretty bleak vision of a world where you had to grab for whatever chance at redemption you could find.

Not much help for a man who knows he wants and needs redemption but isn't sure how he'll recognize it if it shows up.

When I arrived at Phillip's, I expected the gate to be locked up tight and was a little surprised that the padlock was gone. I'd figured on slipping my letter into the mailbox in flagrant disregard of that federal law on unauthorized use of mailboxes, but since this gave me the chance to avoid a life on the run, I gratefully drove on down to the house.

The new pile of bottles had grown by leaps and bounds since I'd last been here, and seeing that gave me a kick to the stomach that almost doubled me over. "God help us," I whispered per usual before cutting the engine and sliding out the door and past the truck Phillip and I had once dreamed of fixing up. The hood was open, and the carburetor and starter lay piled on top of the engine block.

I knocked on the door of the trailer, which rattled in the frame as always, then listened intently. Nothing. "Phillip," I called. "Phillip, it's me. John. I just want to talk to you."

Nothing.

I wedged the letter in between the doorknob and the doorjamb, where he couldn't go in or out without it coming to his attention, if only in the form of a falling slab of paper that he intended to ignore, and headed on to my next delivery.

Michael's truck sat crossways in the yard in front of his and Gloria's place, although I knew that meant nothing, since his welding job was right around the corner and he could walk to work.

I repeated the same hailing procedure, adding Gloria's name for good luck, invoked the spirit of Christmas, even said I had presents for him (which was a blatant lie, since I intended to make him come out to the farm if he had any thoughts of collecting, although he had no way of knowing that).

Silence.

I opened the metal flap to the mail slot with a grating *creak* and slid the letter into another place I could not enter myself.

Story of my life.

At last I pulled up in front of Samantha's house on Prouty Street and sat for a moment looking up and down the street at the familiar houses, wondering, now that it was too late, who might see me parked out there. With any luck, in thirty seconds I might be back in my truck and headed to practice a little early. As I walked up to the front door, I resolved to take advantage of my extra time by shooting a thousand free throws—I'd been uncomfortable with my shot ever since I hurt my ankle—and then maybe a hundred three-pointers before the other guys got there.

That was my plan. But lo, I knocked the third time, and the door was opened unto me.

"Johnny," Samantha said, and the sound of my old name in her mouth almost made my knees give beneath me. She saw the letter in my hands and smiled. "Mailman?"

"Herald," I said, and held the letter out to her.

"Come on in," she said. "You had lunch yet?"

"No," I said.

"Let me fix you something." She took my hand and pulled me inside, or at least so it seemed to me later when I thought about it;

surely I hadn't passed so easily over the threshold on my own accord. She led me through the sitting room, past that same lumpy plaid sofa where we used to fearfully explore each other late at night after her parents thought I had gone home, then on into the kitchen, where she sat me down at the table in her father's place. "I hope you're not sick of turkey."

"Haven't had any yet," I said, and turned in my chair to see her better.

I watched as she pulled some leftovers out of the fridge, arranged them on a plate, and put them into the microwave. Over the whine of it heating, she said, "You know, somebody's bound to see your truck out there."

"Maybe so," I said.

"Are you prepared to accept that possibility?"

"I don't know what I'm ready to accept," I said. The sight of her brought physical pain, an angry tug deep in the core of my being. "You look great," I said when she caught me staring. I shook my head. "I can't believe how great you look."

"Oh, please," she said, although she was not displeased. The oven beeped and she brought my plate over—turkey and dressing, green beans, broccoli—and set it down over my shoulder.

"I can think better," I said as she hovered over me, "if you sit down."

She pulled up the chair to my right and settled in facing me. She opened and scanned the note I'd brought, then looked up at me. "Okay, Johnny. What does this mean?"

I speared some broccoli and avoided her eyes for the moment. "Why did you leave Bill?"

"I asked first."

"I need your answer to give you mine." I finished chewing and waited on her.

"I've been in love with you since I lost my first tooth," she said. "You remember that?"

I did—first or second grade, out on the playground. I helped her pull it. She was crying, and then the tiny piece of porcelain was in my hand, my fingers smeared with her blood, red and sticky, and she stopped crying and smiled, a smile with a hole in it, and that was when Samantha Mathis crawled inside my heart and took up residence. "I remember."

"I think I loved Bill, too, or I learned to. He's not you, but he's a good man, in his own way. But he got so caught up in other things, and after the girls were born, he wouldn't pay attention to me. I tried to get his attention. I tried all kinds of things."

She glanced up at me to try to judge what I knew of these attempts, but I just nodded solemnly, as if to say, *It doesn't matter.*

"I'm not getting any younger," she said. "I want to be happy." She took a deep breath and let it out slowly. "And I think I could be happy with you."

There it was: The promise of joy and the threat of despair. The thrill of victory and the agony of defeat. I looked up from my plate. "How can we possibly be happy if we make so many people unhappy?"

She put her hand on my arm. "I've got it all figured out, Johnny. We could go to Idaho. I've got an old friend who has a real estate agency in Boise. He says things are booming up there. Even if they aren't, I could sell houses right and left. I'm a good realtor."

"I don't doubt that," I said. The pressure of her hand and the wafting scent of her perfume were making me a little dizzy. "But what would your friend think about you showing up with me in your hip pocket?"

I had that relationship right. She admitted, "He knows about you. I've told him."

"And what would I do there while you sold houses? Raise potatoes?"

"Anything you want," she said. "I have some money, and I'll make more. You're not a farmer, Johnny. You could do anything. Or nothing. You could just be. Read. Ski. Go to classes. Learn to paint. Write. You've worked hard enough. Long enough."

A picture of myself on skis in an artist's smock flashed before my eyes. But I couldn't imagine Idaho. "Why so far away?"

She looked at me and smiled sadly. "Why would I want to stay close? You know neither of us will be able to show our faces in this town again. No one will talk to me now, and I'm not even a divorcée yet." She saw the expression on my face, which might have been terror, and said, kindly but firmly, "Johnny, you can't have any false hopes about things working out to everyone's satisfaction. Everybody can't be happy. This is either/or." She tapped the envelope on the table. "If I read this letter right, you're tired of living in between. You'll have to make a choice, not count on life to make it for you."

"I know," I said. "But imagine what people will think."

"I don't have to imagine," she said. "I know." She took my hand in between her two hands, squeezed it.

I looked down at my hand, the touch buzzing like a hive filled with bees. Maybe that would be enough—the jolt, the sensation.

Maybe love would keep us together, as the Captain and Tennille used to say.

What they would think was that they'd been right about me all along, that I had never really become a responsible citizen, a good man. Imagining the crushing moral force of all that condemnation made my heart pound, and I could feel my stomach knotting into a coil. "Sam ... Sam, doesn't it scare you to be talking this way? To talk about turning our lives upside down, the lives of everyone around us?"

She shook her head again; she was as calm as I was freaked out. "This is maybe our last chance to set things right. To live our lives the way they always should have been."

When you hear your own thoughts and arguments coming from the mouth of someone else, it's amazing how persuasive they sound.

"Sam," I said, pushing my uneaten food away from me and covering the hand on my arm with my own. "Sam, don't you worry that we'll ... I don't know, go to hell or something if we do something like this? That at the very least, we'll be punished?"

"I worry about what people will think," she said. "But I worry more about what we will think."

"You don't think God has an opinion about husbands who leave their wives?"

"Johnny," she said, sighing, "if there is a God, I don't have the slightest idea what He thinks. He's never bothered to share His opinions with me."

"I've got to get up to the school," I said, getting to my feet and setting my napkin across my plate. "I'm late. They'll be waiting for me to open up the gym."

"Think about it," she said, taking my hand again. "Will you just think about it? Twenty years ago, you would have jumped at the chance to run away with me."

"I can't stop thinking about it," I told her.

We walked back through the living room, and she paused by the couch and said, "Do you know how many times I've wished you'd gotten me pregnant instead of her? As scared as we were back then that it could happen, we would have been okay, wouldn't we?"

"It would have changed some things," I said slowly. "But not everything. Who you marry is only one part of happiness."

"Still, I wish it'd been me," she said. "Johnny, why did you go to Michelle that night? Why couldn't you wait for me to come back?"

I opened my mouth to defend myself for the hundredth time, but I saw that her eyes were rimmed with tears, that I was not the only one carrying the ancient hurt, and I had to swallow a lump that had formed in my throat before I could answer. "I'm sorry," I told her, again. "You know I didn't plan things to be this way."

We had reached the door. She brought her lips up toward mine, but I turned my head, accepted only a kiss on my cheek and a hug that brought her body into uncomfortably close proximity.

"Think about it," she whispered. "Please think about it."

"I will," I said, as though I hadn't been all along. All day, every day. "I'll see you soon."

And I hurried out to the truck and on to the gym, where my teammates were indeed waiting, their engines running, for me to get there and let them in.

"About time," Bobby Ray said as he and Oz crowded into the gym behind me. "Where you been?"

Bill Cobb followed us in silently. I nodded greetings, and he may have given me the barest nod in return.

Or maybe not.

"Todd Culpepper said he'd play with us," Bobby Ray said, referring to one of the senior subs on the '75 team. "He's supposed to get into town tonight. But he says not to expect too much. Says the years have not improved his shot."

"We'll run him at small forward," I said. "In the meantime, maybe we could do some shooting, get warmed up."

"Okay," Oz said. Like the rest of us—except for Bill, who was wearing our new team warm-ups that simply unsnapped and fell around your ankles—he was sitting in the bleachers pulling his sweats off over tennis shoes.

We grabbed a couple of balls and went down to the west goal to shoot and rebound for each other. We talked a little about the holiday, about presents gotten and given, about family visiting or vamoosed—all except Bill, who shot in silence from the free throw line, one free throw after another, while the rest of us threw up three-pointers and put back misses from down near the basket.

"How are the girls?" I asked him, but he just turned a cold eye on me and said, "Why don't you worry about your own family?"

"Hey, easy, hoss," Bobby Ray said, stepping toward and between us. "We're just wondering how things are. We know it's a tough time."

"Tell him," and he meant me, although he didn't so much as look at me, just twirled the ball in front of him as he got ready to shoot another free throw, "tell him to keep out of my business and away from my wife."

Now Oz moved beside Bobby Ray. "Bill, I know this is—"

"He was there," Bill said. "Today. At her house," and now he turned to look at me, his expression ugly with anger, and I thought he was going to bounce that ball off my face. "If she'd known what he really is, she'd have forgotten about him years ago. But she can't see."

"What can't she see?" I asked, moving closer to him. And watching that ball. "Tell me, Bill. You've always been an insightful kind of guy. I'd like to hear about myself."

Bobby Ray and Oz began to look distinctly uncomfortable as each of us stepped closer to them.

"She can't see anything except the kid she grew up with." We were just feet apart now. "Not the grown-up failure who never got out of town."

"Failure," I said. It was one thing for me to think that; it was another for Bill Cobb to say it. I could sense heat rising on the back of my neck, imagine the crimson rushing up into my cheeks, feel the tension as my jaw clamped tight. Now Bobby Ray raised his hands and waved them like he was trying to stop traffic, and I assumed Oz was doing something equally futile at his end.

"You've never amounted to anything," Bill said, tossing the basketball to one side and pointing his finger at me—if not for our two friends, we'd have been face-to-face now, or worse. "And you never will, John. You never even went to college. You can't do anything. You're a failure. A nothing." I heard the ball bounce twice, three times, roll against the bleachers behind me.

I let out a laugh, and it was not a pretty sound. "Bill," I said, "you're not smart enough to recognize a failure when he stares at you from the mirror every morning. I don't believe you can even *spell* failure." I raised a finger to his face. "What do you call a man who can't keep his family together? Who can't keep his wife happy? Who doesn't even know how much it would have meant to her if he'd ever asked her to dance?"

Well, that hit something. Bill shoved Oz and Bobby Ray, who tumbled over me like water over a dam, and I went down beneath them—and wouldn't you know it, a sharp pain shot up my leg again. I let out a groan and tried to push my friends off of me.

When I looked up, Bill was standing over me with his fists clenched, but when he saw me hobbling to my feet, he groaned, opened his hands, and said, "Not your ankle."

"Yes, my ankle, you stupid—" I began, which brought Bobby Ray and Oz scurrying in between us again, although there was no reason anymore. Bill turned away, shaking his head, and I hopped off to the concession stand to get some ice, which was what I should have done the last time this happened.

It's hard to sustain a practice when the off-court intensity outshines the on-court play, and nothing got accomplished after that. Bill had disappeared by the time I came out, Bobby Ray apparently had gone after him—maybe to try to keep him from doing a Phillip on us—and Oz remained behind to minister to me.

"Is it swollen?" he asked.

"Not yet."

We sat in silence. The loudest noise was the drip of melting ice onto the floor beneath the bleachers.

"Were you really over at the Mathis place?" Oz asked, as though he could not—would not—believe it of me. He just looked at me, the most decent man I knew, and I felt hot embarrassment rising in my cheeks.

"Yeah." I nodded. There was no point in protesting my innocence. Even if I hadn't been there doing what everybody might think, innocence is a relative term. I was guilty of other, perhaps equally damaging things.

"It's wrong, John," Oz said. "No good'll come of it."

I turned to take a good look at Oz. I remembered the boy he had been—gangling, reclusive, a social misfit. That boy would never have dared to say these things to me. I guessed it was almost as difficult for the man, so I didn't argue, and I didn't get angry. I just said, "Thanks, Jim," and patted his shoulder. "You're a good friend."

Oz patted mine in return, exhausted, I think, from the strain of carrying on a running discourse, and climbed to his feet.

Light was failing by the time I felt ready to leave the gym, and I drove home gingerly, trying not to put too much pressure on my ankle. As I listened to the stereo and thought about Sam's proposal—for such it seemed to me—I finally understood the message Bruce Springsteen had been trying to pass on to me in his music: These things I thought I wanted could only be found in the darkness at the edge of town.

If I really wanted to have Samantha, I would never stand in the light in this town—or maybe anywhere else—again.

Was I ready to spend the rest of my life in darkness? Were there enough pleasures and joys to compensate for that?

After getting off the blacktop, I drove the section line road toward the house, and there was enough daylight left for me to see that the gap closest to our house, the one leading down to the pond, had been left standing open. I pulled the truck over, looked up and down the road to make sure no cattle had wandered out, and then closed the gap and drove home.

Dad had always told us that a man never leaves a gate open. Never. The way he talked about it when Trent and I were kids, you might have believed it to be one of his articles of faith: Serve God, save your money, and always, always, close your gaps behind you.

Had he been unable to close it? Or had he simply forgotten?

Either way, it sent a sliver of pain into my heart.

"We're having fish," my mother announced when I walked in, as if the aroma of frying catfish wasn't sufficient to inform me. "Your father had a good day at the pond."

"Great," I said. "The girls back yet?"

"They called and said they'd be in around seven."

I was not displeased that they were taking their time. It was actually shortly before eight when headlights came down the driveway and they came in jabbering and giggling about the sales they'd raided and the money they'd saved.

"To be truthful," I said, "it's impossible to save money by spending it."

"You're always better off saving than spending," my dad affirmed from the recliner. "That's sound advice."

"We got some really cute stuff," Candy said. "And wait 'til you see the baby clothes—"

My dad looked at her with horror.

"—for Michael and Gloria," she finished.

That night after everyone had cleared off to bed, things were quiet, strained in our room. Michelle asked, "How was your day?"

"Not so good," I said. "My mail delivery was pretty much return to sender."

"Practice?"

"We didn't get much done. I hurt my ankle, although it's feeling a lot better." I had it propped up on a pillow.

"Where'd you go for lunch?"

I remembered our promise, the most abiding promise we had ever made to each other—absolute truth, no matter how potentially hurtful.

I remembered the nighttime confidences shared, the trust Michelle had always had in me, the love she had always had for me.

I remembered all this. I remembered it, and I took a deep breath, and I opened my mouth to speak.

"I had lunch at KFC," I said.

"See anybody you knew?" Her voice seemed deliberately light, as if it were a matter of no consequence, as if my answer wasn't about to commit me to everlasting damnation.

I shook my head. I didn't dare to try my voice. It suddenly occurred to me that I'd been lying to her all along, all these years, that not telling a lie was not the same as telling the truth, that the things left unsaid, the desires and wishes I had kept secret from her—or tried to keep secret—were also lies, and that by finally uttering a conscious untruth now, I had simply put myself in the place where I must have truly belonged all along.

Darkness.

What Could Have Been

"Let's go up to school and shoot some baskets," B. W. offered when he saw me moping around the house, watching a talk show about wives who had affairs with other women. Michelle was up at school helping decorate the cafeteria to look like the retro restaurant in *Pulp Fiction*, which she had seen seven times that previous fall and claimed had changed her life; my parents were getting in the last of their visit with Candy and Arturo before they ventured across the Texas Panhandle and into Nuevo Mexico; Lauren was in her room with headphones on, listening to Michael W. Smith, a hunky Christian singer with a perpetual five o'clock shadow and eyes that smoldered out of one of the posters over her bed in such a way that they might evoke more complex feelings in young girls than simple devotion to God.

"You sure?" I asked him. "I know you've got other things you'd rather do. And this is pretty interesting stuff." It looked like two of the wives were getting ready to fight—or kiss.

"Dad, this is trash," he said.

"Right. But interesting trash."

"I've got to get out of this house," he said in a stage whisper. "And clearly you need to too. The sooner the better."

The gym was cold when we got there and smelled of ammonia;

the cleaning staff had apparently given it a once-over the night before, the obligatory cleaning during the Christmas break. The floor, too, had been waxed, because it was both glossy and slippery.

"I can see myself in the shine," B. W. said, dribbling out to center court. I would have thought he was too young to remember those commercials.

"You just want to shoot, or you want to play one-on-one?"

"Let's warm up and then play a game or two."

We dribbled to the west basket. "You doing this for fun or to humor your old dad?"

"A little of both." He sank one from the top of the key and watched as it bounced almost straight back to him, propelled by his beautiful backspin. We shot for about ten minutes until we were warmed up, and then we played three games of one-on-one, the three games necessary because I won the first on the strength of half a dozen deep outside shots that fell before B. W. was convinced he was going to have to guard me out there. B. W. won the other two, as he should have; he'd been playing better ball than I since he was fourteen, and at first that was a hard thing to swallow, although I suppose if one has to lose something to someone, to lose to a talented son at least means you can take pride in his accomplishments.

And, I thought as we dribbled, laughing, over to the bleachers after the last game, all this could be lost—the simple pleasure of a basketball game with a dutiful son, the joy of seeing children blossom into adults with skills and talents that mark them as special, the wordless rapport possible with those who share the blood coursing through your veins.

Afterward, we thought about showers, but the locker rooms would have been as cold as the gym, since no one had been in to turn on the heat, and so we decided just to sit and cool off a little before going outside.

"Hey, Dad, how you holding up these days?" B. W. wanted to know after we'd sat for awhile, panting in silence. "Isn't it hard not seeing Michael?"

I nodded.

"I'm sure it'll change someday. He's not gonna be like this forever. He'll come back to the family. I mean, he did want to see Gram and Poppa when they got into town, and he's been seeing Grandma and Grandpa Hooks every week or so. Grandma said sometimes he and Gloria come over for lunch on Sundays."

"He always did love roast beef," I said. We used to go over to the Hooks' every Sunday after church until the kids got too old or we got too busy or something of the sort, and it became occasional instead of regular. Maybe not all traditions were bad; one could do worse than roast beef.

"I think everything's going to be all right," he said, and he waited for me to agree. "We're just going through some rough times right now. As a family, I mean."

"You may be right," I said. "I hope so." Then I laughed—more of a disgusted snort, really. "Your mom says that Phillip One Horse and Michael have been spending some time together. I can't get close to either of them, but they've managed to find each other. Crazy."

B. W. rose to his feet. "Should we check up on Mom before we go?"

"We're not going to make a very good impression on the other folks there," I said, indicating our sodden, stinking selves.

"I know," he said. "But she said she was worried that everything might not be ready." I don't know how much he knew, but B. W. was a keen observer. "This dance is pretty important to her, you know."

"Yes," I said. "It is." I took a deep breath, let it out slowly, tried not to think about walking into a room where my wife and my potential lover were hanging crepe paper. "Okay. Let's go over and see how things are going." We put on our sweats and jackets and locked up the gym before walking across to the main building and into the long and cavernous hall heading to the cafeteria.

"Sure looks different with the lights out," B. W. said, and it did. The halls that looked laboratory sterile under fluorescent light looked downright spooky. Our footsteps echoed, and if I didn't know the walls were lined with steel lockers, I could almost imagine we were wandering into some monster's den.

Then when we turned the corner we picked up light and music coming from the cafeteria and walked gratefully toward it. Although you may know rationally that mad killers are almost exclusively a creation of Hollywood screenwriters, it's still hard not to imagine one creeping up on you in the iron dark. We stepped into the cafeteria, which was bright and frenetic—although not, it turned out, as bright and frenetic as it needed to be.

"Hey," Michelle called from up a ladder where she and June Four Horse were hanging balloons. Across the way, doing something with the skirting of tables against the wall, was Samantha, who looked up, smiled, then turned back to her work. Caroline Osbourne and a few other ladies (and some duly-deputized husbands) hung banners, carried chairs, fiddled with the sound system, which was blazing "Dancing Machine," the Jackson Five from back when Michael Jackson seemed cute and normal.

Michelle climbed down and crossed to give us head-averted hugs for the sweat impaired. "I'm so glad you're here. We've got a problem. I need you to run to the City."

"What for?" It seemed a little late to set off on the hour and a half one-way trip to Oklahoma City when the dance itself was only some hours away.

"The programs for the reunion aren't in from the printer. They said they'd had a holdup because of a job in front of us that took longer—anyway, they're just now finishing them up. They said we could pick them up this afternoon at four."

I checked my watch. "Which means leaving right about now."

"Why don't you let me go after them?" Sam called over from her tables. "I'm not really doing anything important. I'm sure John has better things to do than fetch programs from the City."

"That'd be real nice of you," Michelle said in the tone of voice that means it's decided, but then she pursed her lips and thought a moment. "Except this printer is sort of hard to find—it's down in the Bricktown part of town that wasn't anything but abandoned warehouses when you moved to Texas." She looked at me as though she'd had a brilliant idea, and when she spoke, her voice was brilliant, although the joy didn't reach her eyes: "John, maybe you ought to go with her, help her find her way."

Sam, B. W., and I all turned to look at Michelle. Probably everyone else who heard did too. "Well," Michelle said, meeting my gaze, "*I* can't go. There's still too much that has to be finished up here. And if you take Samantha's car, B. W. won't have to sit around up here all afternoon because he doesn't have a ride home."

"I don't mind," B. W. said. He looked back and forth between us. He knew something big was happening.

Michelle put her hand on my shoulder; someone who knew her less well might have even seen the movement as playful. "Please, John," she said. "Help Samantha." Her face was grave and her eyes bright.

I turned to look at Samantha, whose eyes were shining too, if not perhaps for the same reasons, and then back to Michelle. "Okay," I said. I looked at her again.

Michelle nodded softly—she was sure, whatever her reasons—and wrote down the address for us. I gave B. W. my keys, answered his "See you at home" with another quiet "Okay," and gave Michelle a quick hug when she came back.

"See you in a little while," I said. She didn't say anything.

Then I followed Sam out to her car, that big blue Buick Century, accepted the keys from her, and slid into the thick cushioned seat behind the wheel.

"She knows you don't have to go with me," Sam said as we clicked our seat belts shut. "I can find an address on my own. I'm a realtor. I find addresses all day every day."

"Yup," I said.

"But she's sending you with me anyway."

"Yup." I started the car, and we glided out of the parking lot. It was so quiet inside the car that I could hear Samantha breathing.

"Do you know where we need to go?" she asked as I headed south out of Watonga toward the interstate.

"No idea," I said. I laughed. It was crazy. "There's absolutely no reason for me to be going."

We sat in silence again as I drove south through Geary, around the curves and up the long hill leading up out of the Canadian River Valley on old Route 66. Sam was deep in thought, and I remembered from the distant past that when she was trying to solve a problem, she preferred quiet to chitchat. She'd hold it in her head like one of those Rubik's cubes, turning it this way and that, trying to picture it from all the angles.

I looked at her there, next to me, the two of us driving away from everyone in my old life and in the direction of something I didn't know yet. I had always wondered what it might feel like, and now that I was doing it, it was strangely unsettling, good and bad feelings mixed like volatile chemicals in the beaker that was my stomach.

"Do you think she knows that you and I might just keep going and never come back?" Sam asked, still turning things over in her mind.

"I think she knows."

"And yet she put us in a car together." She shook her head, turned the cube to another angle.

I nodded as I slowed to turn the big Century onto the ramp leading to the highway. The car accelerated like a Saturn V rocket—as slow as geological time at first, and then as the huge mass built up speed, like something you'd have to crash into a nearby planet to bring to a halt.

At last Sam shook her head and said, "I give up. It'll come clear to me soon, I think. For now, I just want to enjoy being here."

She snaked her hand across the seat, found mine, and gave it an affectionate squeeze before I raised it to tune in something more appropriate on the stereo. Sam was listening to a country station, 101.9, which was playing Garth Brooks's "Friends in Low Places," and while I'd been known to listen to country when forced to, mostly when I was dancing to it, it was not my music of choice, certainly not the music Michelle and I listened to at night as we read or wrote. I found an oldies station, which seemed an acceptable compromise, especially when the Cars' "Drive" came on three songs into a half hour of commercial-free light rock.

"The Cars. Remember our last dance?" she asked. "I've thought about it some nights, late, staring up at the ceiling, remembering your hand on the small of my back—"

She broke off as I swerved back up onto the highway, which I had neglected to pay attention to for the past few seconds and as a result failed to notice the slight curve. I laughed nervously and cleared my throat. It had become suddenly very warm in the car, and I tugged the collar of my sweatshirt to vent a little heat.

"Good to know I can still have an effect on you," she said. "John, do you ever think about me that way?"

"Sometimes," I said, although I immediately felt that I must say, "It's not Michelle's fault. She's a wonderful lover. A wonderful wife." Okay, that wasn't at all awkward. "I just remember, that's all."

"I like the way you stick up for her," she said. "I've never hated her. I've always been jealous. But I've never hated her."

I smiled. "I wish I could say the same thing about Bill. I've hated him since the first time you went out with him."

"Well," she said, "you never liked him much to begin with.

I remember of all the guys, you liked Oz the most. You said you thought Oz would always be your best friend."

"Turns out I was right. Although I wish I'd treated Phillip better," I said, passing a slow-moving pickup. "Maybe things could have turned out different for him if I'd been a better friend."

"Some people are meant to amount to something," she said, "and some never will."

"What have I amounted to?" I asked.

"You've done the best you could with the hand dealt you," she said. "You made one mistake."

"Maybe Phillip just made one mistake," I said.

She shook her head. This was not the way she saw the world, I guessed. There were good people and bad people. Bad people made their lives bad. Although bad things happened to good people occasionally, it was not because of who they were. That's just how things were.

"I don't want to argue," she said. "Phillip is small potatoes."

"Not to me," I said, and now I was feeling a tightness in my gut that would shortly translate into anger. "That's one of the things I've learned by coaching: People are all valuable. Anybody can make a contribution if they find their niche and develop their talents."

"That sounds like a wonderful locker room speech," she said, and I could feel her steering us to safer territory. "I know you're a good coach. Would you like to keep coaching?"

"I don't know," I said. "My future's a little uncertain just now."

She smiled and laid her hand on my leg, our momentary rift mended. "Whatever you want to do is okay with me," she said. "Johnny, can I come a little closer?"

"I'm stinking like a dog over here," I warned her.

"I don't care. Can I?"

My hormones screamed yes; my few still-functioning brain cells shouted no. "Not just yet," I said. "I'd like to make this decision without undue influence."

She nodded and gave me a mischievous grin. "And you think that if I slide over there next to you, it's going to be harder to make?"

"Something like that," I said. I could feel sweat beading on my forehead.

We reached the outskirts of the city, had to drop our speed down to fifty-five, began to hit a little congestion (of course, to someone from Watonga, a six-lane highway with more than three cars in sight means congestion), and looked for the buildings downtown that would signal our imminent exit—the First National Bank building, a trimmed-down version of the Empire State Building; the Liberty Tower, a featureless black rectangle; the Myriad Gardens, crowned by a circular glass greenhouse full of tropical plants where a cousin of Michelle's had gotten married a few years back; and the Myriad itself, a collection of squares and mirrors that served as convention hall and concert venue and where Michelle and I had seen Springsteen in the early eighties, one of the holiest nights in my life.

We took a likely exit, made a right at the Myriad and went under the railroad line. We found the printer the next block over. After loading the box of programs in the trunk (and they looked great; Michelle had outdone herself on the arrangements for this thing), we began to think about grabbing a bite to eat, since neither of us had had lunch.

"Let's go up to Twenty-third," I suggested, and we drove up Classen Boulevard, turned left onto Twenty-third Street across from what used to be the Soul Boutique back in the seventies, and pulled through an Arby's drive-through a few blocks west.

I ordered two beef and cheddars, two orders of potato cakes, and a mocha shake; she got a regular roast beef and a water, no ice. Then I got back onto Twenty-third headed west.

"We're going to need some gas," I said.

"That's not all we're going to need," she said. "We need to decide what we're going to do." She tore little bites off her sandwich, and she licked her fingers after each one, catlike.

"There's a Texaco," I said, and pulled into it. "What does this thing take?"

"Gas," she said, handing me two twenties, and I could read her frustration with me, with us, with the whole situation. I pumped what seemed like a thousand gallons into the Century and also paid for the discount car wash you get with a fill-up.

"I thought your car could use a wash," I said. The dark blue did show road dirt. I pulled around to the wash, punched in the code, and idled forward into the wash bay until the little red stoplight signal came on. Water began to dribble, then to pound against the roof and doors and hood and windows, and then the rotating brush swooped down with a rumble, closer and closer. My body picked up the trembling, and Sam felt it too, for I looked across at her and each of us was holding our breath, and the look on our faces was mingled fear and fascination, and then she leaned toward me and put her hand on my right leg, just above the knee, and we were in each other's arms as the world itself rumbled around us. Her fingers were in my hair and mine were slipping to her back and pulling her closer, closer. My lips found hers, and I kissed her greedily, hungrily, as though she could feed me what I lacked, as though I could ingest the years I had lost, and the water pattered against the car like it had on spring nights in my old Chevy truck back in 1975, and I could almost feel the way it could have been between us all those years.

I saw us going off to college together, myself in law school, in a practice with that mahogany desk and a corner office, saw our family at the dinner table, and of course they wouldn't look like the kids we had now, they'd be some other kids.

I saw us in bed together, those lips on mine, as they were right now, for real, in the present.

I saw the life we never had, all the way to our twentieth high school reunion, where Michelle was decorating the cafeteria for a dance.

And then the water stopped and the dryer howled, high and mournful, and I pushed myself away from her.

"I'm sorry," I said. I pushed her mouth away from my neck, where it had returned, and she withdrew slowly to her side of the car with a sad smile.

"Don't be sorry," she purred. "That was wonderful."

I shook my head. "Yes, it was. And yes, I do. Have to be sorry, I mean. I can't be anything but sorry. For you. For me. For the past." I let out a breath, my hope of a different future whooshing out of my body, and then shifted out of park and eased the car forward into the flow of air howling from the dryer. The water on the windshield streaked and smeared like the brushstrokes of an Impressionist painting, like a world that could only exist on canvas.

"You're not going to leave her," she said, and it was clear by her tone that she could not quite believe it.

"Leave them," I said. "But no. I'm not."

Her hand was on my arm for a moment, then gone. "Why? Can you tell me why? I could make you happy, Johnny. We could have a good life together."

And maybe she could, we could. For so long, I wished I could have had her, wanted a life with her. But now I just murmured, "What could have been is the greatest enemy of what is," and when Samantha gave me a quizzical look, I said it in another way: "Twenty years is plenty long enough to mope over what might have been."

"It could still *be*," she insisted. And now there were tears in her eyes, but I suddenly saw—just as the windshield suddenly cleared with a flick of the wiper switch—that you could want something your whole life but realize in the moment of achieving your desire that it couldn't save you the way you always thought it could, that it could in fact change you irrevocably into someone you didn't know and would not want to be.

"I just can't do it," I said, the world growing clearer to me with each word spoken. "There are too many people who stand to get hurt, people who love us, people who deserve better."

"What about what we deserve?" she asked, and I could barely understand her for the tears.

"You know," I said gently, "I'm starting to think that I've gotten what I deserve. Better than I deserve. And that I should start learning to be thankful for it."

I pulled completely out of the wash bay and up to Twenty-third Street, waiting for a break in traffic.

"She knew you wouldn't leave her," Sam said, realization dawning as I accelerated into the road. The cube had fallen into place. "She knew that when it was staring you flat in the face you couldn't do it." She turned to look at me. "That's why she sent you."

"Then she knew more than I did," I said, thinking, not for the first time, about how often that was true. "Part of me wanted to take you and head for the distant horizon." I sighed. "Part of me still does."

"I wanted you to," she said. "I guess part of me will always feel that way."

"I hope not," I said, looking across at her, slumped in the seat. "You have a family that loves you. And a husband who wants you more than he can possibly express."

She knit her brows. "I thought you hated Bill."

"Well," I said. It was true that I was hard-pressed to think of a single thing I liked about him, but at last, one occurred to me: He loved this woman, and her loss had broken him in the same way I had once been broken. Finally I shook my head. "Not anymore. I've hated Bill Cobb for too long to no good purpose."

She shook her head and sat silently. As we pulled up to the light at MacArthur Boulevard, I heard her repeat, "What could have been is the greatest enemy of what is."

I nodded slowly. "Something somebody told me once."

"Good advice." She sighed. "If you can live up to it."

The light turned green, and the enormous weight of the Century began to move forward. "We can," I said. "We will."

When we finally reached the high school after a drive full of reflective silence, Michelle's little car sat forlorn and alone in the parking lot.

"I'll take the programs in," I said, popping the trunk. "Why don't you go on home and get dressed."

She slid across to take over the seat I'd just vacated, and I walked back to the trunk and lifted out the box of programs.

"Johnny," she called out the window as I closed the trunk and turned for the school.

I stopped momentarily in my tracks. "Yeah," I said.

"Michelle's a lucky woman."

I shook my head and found tears burning the corners of my eyes. "No," I told her. "I'm a lucky man."

The Century eased out of the parking lot, and I walked briskly through the silent hallways, my footsteps echoing, to the cafeteria, where Michelle sat, alone, head down, on the edge of the stage. Her shoulders were shaking, and I could see that she was crying so hard that she hadn't heard my approach.

"Hey," I said, and the look that spread across her face when she saw me is the look I hope to see on the face of Jesus at the moment of my death. I set the box down and headed for her like she was a finish line.

Which, of course, she was.

"I'm sorry," I said as we stood looking at each other. "So sorry for all the pain I've brought on you. I can never make it up to you. Never. But I'm ready to try."

"Oh, J. J.," she said, taking me by the arms, feeling me as if to make sure I was really standing there. "You just have."

And then she was in my arms, and I was swinging her through the air, light and free, and the world had never ever looked so good.

"Why did you come back?" she asked when I finally set her back down on terra firma.

I looked at her and winked. "We better run home and throw on our fancy dancin' duds," I said. "I don't want to miss a minute of this dance of yours."

She nodded and took my arm and led me out to the car, and she stared at me all the way home with a look of bliss on her face that I returned every few seconds.

I can't remember much else about that evening except that I danced every dance with Michelle, waltzes and two-steps, twists and disco, until my feet were tender in my boots and I feared blisters.

"We don't want to ruin you for your game," Michelle said, leading me over to the punch bowl with her arm around my waist.

"I could care less about that stupid game," I said, and I discovered to my surprise and instant relief that I actually meant it. We sat down in a corner far from the dance floor and observed our classmates, graying and balding, rail-thin or losing the battle against obesity, faces lined with years of life's pain and laughter, as they danced to songs we had known when we were children—for that's what it seemed to me we had been, children, at least in our understanding of life and how it was all supposed to work.

"Look at that," Michelle said, pointing discreetly, and I followed her finger to see Bill Cobb cross the room to Samantha, bow, and ask her to dance, to see her blink rapidly, bite her lip, and accept, to see them walk onto the floor and begin to turn, both of them rigid as posts, although his arm was on her waist, and her hand sat upon his shoulder.

"Look at that," I said.

"Things could work out after all," she said, and she spoke as an authority on the subject. I leaned across the table, kissed her long and hard, and stood to my blistered feet.

"Let's go home," I said.

"What?" she said. "And leave all our friends? Do you know how long it's been since we've seen some of these people?"

I pulled her close and whispered into her ear. "Do you know how long it's been since I made love to the only woman in the world I desire?"

She looked up at me. "I don't know that I've ever been the only woman you desire, if that's what you mean."

"Well, there you go," I said, and when I whispered a suggestion that we ought to go make sure the coach's office was locked up safe and secure, she giggled like a teenager.

"You know, John," she said, "I've always thought we'd be together someday."

"And you were right," I said. "Absolutely one hundred percent right." I took her hand, pulled her up from the table, and led her across the dance floor, out of our past and into our future.

What Is, or
Back on the Tractor

And there is little left to tell, although of course there was much that later happened. Much of what had occupied my mind waking and sleeping proved to be so much smoke when I at last woke up and began to see the world more clearly. Phillip did not show up for our exhibition against my varsity team the day after the dance, but we did go ahead and play, after a fashion, with the help of our second-stringers. My varsity beat us handily, as they should have, although we old men did not disgrace ourselves, and I actually played fairly well until the second half, when I benched myself. I told the guys that my ankle was hurting, which, indeed, it was, if only a little. What perhaps was most important, though, was that we made enough money off gate fees and donations that the Watonga basketball program will be able to go a long time—certainly the rest of my coaching career—before having to beg Bill Cobb for anything else.

Although we continued to play unevenly for the rest of the season, my Watonga High team actually finished with a winning record and, by virtue of a huge last-second win over the Okeene Whippets, we went to the district playoffs, where Seiling beat us handily, as they should have. B. W. was recruited by a dozen colleges, but he has stuck to his resolution of going to forestry school in Montana, and Michelle is determined that we will go up this spring break—all of us—to find a place for him to live next fall. For the drive up, she has made reservations for us at a condominium in Winter Park, Colorado, where the youth of our church have gone on ski trips during past spring breaks. B. W. has told me about his first time skiing and gleefully shown me a map of the slopes at Winter Park, of ski runs called Runaway and Feebleminded. When I ask if there's a slope called Fall Down and Break Your Fool Neck, he and Lauren laugh and laugh and just say they can't wait to watch the old man eat snow.

Michelle and I have talked at length about our next twenty years of life, and the upshot is that, this fall, I'm going to start attending classes at Southwestern State University in nearby Weatherford. Mrs. Edmondson, Watonga's eleventh-grade English teacher, is getting along in years and will step down in the not-too-distant future, and it is my thinking that Watonga juniors deserve a good English teacher at least as much as the seniors do. Michelle says she could not be more proud of me, and although money will be tight, I look forward to our future together with the joy I might have been feeling all along.

Still, as I have said before but never understood so well as now: better late than never.

There is one thing more, a sad thing, I must tell. One February morning, some few short weeks ago, Michelle's mother called. Lauren answered the phone and then turned to us and said, "Grandma's crying."

Michelle took the phone from her, said "Mom," listened intently for a moment, and then her face crumpled and tears welled up in her eyes and she lowered the phone and slid to the floor, and I ran across the room and gathered her into my arms.

"It's the baby," Michelle sobbed into my shirtfront. "They lost the baby. Michael and Gloria. She had a miscarriage." She looked up into my eyes. "Gloria will be okay. But they lost the baby."

I held her tight and felt my own eyes fill. "It's okay," I said. I looked up at Lauren, who was biting her lower lip, and held a hand out to her. "Everything will be okay."

Lauren hung up the phone and then we sat on the floor, the three of us, holding each other. Michelle looked up at me finally and said fiercely, "Don't tell me it's for the best. Don't you dare tell me this is going to be better for them than having that baby."

"I wouldn't say that," I said. "I don't even think that. Not anymore."

She sank her face into my shoulder, and her muffled voice was soft in my ear. "I know they can have another. But I was so ready to be a grandma. Is that selfish?"

"You wanted them to be happy," I corrected. "The grandma stuff was just a happy by-product."

It took awhile, but at last Michelle stopped crying, although she was still shaking her head. "Why does something like this happen?" she asked. "Why couldn't things just go smoothly for a little longer?"

"There's a reason for everything that happens," I said. "There's gotta be."

She looked up at me. "Do you believe that, J. J.? Really truly believe that?"

"Yes," I said, and despite the somberness of the moment, I felt suddenly at peace. "Yes, I do."

My crisis of faith—if that was what it had been—was finally over.

That afternoon an old Chevy pickup topped the rise and headed down the driveway toward the house, and Frank, who for once was standing guard duty instead of his usual practice of wandering the pastures looking for rabbits, let out a low baying noise—*ah roo roo*.

When the truck pulled up in front, I stepped out onto the porch to say howdy.

Phillip One Horse emerged from the vehicle, which on closer inspection proved to be the selfsame Chevy truck he and I had worked on those cold winter afternoons back when he was helping me out around the place.

We stood there for a moment, him in the open door of his truck, me on the top step of my porch. "I didn't think that thing would ever run again," is what I finally said.

"Well," he said, "it didn't run without some help. You were right, you know."

"Right?"

"It was the head gasket. Simple enough to fix once I finally knew what needed to be done. Hop in." And he motioned to the passenger side with his head.

I smiled sadly. "I'm happy to see you, Phillip. Really. Happier than I can say. But we've had some really hard news today. Can I take a rain check?"

"I know your news," he said, and he motioned with his head

again. "My grandmother sent me. She told me I ought to take you to your son."

I shook my head. There was the tragedy of it all. "I think your grandmother must have her wires crossed. Michael won't see me. And even if he would, I wouldn't know what to say. There's too much distance between us."

Phillip stepped closer to me, and his voice was low but full of feeling. "Words are not the most important things we offer those in pain. It's standing behind those words, John. Being there. Not giving up. You should know that. You should know that better than anyone."

"But he won't see me," I repeated. "I've—" I stepped down, took him by the shoulder. "Listen, Phillip, you go. Tell him how sorry we are—"

"I will not tell him," he said, and he took a step backward. "If you have a message to give your son, then come with me."

"But I don't," I said. "I can't think of—"

"It's okay, John," he said. "I know the words of your heart." I felt his strong hand take my arm, and he would not let me go. He tugged me to the truck and up into it and closed the door behind me.

There was much I wanted to know, much I wanted to tell him, but when I asked how he had been, he simply said, "We can talk later. Now is a good time for silence. A good time to pray, if you believe in it."

And I did pray, as hard as I've ever prayed in my life. I thought that I'd even uncovered some strength, but when we pulled up in front of the little frame house where Michael and Gloria lived, my courage fled like air escaping a balloon.

I had the image of myself standing at that door, knocking, knocking, and nobody answering. "He won't talk to me," I said, a third time.

"Have faith," Phillip said, and he came around and pulled me from the truck. We went to the door. Phillip knocked, and we waited for what seemed years before Michael opened the door and looked out at us through the tattered screen. He had lost weight, and his eyes had shadows beneath them, but even with the evidence of life's hard use, I thought he had never looked so handsome, so grown up.

Whatever he had been when he left us, he was a man now.

Michael did not turn on his heel and shut the door in our faces, but neither did he open the screen to us.

He stood there; he did not look at me, and he did not speak.

"Michael," Phillip said, "we know there is nothing we can say at a time like this. We have just come to weep with you."

Michael raised his eyes to mine. He searched my face for something that would tell him what to do, what to think. I don't know what he found there. All I know is that, at last, he opened the screen door and ushered us inside.

I will not say that all our problems are behind us, or that we have made up in weeks for years where we did not listen to each other and did not understand each other. But I can say that last Sunday we met Michael and Gloria for dinner at the Hooks' home after church, that Michael shook my hand, and that both of them were noted on occasion to smile, despite our presence.

And now I sit inside the sun-warmed tractor cab on a chilly March afternoon. I have no reason to be here. I was walking past, I saw the tractor, I climbed up. Maybe I wanted a temporary refuge from the howling north wind; maybe I was seized by a perverse impulse to once again look out at my farm through these dirt-streaked windows.

At first glance, this does not look like an appealing world. Rodents have made their home somewhere in here over the winter, for there are rat droppings at my feet; every surface is covered with red field dust; a discolored plastic spit cup from the long-ago days when I used to chew Red Man is wedged down between the instrument panel and my chair. Then, from underneath the seat, a fly buzzes, as if newly born into existence, and I watch with some interest as he stirs into flight, bounces off some windows, settles on the steering wheel in front of me after his adventures to rest in the sunlight and get his bearings.

Maybe he can see that there is a larger world outside, a world where he could fly endlessly. Maybe he even knows that there is a way to reach that world if he is only willing to do whatever it takes to get there.

But it is also a cold world out there, and the winds howl like wolves, and he could easily be carried off, never to be seen again.

Here there is warmth, there is light, and, within certain definable boundaries, there is freedom.

"Stay put," I advise him, a message from God. Then I zip up my coat, pull on my gloves, and prepare to step briefly back into the cold before going back into my warm kitchen to kiss my wife, to hug my children, to take up again my wondrous life.

ACKNOWLEDGMENTS

This book took me some fifteen years to write (or to write right) and only took shape because of the help of some people who may not have ever known they were helping. I particularly want to note the two farmers in my life, both now gone, who taught or told me specific things I needed to know to write this book: my grandpa, Chuck Godwin, and Dale Randolph, my late stepfather. Because of them, I have driven a tractor, plowed a field, stacked hay, fed cattle, and learned the tiniest bit about what it is to be a farmer—enough to supplement it with research and imagination into the book you hold.

I'm grateful also to the other members of my Watonga-based family—my mom, Karen, my grandma Rose, and my stepdad, Dave—who have welcomed me over the years to the patch of Oklahoma ground we call our farm. The Tilden farm is very closely based on our land, as sharp-eyed observers in my family will note. I am grateful for the real people of Watonga, an awful lot of whom I seem to be related to in some degree. This is a novel, but I have tried to be as accurate as I could in depicting this fictional Watonga circa 1994. I have changed things as they've been necessary for the story, though, so please don't assume that any person, place, or thing depicted in the book necessarily has a real-life analogue.

Well, except for the Hi-De-Ho, of course. I could never make up a place as good.

The Reverend Dr. Raymond Bailey unknowingly gifted me with the "weep with you" line in the last chapter during a sermon he preached fifteen years ago at Seventh and James Baptist Church in Waco, Texas, and I thank him. Sometimes things we say take a long time to bear fruit—but they do, eventually.

I give thanks for my agent, Jill Grosjean, who has stuck with me through thick and thin. It's been awhile since the last novel. Thanks, J—and may the bookselling gods assure that this novel gets filed in the right part of the store so people have a chance to find it.

Thanks, as always, to Joe DeSalvo, Rosemary James, and the Pirate's Alley Faulkner Society in New Orleans. They gave me my first big recognition, encouraged me in lean years, and celebrated with me in flush.

I am grateful to be working (again, in many cases) with the wonderful folks at David C. Cook. Thanks to Don Pape, who directed his staff to get a book from me. Thanks to Andrea Christian, Steve Parolini, Kate Amaya, and Terry Behimer. It's a joy to be back with you all, and I look forward to the next book.

Thanks to Baylor University, my employer, which has given me good work to do for twenty years, and to my students, who keep me energized and interested. Thanks to the College of Arts & Sciences and the Provost's Office for sabbaticals and research leaves that made this book possible, to my deans Wallace Daniel and Lee Nordt, and to past Baylor provosts David Lyle Jeffrey and Randall O'Brien for their support of my writing. This book was completed during my 2008 research leave. Thanks to Maurice Hunt and Dianna

Vitanza, my department chairs, for their encouragement and for a schedule that makes writing, speaking, and other authorial duties possible.

Thanks to the Episcopal Seminary of the Southwest for a space to write and for many other things as well. Thanks to my classmates and colleagues there. Thanks to my community of faith, St. David's Episcopal Church in Austin, Texas, and to the communities of faith that have sustained me during these years, especially St. James' Episcopal in Austin.

Thanks to the Right Reverend Greg Rickel, who always looks across the table and asks me, "So, what's next?" and to the Most Reverend Rowan Williams, who kept telling me he was waiting for the next novel.

I am thankful for my boys, Jake and Chandler.

And I am thankful for Martha, who is the kindest person I know.

This book was written and rewritten at Baylor University in Waco, Texas, and in Austin, Texas, and edited at Ghost Ranch in northern New Mexico. Many thanks to Jim Baird, Program Director, and Carole Landess, Host Companion at the Casa del Sol retreat center, for arranging a place to work.

I listened to Bruce Springsteen, Bruce Hornsby, Eliza Gilkyson, Shawn Colvin, Gin Blossoms, Dixie Chicks, Jon Dee Graham, Coldplay, Bob Schneider, and U2 while I wrote and rewrote this novel. Thanks to all of those artists for their inspiration, and for comfort in dark times.

Let's imagine this is the back of a CD: Greg Garrett plays Martin, Fender, and Epiphone guitars and Hohner harmonicas.

Speaking of music, I'm going to go out on a limb and claim that my band, Lavabo, is the only roots/Americana group in Austin, Texas—the live music capital of the world—made up entirely of Episcopal priests and preachers. The folks I've played music with in recent years are the Reverend Cathy Boyd, the Reverend Ken Malcolm, the Reverend Kevin Schubert, the Reverend Lance Peeler (now gone on to the Pacific Northwest), and, following the departure of the Reverend Anthony MacWhinnie for the Gulf Coast, a bassist to be named later. You should hear us. Seriously.

Finally, thanks to all of you who buy my books, come to talks, signings, and teachings, or who have let me hear from you over the years.

I write first for myself, as every serious writer ought to.

And then, when I am finally happy with something, I give it to you.

Thank you for reading, and may God richly bless you.

Greg Garrett
Christmas 2008
Casa del Sol, Ghost Ranch
Abiquiu, New Mexico

... a little more ...

When a delightful concert comes to an end,

the orchestra might offer an encore.

When a fine meal comes to an end,

it's always nice to savor a bit of dessert.

When a great story comes to an end,

we think you may want to linger.

And so, we offer ...

AfterWords—just a little something more after you

have finished a David C. Cook novel.

We invite you to stay awhile in the story.

Thanks for reading!

Turn the page for ...

- **Discussion Questions**
- **An Interview with the Author**

Discussion Questions for Shame

1. John Tilden is the main character and the narrator of *Shame*. How does it affect our experience for him to tell his own story?

2. Several chapters at the beginning, middle, and end of the novel highlight John's strange journey, symbolized by his time on the tractor, moving but never getting anywhere. In what ways can we see that John is on a journey even though he never leaves town?

3. Why is the novel called *Shame?*

4. How does the major setting of the novel affect the action? The characterization? Would this story feel different in an urban setting?

5. Why does John still feel so affected by the past? How does this shape his present and future?

6. John says that he truly wants to be a good person. What are his best qualities? What are his worst?

7. Dreams are important in the novel. How do they reveal John's inner conflicts? How do they reveal things about John and his history we might not otherwise know?

8. The device of using letters in a novel has been used since the first epistolary novels hundreds of years ago. How does the author employ them in this book?

9. In what ways does the setting (the early 1990s) seem alien to us as readers? What technological advances and other changes have altered the way we live in the years since the 1990s?

10. How does the author use music, television shows, and other popular culture artifacts to help tell the story?

11. John says he feels that he may be experiencing more than a simple midlife crisis—that what he's undergoing is also a crisis of faith. Is this true? How does John change spiritually as a result of the events of this story?

12. Fatherhood is a central theme in the novel. Judging from the relationships we see in the book, what does it mean to be a father? More broadly, what does good parenting look like?

13. How is friendship an important theme in the novel? Which characters prove to be true friends to each other?

14. Who are John's heroes or role models? What do these choices tell us about him?

15. What do you consider the most important themes in *Shame?* What does the book seem to say about them? What did you carry away from your reading of the novel?

A Conversation with Greg Garrett

Q: Tell us a little about the writing of *Shame*.

This novel has a long and interesting history—if you're fascinated by me and my life, that is. The short version, for folks who don't share that fascination, is that I wrote the first draft of this novel during the early '90s, around the time when it is set. I loved the characters but didn't feel like I'd mastered the art of writing a novel yet. So I put it away for what I thought would be a short time, but, given the adventures you would learn about in the long version, it turned into years. After I wrote my novel *Free Bird* I felt I had broken through and finally learned how to be a novelist. So a couple of years ago, when I found myself with some writing time on my hands, I came back to *Shame*, rewrote it using everything I know, and, with my editor Steve Parolini's help, turned it into something I was really proud of.

Wow. And that's the short version. Maybe we should just stick with that.

Q: Is this novel particularly autobiographical?

John Tilden is less like me than any other main character I've written a novel about, although there are certainly some autobiographical elements. As I mention in the acknowledgments, the book is set in a place I've known since childhood, a place where you could find my mother, grandmother, and many of my relatives. Our actual farm outside Watonga, Oklahoma, is where John Tilden lives, and that was important in writing about John. Our day-to-day lives are so different that I really felt like I needed the grounding of knowing exactly where John was brushing his teeth, feeding his cattle, sitting by the pond, because I had been there myself.

In most of the details of our lives, we're different, though. I left the small town where I graduated high school, got ridiculously overeducated, and live now in Austin, Texas, a large city that has foreign films, sushi, and

Episcopalians. I teach at a major university, I travel all over the world. I guess if John were real, I'd be living his dream life. Maybe I'd have to arm wrestle him for it. Perhaps we're more alike than I thought.

Q: What made you want to write a novel about a farmer and small-town coach?

The superficial details of John's life—farmer, coach, husband, father—were actually less interesting to me than the sloppy inner life—his wants, hopes, desires, dreams. John has been deeply unhappy, wishes his life had turned out differently, and wonders whether it's too late to make a change. I think all of us wrestle with that "road not taken" question at one time or another. I was certainly wrestling with it in my own life when I was writing the first draft of the novel, and so I really resonated with John's story.

But what I loved most about telling John's story was that, restless as he is, unhappy as he sometimes is, down deep at his core John is a genuinely good person. I admire him, I like him, and I hope readers will feel the same. I had written about lovable scoundrels in my first two novels; in this story, I wanted to talk about what it takes to be a solid family man—to do the right thing, as unflashy as that might sound.

Q: You've published a number of short stories set in and around Watonga. Are they related in any way to *Shame*?

Over the years I've published about a dozen short stories about Cheyenne Indians who live in and around Watonga. Ellen Smallfeet is a recurring character in those stories, and Michael Graywolf was in one of the very first I published, in the *South Dakota Review*. Phillip is also in several stories. He's one of my all-time favorite characters, because I see a lot of myself in him (dating back to all the stuff I left out of the short version awhile ago). In particular, I think the long story *Bridges* is one of the best things I ever wrote. It retells the action of *Shame* from Phillip's perspective. That story shows us John and Michelle through Phillip's eyes, which is cool if you love those characters as I do, and it's a story that breaks your heart for Phillip all over again because you hear in his own words what he's been through.

I guess you could say all the Watonga things I wrote in the 1990s were early stories investigating what William Faulkner said every writer needed, a little postage stamp of land to call his own. Watonga, the farm, small town life, and the mix of white, black, and red people were things I knew about from my earliest childhood, and I thought they were elements I could write about in a way that nobody else could. Writers need material, and the Cheyenne stories showed me that I could tell great stories about this land and the people who walk it. When it came time to write a novel, I knew I could set it in rural Oklahoma and write something universal that people would want to read about.

Q: *Shame* is your third novel, following *Free Bird* and *Cycling*. Those novels received some critical attention and even acclaim. It certainly wasn't like people suggested you should stop writing fiction. So why has it taken you six years to publish another novel?

After *Free Bird* achieved some pretty considerable notice (Top Ten lists, film interest, that kind of thing), *Cycling* came out in 2003 and was well reviewed, if (*sigh*) generally misfiled by booksellers next to the latest book by Lance Armstrong in the sports section. I heard from angry guys who bought it accidentally thinking I was going to help them with their road training or something, but instead, there was all this stuff about this guy who couldn't seem to get his life together. Suffice it to say that the book never really reached its target audience, although I also hear from people who have read and loved it. I think the wait would not have been quite so long if *Cycling* had found the audience we expected for it, because there would have been a desire from more than just a few readers who happened to stumble across it.

But the bigger reason is that over the last six years I've been doing a lot of new things: I went to seminary full time for three years, wrote a number of nonfiction books, taught, lectured, and traveled, and my life started taking me in a number of different directions. When I published my first two novels, writing fiction was the primary demand on my writing time. Now there are a number of demands. But I don't ever want to stop writing fiction—I love telling stories about characters who interest me, and being taken away into their worlds.

Q: What stories do you want to tell next?

I don't know. I've been writing pretty hard for the past couple of years, and one of the things I'd like to do is slow down a little and let some stories unfold in my head. You can't rush a novel into being—or, at least, I can't. I'd like to write a children's novel—or several of them—with my son Chandler. We've been throwing ideas around and plotting a series. I've given thought to a literary detective novel and a novel about a shipwrecked sailor fished out of the sea. And I have a novel finished, I think, about an oncologist who makes some very bad decisions involving one of his patients, a Dallas gangster. Mostly I just want to keep listening for the voice that's going to start speaking into my ear and telling me about somebody's life. That's how all three of the published novels started—I wrote down a first sentence that came to me. And then a second. And then I was off to the races. So to speak.

I've got nonfiction projects that people want me to write, and so it looks like there will be Greg Garrett books on the stands for the next few years. The novels are just for me, though, and they take as long as they take.

But not, I hope, another six years.